S. E. Tolsen is the pseudonym of husband and wife writing team, Emma Olsen and Vere Tindale. Emma was born in Wellington, New Zealand and Vere in Johannesburg, South Africa. They are both graduates of Victoria University, New Zealand. *Bunny* is their first novel and was adapted from their screenplay *Crepuscular*, which was a nominee for Best Feature Screenplay at the 2018 Renegade Film Festival. They live in Brisbane, Australia.

bunny
S.E. TOLSEN

Pan Macmillan Australia

Pan Macmillan acknowledges the Traditional Custodians of country throughout Australia and their connections to lands, waters and communities. We pay our respect to Elders past and present and extend that respect to all Aboriginal and Torres Strait Islander peoples today. We honour more than sixty thousand years of storytelling, art and culture.

This is a work of fiction. Characters, institutions and organisations mentioned in this novel are either the product of the authors' imagination or, if real, used fictitiously without any intent to describe actual conduct.

First published 2023 in Macmillan by Pan Macmillan Australia Pty Ltd
1 Market Street, Sydney, New South Wales, Australia, 2000

Copyright © Vere Tindale and Emma Olsen 2023

The moral right of the authors to be identified as the authors of this work has been asserted.

All rights reserved. No part of this book may be reproduced or transmitted by any person or entity (including Google, Amazon or similar organisations), in any form or by any means, electronic or mechanical, including photocopying, recording, scanning or by any information storage and retrieval system, without prior permission in writing from the publisher.

A catalogue record for this book is available from the National Library of Australia

Typeset in 12/17 pt Sabon LT Pro by Post Pre-press Group, Brisbane

Printed by IVE

The authors and the publisher have made every effort to contact copyright holders for material used in this book. Any person or organisation that may have been overlooked should contact the publisher.

The paper in this book is FSC® certified. FSC® promotes environmentally responsible, socially beneficial and economically viable management of the world's forests.

In memory of Dr Vernon Naidu, Leon Hampson-Tindale and Lucy Olsen. Thank you for everything.

To a drinker the sensation is real and pure and akin to something spiritual: you seek; in the bottle, you find.

– Caroline Knapp

bunny

1994

PROLOGUE

A doorbell rings. Silas scampers to the front door. Lou Lou inhales deeply. She is all too aware of his incessant pacing from the master bedroom, but she's at her vanity mirror and eyeliner doesn't apply itself. Polished floorboards creak as small feet thump over them. Lou Lou flicks her wrist upwards – the perfect cat eye again. It may not bring in any income, but if Lou Lou knows anything, it's how to look fuckable. She stares at herself in the mirror and exhales. If she'd been more ambitious, she could have been a movie star. She takes a moment to enjoy herself, to enjoy how beautiful she feels. *Let him wait.*

Adjusting an oversized melamine bangle and holding on to a gin and soda that's already taking effect, Lou Lou strides down the hallway like a woman who knows how to walk in six-inch heels, knowing that it's going to be the same shit with Silas again. Being a single mother in her late twenties is a fate Lou Lou can almost not bear to endure – if it hadn't been for Bunny, she's sure she would have strangled Silas with the cord of her beloved Conair hairdryer by now.

As she approaches the front door, a spindly child's body covered in happy dinosaur–print pyjamas tries in vain to block her departure. His six-year-old arms reach out towards the walls on either side of him as if to brace himself, but they're too short to touch both sides.

Lou Lou is momentarily struck by the endearing, almost amusing quality of a child assuming such a dramatic pose.

And it is endearing.

Except for the child's eyes, clearer and more piercing than normal. Anger and guilt twist in Lou Lou's gin-filled gut.

'Mom, please don't go tonight,' he says with quiet urgency. '*Please*.'

Silas looks at his mother, dressed again for a night out with men. Lou Lou drains her highball glass and deposits it on a side table as she sashays towards him. She sighs heavily and purses her lips. For her, this whole motherhood game has already had too many innings.

'Sweetheart, Mommy deserves her playtime too sometimes, and tonight is Mommy's playtime. Okay?' Her tone is warm, but there's a brittle quality to it.

'But Mom . . .' Silas's eyes dart towards the hallway behind Lou Lou, checking for *her*. 'I'll be alone.'

'Silas, darling, you're not alone. Your Aunt Bunny is here. Okay?' Lou Lou ends the conversation with syrupy finality. He's a child with an imagination that finds monsters in the most serene of surroundings. She knows that life will knock her sensitive boy sideways more than a few times and because of that she wants to provide comfort when he needs it. She also wants to get to the fucking door. Her jaw tightens as she watches his eyes slip to the wooden floorboards between her feet.

'But Momma, she's sad tonight, and she acts different when she's sad and nobody's looking.'

'Enough, Silas!' Lou Lou's voice flashes like a cold white thunderclap.

Silas drops his arms to his sides. His fingers squeeze his thumbs into his fists as his shoulders hike up protectively. His gaze is frozen on a knot of wood in the floorboards. He's stared at this same knot many times before when Lou Lou has left for one of her 'dates' (sometimes she'd come back in the middle of the night, sometimes she'd come back two days later). If he stares at the knot long enough and softens his gaze, its swirling imperfections morph into a rosebud.

'Jesus, Silas, you wanna pull this shit every time I go out?' Lou Lou doesn't wait for an answer from him. 'Go to your room. Go to bed. Get!'

Silas stays put, gauging the right time to move; too early or late and there might be consequences, especially after Lou Lou puts down a few too many empty glasses.

A softly slurred voice from down the hall caresses the tension. 'Relax, Lou. It's fine.' Out of a doorway drifts the owner of the soft voice – Farrah Fawcett's doppelgänger cradles her own gin and tonic in a coffee mug while her fingers lightly rub a delicate gold crucifix around her neck.

The voice soothes Lou Lou like a magic incantation.

'Let me take him,' she says as she steps forward to end Lou Lou's frustration.

Silas, defeated, allows his mother to steer him towards the woman, who stops toying with the crucifix and rests her hand on Silas's left shoulder. Lou Lou ruffles his brown locks before gently resting her hand on his right shoulder.

Dwarfed by two women who resemble models that have just stepped off a *Vogue* cover shoot, Silas looks like he's being blessed in a revivalist church, where the only nice clothes in the congregation belong to the pastor.

'You see how much your Aunt Bunny loves you, Silas?'

Bunny's hand feels feather soft. Lou Lou's fingers slowly press harder into his shoulder blade until he replies, 'Yes, Mom.'

Bunny smiles down at him. 'Come on, we'll watch TV.'

The doorbell rings again, causing both women to release their grip on his tiny frame.

'Coming!' Lou Lou calls, sounding just as sweet as pudding. She whirls around and opens the door as if she's winning an award. Outside stands a man chewing gum and smelling like Old Spice and three one-night stands spaced over a month. He ignores Silas and raises his eyebrows in greeting to Lou Lou and Bunny. 'Things okay? Heard yelling.'

'Don't ask. Let's go, hon,' Lou Lou says as she leaves, slamming the door shut behind her.

Bunny looks down at him and smiles as Silas's eyes crawl up to meet hers. Her face falls into a grin that reveals the gap in her front teeth. He fixes his gaze on the gap as it exposes a sliver of her increasingly pickled tongue, and feels overwhelmed by vertigo. His peripheral vision picks up her lacquered red nails impatiently dancing along the rim of the mug.

Silas knew that when Mom and Bunny had their 'drinks' at night-time, this meant that he had to be quiet because they were 'very tired'. Their drinks were different to his – sometimes he sneaked a sip when they left their glasses to answer the phone.

In it was what looked like water, but with tons of ice and a piece of lemon with fizzing bubbles that floated to the top. It reminded him of the NYC snow globe his father had bought him before he left. In the centre of the globe was a girl with a red jacket forever skating; if you shook the globe in an angry way, her face disappeared behind the trapped snow.

But Aunt Bunny got so sad sometimes after her drinks. It was a different kind of sad and happened only when Mom wasn't at home to be with her. One time he followed her, and she kept checking rooms as if she had lost something important. She stopped in the hallway like a compass that couldn't find north and when he looked up at her face, her eyes looked straight through him and seemed to gaze through the floor behind him – down into the earth and out the other side of the world.

'What are you looking for?'

She jumped in fright like she didn't know he was there, even though he was right in front of her. That's when she dropped her glass and started crying. Then laughing in a way that sounded sick in his ears. Then screaming. Silas cried and tried not to move.

And that's what he's afraid of happening tonight.

She looks okay at the moment though, standing in the doorway, smiling down at him.

She caresses his hair as she shepherds him into the lounge. These moments are the ones that confuse him and make his stomach feel twisted, because right now, he feels safe. Loved, even . . . But then there's that *other* feeling there too.

Silas wants to go back to his room, but he's too nervous to ask permission, so he sits on the couch and watches TV – a rerun of an old *Baywatch* episode that Silas has seen before. One of the lifeguards is possessed by a ghost so the other lifeguards try and help her. The possessed lifeguard is a pretty blonde woman named Summer.

Bunny drains her mug, hops onto the couch next to him and twirls one of Silas's brown curls around her finger. He fixes his eyes on the TV and pulls his knees up under his chin, clasping his arms around them. She reaches out and gently tickles his ribs with her finger. He can't help but squirm. The phantom of a smile floats over his face, but he's still artificially engrossed in the TV.

Summer is about to jump off a balcony with a man who loves her, but he's actually a ghoul.

Bunny tickles Silas again. His eyes flick towards her for a moment but he wills them back to the TV. He's practised in this now.

Summer hasn't jumped, but the man has. He's falling.

Bunny's finger finds a new spot on his ribs. He lets out a little *peep* as he squirms again. A shy smile breaks through. *Maybe she's okay tonight.*

'Finger wiggles, Silas giggles,' she says in a sing-song fashion.

'Stop!' He chuckles as he squirms.

'Finger wiggles, Silas giggles.'

'Bu-nny!' He squeals in delight as he rocks away from her tickles.

Silas closes his eyes and laughs as he tries to stop Bunny tickling him. Her finger freezes for a moment: he feels it become stiff and straight. Then Bunny's finger drives into his ribcage with such force that he slides sideways along the couch cushions. A sharp, searing pain tears across his ribs. He can feel Bunny's nail dig into the soft flesh between two ribs like a Roman spearhead. He howls and scuttles backwards into the opposite corner of the couch, clutching at his side. Hot tears of pain and surprise blur his eyes.

Bunny is frozen, finger still outstretched like a lance. She's looking at him dumbly, almost empty. A muddy mixture of fright and malice tumbles over her face; two flashing sides of a spinning coin. She examines her finger as if realising for the first time that it's part of her body. She looks back at him confused – sheepish, even. Silas clamps a hand over his ribs and holds his breath in terror. They regard each other like two statues in the flickering light of the television.

Bunny's gaze drifts in thought; he watches her mind slowly turn inwards and shut out the world as she gradually rises and floats out of the room. Her near-silent footfall sounds like a solitary dry leaf rustling away down the hall.

Silas holds his breath for as long as he can, but his galloping heart demands air and his mouth springs open. Ragged, heaving breaths burn down his throat as he tries to remain quiet and stifle a sob.

She's walked into the kitchen this time. He hears her opening drawers then banging them shut – jangling metal objects collide in her search. He lifts his pyjama shirt to discover a fresh bruise surrounding an angry red crescent between his ribs. A tear of blood crawls down the gentle dunes of his ribcage and into the waistband of his pyjama pants. From the kitchen comes the crisp sound of a cork popping out of a bottle. Soft footsteps approach; he drops the shirt over his ribs and presses the cloth to soak up the blood.

Bunny rounds the corner of the doorway, carrying a freshly opened bottle of wine. She fills her mug to the brim before nestling herself back into the corner of the couch. She hikes her knees up to her chest to mirror Silas before turning her face to watch him.

Silas's young mind can't read the expression on her face. She seems to be warily examining him, as if he is now some foreign thing. Bunny empties her mug in one long drink. Silas huddles his back into the couch and tries to focus on the TV screen. He can't follow what he's watching. The only visual he can discern is multiple children dancing and their elation: *Rice Krispies! Snap! Crackle! Pop!*

Silas glances back at Bunny; she returns the favour. Her eyes are foggy, like the bathroom mirror when Silas has finished with his bath – lingering condensation needing to be wiped clean. The only part of her that moves is her thumb and forefinger as they twirl the crucifix around her neck. She twirls it until the gold chain looks like a glistening rope, a rope that is slowly creeping from her décolletage to her throat like a tiny noose. He thinks he hears her whisper. But when he turns to her, her mouth is shut.

The waning adrenaline in his body slowly turns him into lead. His ribcage aches as his eyelids droop, lulled by the soft shapes of the television dancing before them, and without him realising, they close . . .

A staccato rhythm of noise and silence gently nudges Silas out of sleep. He turns over, returning his gaze to the TV, and the small movement re-ignites the pain in his ribs. It's changed from a raw, sharp pinpoint to a wide, dull glow. His eyes float open, sensing a change in the lighting. The rhythm of noise and silence is also one of light and darkness. His brain pieces it all together. His eyes focus as his head scans the room.

The lights are off. Not just in the lounge, but in the entire house.

Darkness except for the TV switching ON, OFF, ON, OFF; *Kramer is yelling and Jerry is calming him down . . .* they disappear . . . *Jerry is confused and Elaine is yelling . . .* they disappear again.

A finger of glowing moonlight shines in through a crack in the floral drapes, breaking up the darkness with timid illumination.

Silas turns to the opposite end of the couch. Aunt Bunny isn't there, but her mug is, and so is the bottle. Both are empty now. A tiny movement draws his attention to the hallway entrance. His eyes are unable to see what it is in the near-dark.

He squints from the corner of the couch. *What is it? It's*

almost ceiling height. It moves. The TV switches on again, bathing the room in pale light, just enough for him to see the start of the hallway. In the top corner, near the ceiling, a hand holds the TV remote. Something behind the hand catches a glint of reflected light from the television screen. It's the top half of Aunt Bunny's face.

'Playtime,' she whispers.

The TV turns to black as her hand releases the remote, sending it tumbling to the wooden floor. It erupts in a fountain of batteries, but before the batteries have time to clatter onto the floor, manic giggling erupts as bare feet thump down the hall. Silas hears her swinging open another door and pounding through it.

A thought creeps through his mind. *She was almost up to the ceiling. How did she get so high up?* His body is moving without him needing to drive it. Some deep part of him with the voice of a man speaks in his head. *You need to hide now, hide now, Silas.* He listens to the grown-up voice.

He edges towards the doorway and peeps down the hall. There's no crack in a curtain to let any moonlight in here. The light switch is further down the hall on the opposite wall. He creeps into the black hallway and is overwhelmed by powerlessness. He had the same feeling once when Lou Lou took him to New Jersey one summer and he got caught in a rip current. He had swum too far from the shallows and as the water pulled at his legs and turned him away from the shore, he realised he might not be alone in the inky blue abyss below him . . .

He reaches the light switch and flicks it on; his happy dinosaur–print pyjamas appear almost fluorescent under the brightened light. At the end of the hallway passage is a flight of stairs leading up to the second floor, and at the other end is the kitchen, bedrooms, an unused sewing room and the front door. The door to the kitchen, where Bunny ran into, is open. It's the heart of the house and has adjoining doors to other rooms. *Listen for her. You're safer if you know where she is*, the grown-up voice says inside his head. Silas stands still and listens.

'Wha!' Bunny's head pops out of a far doorway like a jack-in-the box, then disappears again. Silas hears her giggle as bare feet slap away through an adjoining doorway.

NOW. Silas vaults up the stairs two at a time. He whirls around to close the door. *No, she'll know you're in here if you close the door. Give her more places to look.* He leaves it open and dives towards his bed. *Not the bed, it's the first place she'll look. The dresser. Under the dresser.*

Downstairs, bare feet thump across the floor, weaving from room to room. A crow of manic laughter rises through wooden floorboards. Silas crawls towards the dresser, a hulking thing on thick wooden legs, with claws that look like eagles' feet carved at the bottom. He twists himself underneath its protective girth, breaking through cobwebs to reach the back, as far from the edges as he can get.

The pounding downstairs stops.

In his mind, Silas sees a feral black dog with blood-matted hair, catching a scent.

He hears Bunny run up the hall. She's on the stairs, up the stairs. *It sounds like four legs instead of two.* From under the dresser he can't see the doorway but feels her pass. She's in Lou Lou's room now.

She's running in circles, faster and faster like the stone in David's sling preparing to tear skin and splinter bone. Silas's small body tries to grow smaller, to sink into the wall behind him. Bunny launches out of Lou Lou's room, ricochets off the walls and into his. He watches her feet sprint past the dresser as she tears open the closet with an ecstatic howl. She pulls his clothes off their hangers and tears bags from shelves. She claws the back of the closet where he would have hidden. Slivers of yellowing wallpaper fall to the floor. Bunny wails, dives to the floor and scampers to the edge of the bed, delightedly tearing the covers aside as she pokes her head underneath them.

'No,' she says to no one. Her head slowly retracts from under the bed. She stays on her hands and knees. Silas watches from the gloom under the dresser. Her feathered hair sways in front of her face as she rocks back and forth on her haunches.

The rocking stops.

'I see you.'

It's barely a whisper. He almost doesn't hear it.

'I see you . . . I see you,' she says, louder, clearer, faster.

Bunny slowly turns her head towards him. Silas glimpses a glinting blue eye through the blonde hair covering her face.

'I see you, I see you, I *see* you.'

Her head turns until two eyes bore into him from across the room. They're not her eyes; they're the same colour and shape, but they're not *her* eyes.

Silas pulls his pyjama top over his face to hide from them.

His body shudders as he stares at the flannel weave in front of his eyes. The happy dinosaurs morph into a colourful cacophony of distorted shapes – a putrid kaleidoscope of fear.

'I see you.'

The link between his eyes and those eyes isn't broken by the cheap discount fabric between them.

'I see you.'

He squeezes his eyes shut so tight that his eyebrows feel they may cramp. It works. The connection is broken. Her voice stops. The room fills with silence.

He has a headache from not breathing. He needs to breathe normally but first he must check. He slowly pulls the fabric from over his closed eyes. It slides down from the bridge of his nose and falls to his chest, freeing his mouth. Without his permission, his body steals a small breath. With the top no longer over his face the air is cool and sweet as it washes over his lips.

I'll open my eyes on three.

One . . . two . . .

Silas snaps his eyes open.

'I see you! I see you! I see you! I SEE YOU!' Bunny screams. Silas screams.

Her hands clamp around his arms as she pulls him from under the dresser.

2018

JERRY LEAVES A VOICEMAIL

Silas, early thirties with a leonine mop of brown and grey hair swept behind his ears, sits at a kitset desk, hammering away on a keyboard. The fleshy neon pink drone of John Carpenter's instrumental synth music slithers out of the giant headphones clamped over his ears. The drapes are drawn and a weathered second-hand desk lamp is the only source of light. In the orange halo of its globe lies a cemetery of chewed-up toothpicks in a dish. Silas abruptly stops and frowns at the wall of words on the screen in front of him. Bukowski's impish eyes shine out of his lumpy face from a curling picture tacked to the wall above the screen; the patron saint of writers without an MA. The air has a damp brown quality, like old coffee filters; it's exacerbated by the near-empty glass coffee urn perched atop sundry yellowed paperbacks: *Salem's Lot*, *A Passage to India*, *Ham on Rye*, *Save the Cat!* ®.

A small pit bull–looking rescue mutt rolls lazily onto his back under Silas's chair. Silas's bare foot absently scratches the dog's belly as a moist whistle of air escapes its avant-garde end. He takes another exhausted toothpick out of his mouth and drops it among its fallen brothers before fishing a fresh one out of a cheap plastic container that he swiped from a Chinese takeout restaurant after one too many beers.

He continues reading as he pops it between his lips and begins crushing the pick into soft wooden strings with his teeth.

His eyes are dry, the minute muscles around them tired. The writing, not just today, but months and years before this morning, has been done in stolen time in the derelict hours before the start of a work day in a cascade of meaningless jobs. Silas wrote what bubbled up from the swirling black ocean trenches where his rage and fear lived. He was vaguely aware of a pressure mechanism being vented when he wrote his stories; if he missed too many morning sessions his mind became depressive, (even more) short-tempered, his vocabulary would soften (even further). He'd find himself unable to find the right word in conversation, his mind's eye would see the dustless spot on the shelf in his head where the word had been, but some fucking guy had moved it.

If I didn't write and if I hadn't met you, I'd be dead or in prison, Rosie, he often told her. Rose would smirk and roll her eyes and play air-violin. Then lightly kiss him. Her way of bringing brevity to his maudlin pronouncements . . . However true they might be.

The door cracks open. Fresh air and morning sunlight invade the bolt-hole office. The mutt below him springs up and greets the woman standing in the doorway. She is wearing scruffy activewear that over the past six months has morphed into her pyjamas. She bends down and cuddles the little guy.

'Goober! Poor baby, how long has Dad kept you locked in his stinky room?' Rose says.

Silas places the headphones round his neck.

'Part of that is his fault. I think I can taste dog food.'

'How long?'

Silas shrugs. 'Long. Couldn't sleep.' He nods at the screen. 'It's good, I think.'

Goober scampers off to check the run-down apartment's perimeters. NYC on a budget is shitty (but at least in Astoria you might get enough space for a dead potted plant).

Rose smiles coyly. 'Jerry left a voicemail.'

'You listen to it?'

'Nope. Should we just call him? Make it a surprise?'

Silas gets up, wraps his arms around her and nods.

She inhales and grimaces at the stale air. 'Oh man, let's do it out here so I stay conscious.' Silas laughs as she leads him out of the room and into the kitchen-cum-dining-room-lounge-entrance-hall-office.

Set out on one corner of the kitchen table is a beacon of order in the cramped chaos, the most methodical work surface in the world. A laptop sits at the perfect right angle to the table top with a purposefully placed notepad next to it. Rose's work station resembles a collage of can-do, high-accomplishing Shutterstock images (while Silas's resembles a cautionary tale of writers who fell in love with the madness of other writers who ended up dishevelled and howling). Definitive points on Rose's notepad are neatly crossed out or highlighted. Notes on notes are written in the margin.

Rose dials a number and places the phone on the table between them as they sit opposite each other. Silas has a pregnant look on his face. Rose takes a deep breath that lasts four counts, a technique her tai chi enthusiast of a therapist once taught her.

It rings twice. The cold-iron voice of an older woman answers, 'Contact Agency. May I help you?'

'Hi Lauren, Rose here. May we speak to Jerry?'

The cold voice instantly warms. 'Putting you through now, sweetheart. Congratulations!'

Rose and Silas ripple with excitement like leaves in a sudden gust. Lauren has never been pleasant to them before.

'Uh, thank you, Lauren.'

There's a crackle as the call is transferred, as if music were supposed to start playing but doesn't.

Jerry answers, 'You two assholes get my fuckin' message?' His voice sounds like an old boot stuffed full of rocks and dusted with the ash of unfiltered cigarettes.

'We haven't played it yet. What's it say, Jerry?' Silas beams at Rose.

'Haven't played it yet?' Jerry's hamming it up. 'Fuck you, Si, Where's Rosie? I wanna speak t' Rosie.'

Silas rubs his forehead and chuckles. Jerry ass-grabbing like this is a *really* good sign and all three of them know it. However, Silas has heard rumours that Jerry's ass-grabbing isn't just confined to the figurative. The Twitter accusations/sexual harassment lawsuits haven't come for Jerry yet, but Silas and Rose are sure that they aren't far off. (Although Silas also thinks Jerry is probably one of those guys with an exit strategy involving a well-off gated community in Mexico once allegations become likely to arise.)

'I'm right here, Jerry,' Rose says.

'Oh, thank Christ, the brains. Now, Rosie, listen to me carefully. This is important.'

'Okay, Jerry, I'm listening.'

'Marry me. Silas is no good. He's no good, Rosie.'

Silas and Rose smirk. Jerry's already told them what they wanted to know.

'I don't get to say these words often enough to people, so bear with me, kids, but I gotta actually say them for my own ego.'

'Shoot,' says Silas (when what he wants to say is, *get to the fucking point, Jerry!*).

'They love the script and want to buy it. Paying two hundred against one hundred. There it is.'

'Thousand?' asks Rose.

'Thousand,' says Jerry.

Shit.

Silas and Rose erupt in a silent scream and dance resembling a frantic Martha Graham masterpiece, if Martha were on meth. Goober jumps up on his hind legs and joins in. Rose holds his front paws and dances with him while Silas tickles his belly. His tail whips the air madly.

Jerry continues, 'You've hit the fuckin' jackpot, kids. I know these guys. The guy giving notes isn't a writer, but he knows how to write. Okay?'

The dancing ceases; Goober barks in protest. Silas shushes him.

Rose hesitates. 'What are you saying, Jerry?'

'So, they want an extensive rewrite. They pay you *after* that happens. It's cheeky, but this is your first script sale. Ya gotta expect to get editorially fucked in the ass a bit. Look at it this way: when you eventually get paid, that's what all the money is for.'

Silas watches Rose deflating. He can tell she's imagining

herself forever locked into working the complaints department at Oko-Help. The one time she was bedridden with flu (but still forced to log in remotely), Silas overheard her on her headset trying to explain to an irate customer that she could not 'refund a $4.99 second-hand perm kit' as firstly, it was second hand, and secondly the thirty-day money-back guarantee had lapsed six months back. He wanted to reach through the phone when he heard Rose politely asking the rampaging hillbilly to refrain from threatening language.

Silas waves a hand in front of Rose to catch her eye and points to a large, neatly printed note nestled among old bills on the fridge door:

IF YOU WANT ARTISTIC INTEGRITY, PREPARE TO WRITE A BOOK THAT NOBODY WANTS TO READ.

Rose frowns at the reminder, then wearily nods in agreement. 'Whatever they want, Jerry. What are the notes?'

'I'll send 'em over. They don't wanna touch the bones of the thing. Most are focused on making the story a little bit more, uh . . .' Jerry searches for the right word.

'Marketable.' Rose beats him to it and spits it out like toothpaste foam. 'Younger lead, tits and ass and a wacky sidekick. Fuck. Am I wrong?' Of course she's not.

'Maybe not the sidekick, but in that ballpark, yeah.'

'Can't they just make it the way we wrote it?' Rose asks dreamily.

All three chuckle sardonically.

'How long do we have?' Silas asks.

Jerry rips the Band-Aid off. 'Three weeks from today.'

Silas snorts as he flops down into a window-sized square of morning sunlight on the floor.

'Then they pay us?' asks Rose, the open-plan online retail hellhole becoming more and more of a distant memory.

'Then they pay us,' confirms Jerry.

Goober saunters over to Silas and lies his small, furry head on his chest. It rises and falls with Silas's breath.

Rose leans on the table and does the talking. 'Okay. Okay. Send over their notes and we'll make it work.'

'Fuckin' A you will,' exclaims Jerry in his Al Capone gangster growl. 'See ya in a few weeks with a check, kids. Bye.'

Rose ends the call looking like it's going to be a long few weeks. She leans over the table. 'What are my boys up to down there?'

'Nothing. We're dead,' Silas says as sunlight hits his freckled arms. Goober's wagging tail thumps against the wooden floor in agreement.

Rose shuffles over to her boys and lies down. Goober, sandwiched between them, blissfully drifts off. Silas lays an arm over Rose's shoulder and cups her breast through her top. Silas has always admired the fact that Rose's breasts fit perfectly in the palms of his hands. This instils in him a naive security that the universe, in some aspect, has designed him and Rose for one another. A fanciful thought at best, but one that soothes him.

'We're gonna have to quit our jobs to make the deadline,' Rose whispers.

'I know.' Silas gently squeezes her breast.

'We won't make rent next month.'

'Nope.' He shifts his hand so her nipple catches between

his fingers. Gently, he brings them together. 'Guess we should say goodbye to the apartment properly?' he asks with hope in his voice.

'Si, be serious.' Her nipple is stiffening despite her protests.

'Don't tell me what to do, boss-lady – me an' my girl just sold a screenplay.'

Silas gets up and scoops Rose off the floor and over his shoulder. He marches to the bedroom. 'Goob, stay out here. Mom and Dad have a very important meeting.'

Goober doesn't stay but tries to jump on Silas. 'Sorry, Goob.'

'Stay, Goob.' Rose laughs as she closes the bedroom door behind them.

Goober watches the door click shut and heaves the sigh of a dog unceremoniously and gravely wronged – MomDad pulls this trick from time to time. He lingers for a moment, weighing his options, then trots back to the kitchen/lounge, deciding he will raise whimpering hell in a little while if he is still barred entry. He notes the warm square of sunlight on the floor, walks over, plops down into it, and rolls onto his back to warm his belly.

Silas kisses Rose's eyelids with the naked male tenderness reserved for post-coitus. He rolls off her and onto his back.

'That was fast,' she says good-naturedly.

'Economical,' he corrects her.

He reaches over and hands her a fresh towel from a pile of unfolded laundry.

He lies back and lets the sagging mattress take the full weight of him as he feels reality reassert itself like a brick through a window.

'We'll have to move in with my mom for a while.'

Rose inhales and pinches the bridge of her nose.

'Would you be okay with that?'

'Have to be.'

He stares up at the ceiling as (without himself registering it) his hand glides over a faint white crescent scar between two ribs.

'I haven't seen that before,' Rose says, rolling onto her side.

'What?'

'That.' She rubs the scar with her finger, a small white keloid with the smooth texture of silk.

Silas regards it. 'Hmm, kid stuff I guess.'

'Your mom's place, huh? You know, if we sold everything, we could go to Puerto Rico. My mama would make us warm farina in the morning.'

'Your mother hates dogs.'

'Goober could go in a kennel.'

'Excuse you?'

'Three weeks max.'

'That sounds expensive.' Silas contemplates their current finances. He knows they can ill afford two return plane tickets to Puerto Rico and a boarding kennel for their son.

Silas is all too aware that since Hurricane Maria, Rose has been supposed to be sending money back, not returning to Caguas with her broke boyfriend in tow. He is also aware that Rose has purposefully forgotten to mention that she is living with Silas out of wedlock.

Silas absently rests his hand over the scar again as he speaks. 'Hate to say it, but let's pack, drive up tomorrow. Throw away anything that won't fit in the car. The landlord's gonna keep the deposit but we'll have enough for a few weeks. Not including Valium for us and regular offerings to the gin twins.'

He rolls over and nuzzles Rose's neck. *Reassurance, reassurance, please God reassurance.* A moment of hesitation hangs between them before Rose begins drawing on Silas's back with her index fingernail. *Good, she's okay . . . A house, she's drawing a house*, he guesses without saying it aloud.

'Write, get paid, find a new place and never look back. Plan?'

'Plan,' she confirms. With a muffled whimper, Goober politely demands entry through the closed bedroom door.

THE ROAD HOME

The car interior possesses that icy, early-morning chill that cars have before the engine (or the bodies inside) warm them up. They finished packing late yesterday, and grabbed four hours of sleep before they dropped the apartment keys in the mail slot and piled into the car.

Silas's tired hands shift over the cracked rubber steering wheel while Rose sleeps in the passenger seat in an entanglement of contorted comfort, her feet propped up on a duffel bag stuffed into the footwell. Goober's nose peeps out between the seats from the back, where his small body shares space with an assortment of boxes and his favourite tartan fleece blanket.

Later, Queens!

Rosie and Goob are still in a near-comatose state as Silas pulls into a city-limits 7-Eleven parking lot for a much-needed industrial-sized 7-Eleven coffee. His bleary eyes and dry, early-morning mouth demand this black tar in his empty belly. Rose can't drive (he teases her about being a *real* New Yorker whenever it comes up) and he needs to stay awake.

Am I the only one who misses BUNN coffee urns? his tired mind ponders as the fancy self-service barista machine grinds his double espresso shot. The thought of the unpretentious old urns, coupled with his antiquated sensibilities, descend him into scenes in Tarantino diners full of red-herring dialogue and Baltimore mornings, where cops in *The Wire* pour bad coffee over worse hangovers. An ungodly beeping rips his attention back to the espresso machine as it signals that his diminutive cup of coffee is ready. The pixellated Italian flag animation dancing on the selection screen reminds him of the nightmarish plasticity of the century in which he finds himself. The mewling offer of a prize (if he posts a picture of himself and his coffee) with the hashtag *#SippinWith7* doesn't help matters . . .

He pays at the counter and his drifting eyes spot an old BUNN in the cupboard-sized office behind the clerk – retired from public service and happily glowing a single red LED switch with half a pot of midnight-black drip on the warming plate. The clerk, who looks like he's been working here since the movie *Clerks* premiered, follows Silas's gaze behind him. He walks into the back room, fills a fresh large takeaway cup to the brim, returns without a smile and slides it over the counter.

'Keep the faith, brother,' the old clerk grunts.

'Amen,' Silas says appreciatively to his fellow java-luddite as he cradles the drip coffee. The old clerk grabs the faux-Italian espresso and picks up a small bin behind the counter. As Silas leaves he hears the clerk mumble 'overpriced shit' as he pitches it into the back of the bin.

Silas sips from his cup and lowers his foot onto the tired accelerator pad. The road ahead morphs from working-class suburbs to industrial areas and, finally, into interstate highways.

He imagines floating high above the car and watching it leave the city lights behind, as the old Toyota crawls through the pre-dawn shadows towards the dark, rolling hills of the north east.

In this car is everything in the world that he loves.

WELCOME HOME, SILAS

The sun glares into the car. *Lunchtime? It feels like dinner time*, Silas thinks. The 7-Eleven was hours ago and the coffee in his empty stomach hurls acidic somersaults around his belly.

Rose woke with the mid-morning sun pulsing in her eyes as the light chased the car through the tall pines that crowded the road on both sides. With no time to lose she began paging through script revision notes – which largely consist of Silas's illegible Post-its. They joust over how to make the necessary changes, creating almost-arguments followed by hollow silences. Goober cocks his head every time somebody emphatically raises their voice, the little rescue mutt their ever-present audience. Rose's head throbs from the stress of the last few days. She closes her carefully assembled binder full of notes (including the inserted plastic folders required for Silas's illegible Post-it notes) and leans into the headrest.

'I'm starving,' she says. 'It's got to be lunchtime.'

The dashboard clock stopped working well before they bought the car, so Rose fishes her phone out to check.

'Whaaat? It's only ten thirty!'

Silas rounds yet another evergreen bend and peers down the road. 'If I recall, there's a gas station diner about thirty minutes up ahead. I've never actually stopped there before, but it looked fine from the outside.' It was one of those badly placed stations, doomed to be skipped by travellers who were still full from the last stop and too close to the pretty, long-weekend towns ahead to stop again before arrival.

'There! There!' Rose shouts.

Hidden by the angle of the gently curved road stands the entrance to a dirt parking lot with a long building squatting in the shadow of tall trees. There's a single pump and office on one end and an extension, somewhat resembling a diner, stretching along the other. Behind the long building, leaning into the damp hillside, is what he assumes is the proprietor's ramshackle house.

'That's not the one I was thinking of. I've never noticed this place before.' *How could I have missed it? The entrance is hidden on the bend, but still . . .*

'Don't care. Let's eat,' Rose demands.

'It looks closed,' Silas replies hopefully.

'Nope,' Rose chirps, 'there's an open sign and lights on in the diner.'

The open sign bristles with LED lights, many of them long dead.

Silas parks the car in the empty lot and gets out to stretch his cramped calves. The cul-de-sac traps the moist air so that under the pleasant pine-forest smell hangs a faint note of earthy decay. Rose's head pops up on the other side as Goober hops out, sniffs the pine-needled dirt, and tracks a scent before finding the perfect spot to urinate. His back legs swiftly kick pine needles into the air in a direction that has nothing to do with where he actually whizzed. With the ritual completed, he claims the vacant passenger seat.

'Should we bring Goob?' Rose asks.

'I wouldn't do that to our son,' Silas says, frowning at the diner's murky windows. 'I'll crack a window. He'll be fine. Hell, he'll probably be better than us.'

Silas carefully winds down the window. A large crack in the tired plastic handle that has caught both his and Rose's fingers countless times stands as a reminder of his chronic DIY procrastination problem. Goober kisses the lip of the window with his snout, sampling the gentle breeze.

'Let's go get hepatitis,' Silas says cheerily.

Inside, the diner expands into a fifties art-deco lunchroom with eighties fixtures forced upon it. The discombobulating interior design suggests someone got part-way through a soft refurb before losing the will to live. The only unifying features are the small brown fly spots dotted along the edges of the light fittings.

What appears to be a mechanic in a kitchen apron walks over to a booth before tossing a plate of something sinister in front of an old man draining the dregs of his coffee from a chipped white mug.

The old man lowers the empty mug back onto the table and flicks it with a grimy fingernail. 'Refill.'

'In a minute,' Mechanic replies sulkily, and shuffles back towards the kitchen. 'Sit wherever, menu's above the counter,' he mumbles over his shoulder at them as he goes.

An old woman perched on a stool in a gloomy corner of the lunch counter holds an empty beer glass with both hands. She spots Silas and Rose, and her jowls wobble and her eyes come alive as a smile contorts her face. She wiggles a silent index finger at them as if she were greeting a child. They reciprocate with raised eyebrows and tight smiles before tentatively sliding into a booth by the window.

The mechanic/fry cook shuffles back. Rose notes he's wearing slippers that look like they got soaked and haven't had enough time to dry. He bangs two battered mugs down and fills them with filter coffee. Silas notes the coffee is poured from his preferred old-school urn. Small victories. The old woman ogles them. She's still wiggling her finger in their direction as she gently bangs her glass on the counter.

'Cut it out, Granma!' Mechanic shouts. He continues staring, waiting for a food order.

'Is she okay?' Rose asks politely.

His eyes float over to Rose. 'Nope. What can I getcha?'

Rose scans the faded chalkboard menu. 'Uh, cheese and tomato on brown please.'

'Only got white.'

'That's fine, thank you,' Rose says sweetly as she attempts to kill the mood with kindness.

Mechanic regards Silas again. 'How 'bout you, bud?'

'Same please, *bud*.'

Fuck. It just came out without him thinking, some knee-jerk antagonistic streak in Silas where if you told him to go left, he turned right without knowing why.

Mechanic cocks an eyebrow, vaguely amused.

'Could we get those toasted, please?' Silas asks, with a grin that he hopes will defuse the tiny fuse he may have just lit. The pregnant moment is interrupted by the old woman gently banging her glass again.

'Granma!' Mechanic shouts.

The banging stops. He turns back to Silas, fuse extinguished. 'Toasted. Yup. They come with fries or salad but we got no salad,' he states before he and his slippers scuff off back to the kitchen.

Rose makes sure that he's gone before leaning over the table. 'Don't be a dick to servers. I was a server.'

'So was I. Guy was rude.'

'Why do you always do that?'

'Okay, sorry.'

The kitchen's saloon door flies open with Mechanic carrying a plate of brown mush to the old woman. Her glass-banging starts up in earnest when she sees him coming. He pries her blue-veined fingers from the glass and she resists rather effectively, as one small finger remains clamped onto the cup handle.

'No. Three mouthfuls. Then you get your refill,' he scolds.

The whole scene plays out like a surreal vaudeville. Silas and Rose attempt their best *not watching* faces.

Mechanic pulls out a bottle of Miller High Life from his apron pocket. The old woman spots the amber bottle and the effect of utter glee is instantaneous. She moans – an almost sexual sound. Mechanic points expectantly at the bowl of mush in front of her. Her eyes flick between the Miller and his face. She scowls and wheezes an obscenity before gulping down a mouthful of mush with a shaky hand, and then two more. Mechanic nods before opening the bottle with an opener hanging from the ceiling on a dirty length of string.

The old woman reaches for her drink with both hands, like a baby given a double-handled sippy cup.

'Wait. You always spill,' Mechanic grunts.

He expertly empties the bottle into the glass, leaving a perfect half-inch of frothy head on top. He finishes it off by dropping in a red and white plastic straw. The glass appears clean until the light catches it, exposing a legion of dirty fingerprints that either indicate that this is Granma's *special* glass or that there's no dishwasher on hand – either seems completely possible. She grips the glass with shaking hands, sucking on the straw until half the glass empties. Silas watches her as she closes her eyes and lets the medicine work through her body. Mechanic walks back to the kitchen, presumably to make their sandwiches. Silas absently wonders when the last time was that he washed his hands.

The old woman's eyes flutter open. She takes a serene moment before retrieving a small bottle from the inside of her coat. Silas can't be sure, but from the clear contents, he presumes it's cheap gin or vodka, in one of those small plastic bottles that liquor stores keep behind the cashier instead of out on the floor, because the only people buying them would almost certainly steal them given half the chance.

The old woman cracks the seal and empties as much of the bottle into the glass as she can. She stirs the drink with the candy cane–coloured straw, never taking her eyes off her concoction. *Perfect*, her eyes say, as she sucks the burning mixture through the straw until the glass is empty.

She promptly tucks the bottle back into her jacket pocket before turning her attention to the young couple. As she locks eyes on Silas and Rose staring at her, a wet gurgling belch erupts. Strings of ethanolic saliva frame the pink corners of her small mouth.

'Jesus Christ, don't look over again,' Silas says quietly as he turns to look out the window.

Goober's silhouette in the car beckons like Lady Liberty.

'Shouldn't be too hard,' Rose says into her coffee.

'Can I get a goddamn refill before hell freezes?' calls the old man from the far booth. He holds up his chipped mug, shaking it like a ringing bell – The Last Town Crier of New England demands a refill. A clatter of utensils and slamming of pans, followed by muffled cursing seemingly answers him from the kitchen.

'Should we just go? This place is a bit much,' Silas pleads.

'We already ordered.'

'Fuck it, I'll leave cash, let's just get –'

They lock eyes and fall silent. There's no reason for them to have stopped talking, other than the same preternatural reflex that makes you turn around when a stranger on the train is staring at the back of your head.

'Welcome home, Silas,' whispers a voice from the end of their table. Rose jumps and spills her coffee; Silas jolts, the hairs on his arms rise. From the back of his mind, Silas feels, rather than hears, a dog barking. It's Goober. The old woman leers at Silas with fascination and childish amusement. She has swiftly and silently moved twenty feet from her perch at the counter to sitting at the head of their booth.

How did she move like that? We only looked away for a second. Was that chair there before? The thoughts race through Silas's head as Rose reaches for the napkins.

Silas blinks at the old woman. 'What? How do you know my name?'

The old woman ponders this for a moment, takes a deep breath, and then belch-vomits an oily brown geyser. The liver-coloured tide washes over the table towards them.

'Jesus!' Rose says, more in fright than disgust. They hurriedly scooch along the cracked vinyl cushions until they hit the window. The acrid smell of juniper berries in stomach acid wafts towards them. *Ah, gin then*, Silas's detached sense of humour confirms. He and the old woman have still not broken eye contact, his body frozen under her gaze.

How does she know my name? his mind screams. Another voice in his head speaks from a deep, quiet place; the calm inner voice that is different to his own; the voice that helped him as a child. He has only heard it in times of distress and he hasn't heard it for a long time, but now here it is again. *You know how, Silas.*

'Oh God, let's get out of here!' Rose levitates from her seat. She's halfway into the neighbouring booth when Mechanic bursts through the swinging doors with the coffee urn. 'Calm down, you've had three refills already, you old bast–'

Silas guesses that Mechanic has most likely seen his grandmother indulge in eccentric behaviours before, but projectile vomiting over the few customers that actually came through the doors is probably a new one. He slams the urn onto the countertop hard enough to slop the coffee. 'Aw Christ, Granma, what now?!' His voice wears the frayed tone of a relative who's been tested one too many times by the family fuck-up.

As Mechanic lumbers towards her, the old woman lifts her trembling hand to her face, as if she has just awoken from a nightmare. She clocks her grandson and whimpers, her small frame overwhelmed with exhaustion. Mechanic rubs his grandmother's back. Out of his apron he pulls out a stained dish rag and tenderly wipes her hands. The attention quietens her.

'How did she get over here?' he growls as he turns his focus to cleaning the vomit off the table, inadvertently spreading it further and onto the cracked booth cushion where Rose was previously seated. Silas slides out of the booth, still transfixed by the old woman.

'She walked over, I guess,' Rose says from the neighbouring booth.

It was a strange question to ask, Silas thinks. The answer is obvious enough. Mechanic closes his eyes with anger: Rose's answer has failed to assuage him. He cocks his head as if he's about to let loose on her, but instead he hooks his arms under Granma's shoulders and drags her out of her seat. She whines like an eighty-year-old woman being manhandled, which is exactly what's happening.

'*Voilà!*' Mechanic barks, presenting his grandmother's legs – or rather, what should have been her legs. Instead, two purple stumps with orb-like ends and puckered white scars peek out from below the hem of her stained, sunflower-print sundress.

Mechanic makes an imperceptibly small but threatening move towards Rose. 'Alcoholic diabetes, lady. Why'd ya fuckin' move her?'

Silas picks up on the small movement and edges between

them. 'We didn't move her. How did she know my name?' he demands flatly.

'What? She don't,' Mechanic says as he lowers Granma back onto the chair.

Silas looks down at the old woman. 'How do you know my name? Why did you say that?' he gently asks her as her unfocused gaze flits around the room.

'She don't know your name. Dunno what you're playing at, but just get the hell out.'

'Okay, okay, we're going – right, Silas?' Rose asks him imploringly.

Silas nods as he follows Rose to the exit. His hand hovers on her back, protectively steering her ahead of him towards the door.

'Hold up there!' bellows Mechanic.

Rose's hand embraces the grimy door handle and begins to turn it. Mechanic holds the vomit-covered rag to his nose as his eyes narrow in on Rose and Silas.

'Did you give her *gin*? Huh?'

He's threatening, not asking, as he strides towards them. Silas calmly raises his hands to interject but Mechanic barrels past him, grabbing Rose's arm. 'Did you?!'

Rose's hand rips away from the door handle, making a *THUNK* that perfectly matches the timing of Silas whipping his fist over Mechanic's shoulder and slamming it into his jaw in a tight hook. *Make it a good one. He's bigger than you.*

His hand feels like he just punched a tractor tyre (and it'll feel much worse later). He knows it's a sucker punch, but the guy's got forty pounds on him, and if you touch Rosie, all rules go out the window.

Mechanic staggers sideways, his fingers grapple with a booth, but his hand slides over the old backrest, sending him falling to the floor. Silas stands over the big man.

'The gin was in her coat. She still has the bottle. People like her, they always find a way. I'm guessing you know that.' His voice shakes more than he means it to. He's unsure if Mechanic heard him, or if he even said the words aloud.

Mechanic's gaze confirms that he did. He wiggles his jaw with his hand, but stays put.

'I'm sorry you have to deal with this bullshit. But we didn't fucking move her,' Silas continues as he motions towards Rose for them to leave. He drops a few bills to cover the sandwiches and the green notes flutter to the floor.

The tyres squeal as they fight to hold on to the road. It's an old car and the tread is light.

Backseat boxes rock left then right as if on a small boat in a storm. Goober eyes a box that leans over him ominously.

Silas flicks his eyes up to the rearview mirror every few seconds. As they round another bend it's hard to discern if anyone is following them. Rose turns to look over her shoulder when she hears a car engine behind them.

'Someone's coming!'

He squeezes the wheel, his forearms pulse, his shoulders hike up.

'Si . . .'

Rose looks over her shoulder again.

Silas's eyes flick up to the rearview mirror. He sees outstretched and overgrown tree limbs hanging over the road.

His foot spasms with tension as he applies further pressure onto the foot pedal. His chest tightens, his eyes sting.

'Si.'

He doesn't hear her.

'Si, you're crying.'

His forearms burn. Rose places a hand on his arm. He flinches at the comforting gesture. He inhales sharply as the car fishtails, kissing the edge of the road. They bounce in their seats as the tyres drop into the dirt, before jumping back up onto the asphalt.

'Silas!'

He registers her panic. His foot edges off the spongy accelerator pedal and his shoulders drop as he pulls over to the side of the road and kills the engine.

Silas hears the engine ticking as it cools. The car behind them passes without slowing and for a brief moment the bored face of the kid looking at them out the rear window resembles a flying, framed picture.

'Jesus Christ, Silas.'

He looks at his bruised knuckles, which are now a deep purple – the old woman's stumps flash through his mind. *Same colour*, he thinks. He releases his fingers from the wheel; they creak open as if he's been carrying an overloaded shopping bag for far too long.

'What the fuck is wrong with you?'

'It's . . . it's just that every time . . . every time I start getting near this fucking place, the carnival opens.'

'So, you want to kill us? Slow down next time.' Her tone is composed, but he can hear the underlying rattle of anger.

'I'm sorry.'

The hush of the pine forest only emphasises the silence in the car; the only definable noise is Goober panting, tongue lolling, probably in relief.

Silas slows his breathing by staring through the windscreen at the trunk of a pine tree.

He turns to look at her.

Her face is granite.

He turns back. 'I hate pine trees.' The thought rolls into his head and out of his mouth. Rose's monolithic silence grows, leaving him to gaze at that pine tree while he considers how close he came to crashing the car and killing everyone. If Rose hadn't shouted when she did and made him slow down... *Once they moved your bodies and the car wreck away, your whole world could have been nothing but a quarter-inch-deep welt in a tree trunk, pal.*

Rose shoves his shoulder. He turns to see her pissed-off face. 'Apologise to Goober.'

Silas reaches out between the seats and gently pulls Goober towards him and onto his lap. He hugs him, instinctively smelling behind his ears. Yip, still smells of puppy after three years. 'Dad's an asshole, Goob. He's sorry he almost crashed the car and killed all of us.' Goober's tail thumps against the dashboard, uncaring as long as he receives a cuddle out of it.

'Nice left hook, by the way. Have you been practising tae bo, psycho boy?' Rose asks as she thaws. Silas takes her hand and kisses the knuckle above where he would one day – soon, he hoped – slide a ring.

After a moment of expiation, Silas frowns. 'You heard her say my name, right?'

He has to check he didn't imagine it.

He looks out at the trees and feels all the memories hiding behind them. Rose regards him, checking over the parts inside him, reading the pressure gauges.

'Yeah,' she confirms in a measured tone.

'We shouldn't do this. Move here, I mean. Something's wrong.' He feels like an idiot saying the words out loud, but there it is. Since the diner, something in his balls, and his gut, and the base of his spine, has been insisting that this is wrong. His mother's house, the neighbouring towns, that creepy fucking diner, are all spread out over a few hundred miles – hardly next door to one another. But the one thing that connects all of them is the forest; their life suspended like a giant web in the dark green sea of trees. 'We should find somewhere else.'

'I'll try to be born on the mainland next time,' Rose says with a wry grin.

Silas flinches. 'Christ, sorry, that isn't what –'

'Oh, shut the fuck up!' She laughs.

A family station wagon drives past them leisurely, at the recommended speed.

'Look,' Rose says, 'that old woman was creepy as hell, but . . . if you . . . if you put things into perspective here, most people feel this way when they go home. Home is a time machine – you step through those doors and you're a kid again.' She reaches out and strokes Goober's back. 'Given your family, frankly I'm surprised you aren't bleeding from the ears right now.'

Silas could feel her gently moving bits and pieces inside him back into their proper places, tightening a loose nut here, resetting a circuit breaker there, moving things back into perspective. They were constant structural engineers for one another (mind you, his machine was a little more troublesome).

'Like you said . . . Three weeks and we're done with the script and then we're out of there.'

He blinks and nods. It's all his nervous system can muster for a response right now. She's right, of course.

Rose picks up the momentum, swinging for the bleachers. 'And there are like five people around these parts. That creepy old lady probably recognised you from twenty years ago somewhere . . . Ex-girlfriend, maybe?'

Goober starts barking. His cuddle has been interrupted by MomDad howling with laughter about something Mom said. Before he knows it, he's gently lifted to his spot on the backseat. Dad makes space again so he can lie down. That box isn't leaning over him anymore. He likes lying down in the back, with MomDad close by. The car starts moving again, and the growly warm hum makes him sleepy and warm. *I love warm*, his pure mind says before his eyelids close.

1994

THE VISITOR

'You wanna pull this shit every time I go out?' Lou Lou shouts from the hall.

Oh gosh, better get out there. Bunny takes a sip of her drink and steps into the doorway.

'Go to your room. Go to bed. Get!' Lou Lou shouts. Her fist jerks into an open rigid surface for slapping. *She wouldn't, would she?*

'Relax, Lou. It's fine. Let me take him,' she says in a soothing voice. Lou Lou turns and gives her a grateful smile as she ushers the little boy towards her. Bunny hates that Silas now looks perpetually terrified around her.

It started a few months ago. They used to be thick as thieves, but now, he seems to avoid being near her. She wonders if it's a developmental thing – maybe too much female energy around? The poor kid has nobody else but two grown women for company most of the time. His father leaving like he did hasn't helped, that's for sure. Originally, she moved in to help support Lou and pick up the slack with Silas while they adjusted, but she and Lou both knew she needed to be there, too.

She had nowhere else to go.

After Jonathan had died, his children – the daughter especially – dropped the act completely; called Bunny 'the trophy wife' at the reading of Jonathan's will. She realised afterwards that yes, she probably had been. She loved Jonathan until the end, but a part of that love had also been for the lifestyle he provided. Of course, she paid in kind for as long as he was interested. And in the years after, she had (mostly) stayed faithful and cared for him.

The daughter, that stupid little cunt, didn't ever see that part, of course (midnight bed-wetting and wild episodes of dementia where Jonathan would occasionally lash out at something unseen and catch Bunny with a wild fist). She chose to see only the much younger, little blonde thing her aging father had acquired. Bunny was sure that all the little bitch ever saw when she looked at her was Anna Nicole Smith on the cover of some tabloid. But Bunny knew that Anna truly loved her sweet old man. And Bunny loved Jonathan.

And then one sunny morning Jonathan Mannerheim, one of the last of the anonymous minor-industrialist millionaires of the last century, died.

And it all went away.

He hadn't put her in the will and she hadn't bothered reading the prenup that, years before, his attorney had casually slid across to her and assured her was 'just a formality'. She tried to speak to the attorney, teary-eyed, just after the reading of the will.

He just smiled as if explaining something to a particularly dense child. *'Sweetheart, I represent the interests of the family, of which you are no longer a part. If you would like to contest the will, you're welcome to call another lawyer. But I'm very good.'*

Bunny was out on her ass at twenty-nine, no qualifications, no discernible skills and no résumé. The only thing she had to show for those eight years of marriage was a small wooden box, pilfered from the bathroom, that held Jonathan's fancy-schmancy cut-throat razor (which she took out of spite, because in life, he had instructed her never to touch it). Oh, but she did still have the contents of an old savings account in her name – opened before she met him – and a portion of the jewellery he had bought her, hidden among her clothes as she packed the single suitcase she had been allowed to take with her. Jonathan's daughter had locked the rest away sometime between his passing and her current expulsion proceedings.

Her savings account – well, she had tossed a few hundred dollars of cash into it here and there when Jonathan gave her pocket money. He'd forgotten he had given her a credit card, so she charged stuff to that and stashed the rest in her Secret Little Account. *I'm a cute little Jessica Rabbit hoarding my nuts*, she used to think as she waited in line at the teller window.

A cold knot had grown in her stomach the afternoon she left Jonathan's house. In the most confronting manner that a family of monied New England WASPs could possibly muster, they kicked her out of the Mannerheim estate via a letter from the family lawyer. A bored cop (or maybe he was private security?) loitered outside with the lawyer as they watched her carrying her belongings down the grand front steps.

An hour later, she was standing in front of a strip mall ATM and for the first time in years, she checked the balance of her Secret Little Account (maybe it had earned a lot of interest?). It took a moment before her balance blinked on screen like the green flat-line on a casualty ward ECG:

$ Not, nearly, enough.00

Her hand found the little gold crucifix around her neck, her very first gift from Jonathan. Nervously, she rubbed it as she stared at the balance. She walked back to her car, an old Lincoln sedan the little bitch had allowed her to take that would turn out not to survive that summer. She climbed in and cried. *Oh, Jessica Rabbit, what do you do now?*

She looked up, saw a liquor store across the parking lot, and clicked into autopilot. *I need a drink.* It sounded like a line from a million characters in a million filler TV shows, but in that moment, it was just fine.

A few minutes later she was back in the car with two bottles: gin and tonic water. Jonathan used to order a drink for her on the rare occasions they went out, and it was always a glass of Chardonnay. She would have bought a bottle of that, but she didn't want to have to buy a corkscrew too – it was 11 a.m. People would have thought she was a drunk.

She knew a 'G & T' was not something a drunk would buy, so she went for that instead. She was sure people would assume she was just picking up supplies for a luncheon or some other social event, but just to make sure, she had said so to the old man behind the counter as she paid. He nodded, unhearing, as he stared at her tits. She had walked back to the car and moved it to a secluded spot in the parking area. She didn't know how to mix a G & T – other people had always done it for her. She hadn't thought to find a glass or cup, so she swiftly took alternating sips from the two bottles and mixed them in her mouth. *Wow, this is a bit different to a glass of wine! Thank gosh the tonic's cold*, she thought after the third slug. By the eighth she was crying again, and by the tenth she was leaning into a payphone and dialling Lou Lou's number from a piece of paper in her purse that she was having trouble reading.

And so, here she was, the live-in babysitter to both Silas and Lou Lou.

The bloodletting in their lives seemed to sync up like two particularly heavy menstrual cycles; around the same time that Jonathan died, Lou's husband pulled a disappearing act of the *'I'm just picking up cigarettes, back in five'* kind.

'Things okay? Heard yelling.'

'Don't ask. Let's go, hon,' Lou Lou says as she steps out the door with her date.

Bunny gently shepherds Silas into the lounge to watch TV. He's pale and silent. She caresses his mousy brown hair and feels him wince slightly under the touch.

She slides onto the couch next to him. The first drink of the night goes before she's even settled in. She pours a generous refill this time. Niki Taylor stares back at her from a glossy magazine on the couch's end table. It was the latest *Cosmopolitan* magazine Lou Lou picked up for sex tips and ineffectual career tidbits. *If I had been five foot eight instead of five foot six then I too could have been Niki fuckin' Taylor on the cover of* Cosmo.

When Bunny was thirteen, her mother's friends would say, *'Oh, you could be a model.'* By seventeen it had turned to *'Oh, you could've been a model . . . if only you were taller.'* So she married rich, and she married young. She felt it was the best (and only) career choice she had ever made.

I know what to do, she thinks as she settles into drink number three. She gently wiggles a finger against Silas's side. His body stays unresponsive for a moment until he can't take it anymore. He snorts and squirms away, unable to stand up against the tickle. He almost laughs but stops himself. *I'm getting somewhere.*

A few more will break the ice and get the kid smiling again.

'*Finger wiggles, Silas giggles,*' she croons in a sing-song voice.

He squirms and squeals. '*Stop!*' A radiant smile washes over his face as laughter spills out.

He really is a beautiful little boy. His laughter twangs a steel bass string of love in her chest.

'*Finger wiggles, Silas giggles.*'

'*Bu-nny!*' he howls.

There he is, my happy little fellow. His joy is infectious. Whatever was upsetting him will be forgotten or forgiven and we'll be thick as – thick as – as . . .

Bunny's finger hurts.

It feels like she's rammed it straight into a wall. She examines it. No marks or anything, but God, it's really sore. A small movement at the opposite end of the couch draws her gaze: Silas, huddled up against the corner like a kicked puppy. He's shivering, staring at her with blind terror in his wide, tear-filled eyes. *What's that all about? Did he hurt my finger by mistake and feels bad about it? I'll pretend it doesn't bother me, he'll calm down soon.* Sometimes kids blow things out of proportion. If she doesn't make a big deal about it, then he'll know he didn't do anything wrong, and it will all just be less trouble to deal with.

She rises from the couch to get another bottle. Once in the kitchen, she's struck by the emptiness of the house. *Too many dark windows.* Tonight, they all look like little open doors, leading to bad memories. She brings the bottle back to the lounge and sits back down on the couch and pours. She pulls her legs up for warmth and childish comfort, and watches Silas; he's still cowered there, silently watching TV.

Bunny sips her wine and watches the screen – a *Seinfeld* marathon.

'*The roots in the rock wake me. I bite them. The land is dead,*' a voice whispers.

Bunny turns to Silas. Was it him? It's so quiet, it might have been static on the TV. White noise sounds like whatever your mind thinks it sounds like.

'*The land is dead.*' It speaks again.

It wasn't Silas. She watches his mouth – it's closed. He's watching TV intently. She can tell he's pointedly not noticing her looking at him.

The third time she hears it, Silas's eyes flick towards her for just a second as if she has said something. *Not me, kid. TV static.* She fiddles with her crucifix pendant as she lets her mind drift. Her mug empties, she fills it up, her mug is half empty, she fills it up, she leans forward, the mug is full, she drinks, she fills it up, the bottle is empty – another one in the fridge, she fills her mug. Jonathan used to watch *Seinfeld*.

The static interrupts her drifting mind again. She listens for the origins of the sound and notes it descending from the stairs. *I know what it is: Lou left her radio on.* Somewhere between all the refills and her wandering mind, Silas has fallen asleep.

Put him to bed? No, let him be. She stands and stumbles, catching herself on the couch's worn-down arm with a whoopsie-daisy snort.

She walks down the hallway and up the stairs, following the static-like noise. It's like the call of a conch shell willing you to listen to its internal ocean.

She tops the landing and sways lightly, full of wine and warmth. She steps forward and stops, her left toe hovering above the wooden floorboards.

The noise has stopped . . .

The deep, monkey part of her brain squirms. She intuitively knows that upstairs is empty and not empty.

Her heels edge over the lip of the top stair, wanting to step down and run. *Leave, leave, leave*, she thinks, or does she say it aloud?

'*Who's there?*' she whispers.

A sudden gentle pressure on her breastbone forces her to lose balance and fall backwards. She braces for pain – waiting for her body to slam into the wooden staircase below. But something catches her. It squeezes her tight as the lights go out.

'*A visitor,*' it whispers.

2018

SPINACH

Silas turns off the tarmac and onto a ragged gravel driveway that snakes through the trees. Thick pine trunks that are four men wide – the forest here is old – engulf their small car until sparkles of sun flare into Silas's eyes as the trees thin out to a clearing. Nestled in the centre stands a house that resembles a simple cabin, but much larger. Handsome double-storey windows peep out from the unpainted wooden clapboard of the New England saltbox. A large porch stretches the length of the front of the house (which is atypical of the style – Christ knows why or how Silas knows that, but he does).

A lone figure sits on the front porch in anticipation. She stands, waving madly as the car approaches.

'Gird your loins,' Silas mumbles as he pulls up and cuts the engine.

The woman hops down the porch towards them while expertly balancing a highball in one hand.

'Holy fuck, Ms DuBois broke out of the asylum again,' Silas says to himself. Rose, forever on self-imposed diplomacy duty, turns back towards Goob to laugh.

'See that? Down the steps and not a drop spilled,' Silas states with a *bada-bing!* flair. He deals with anxiety by occasionally turning into a poor Rodney Dangerfield impersonator: project enough energy outwards and hopefully nothing gets back through it, and onto you.

Rose gets out of the car and opens the back door. Goober bounds out to appraise exotic scents.

'Darlings!' Lou Lou exclaims. She halts at the car as if she were the lead in *Anthony and Cleopatra* (which she performed in high school – as the lead). 'My God, look at you!' she says, arms outstretched.

Rose swiftly moves to greet Lou Lou as Silas instinctively shirks away from the maternal clinch. She effortlessly falls into the space Silas has vacated like a choreographed dancer, hugging Lou Lou with enough enthusiasm to move them all past the awkward beat. 'Lou Lou, how are you? It's been a while, huh?'

Lou Lou holds Rose out at arm's length and breathes her in. 'Rose.'

'Thank you so much for letting us stay for a while. We really appreciate it.'

'How could I say no? You two stay as long as you need.'

Whenever Rose spends time with his mother (which has only been a handful of times when she has come into the city), Silas is always struck by how every affected utterance seems to be performed for the benefit of some unseen audience. As if at any moment a bullhorn might holler 'CUT!' and a director who talks with his hands too much will appear from behind a tree, mince up to them and suggest that Rose could be smiling *more*, while encouraging Lou Lou to *go even bigger* . . . '*Like sands through the hourglass, so are the days of our lives*' indeed.

Rose is already being gently steered aside so Lou Lou can

get to Silas. 'And congratulations on the writing! I can't wait to read it!'

Silas grimaces – the script is titled *Evisceration* and is about a visiting reporter sharing a last meal with a man on death row (for going to his ten-year high school reunion and killing everyone). Much of the story recounts his dysfunctional upbringing with two alcoholic women in a secluded house in the woods. In the end, the prisoner's last-minute appeal to avoid the death penalty is granted. He celebrates by plunging the steak knife that came with his wagyu beef into his temple.

Silas nods. 'Yeah, uh, when it's finished.' *And when we're living interstate.*

Lou Lou darts her eyes to both Silas and Rose and finally goes in for a full maternal embrace. He hugs her for as short a time as is polite.

'Oh.' Lou Lou leans forward as the hug breaks, before Silas can move away, and she presses her face into his and kisses him on the lips.

Rose looks like she's just seen a person shitting on a sidewalk.

Silas inhales sharply and catches a pungent whiff of gin as Lou Lou exhales; he instinctively recoils. 'What the fuck are you doing?'

'Oh, darling, I had to! You look so much like your father used to. It was like kissing him again . . . before he *changed*.' Her face hardens, her mask slips for just a moment; behind it is a bitter rage, simmered for too long, that has eaten through the iron pot and run out over her soul like molten glass into a vulnerable eye.

'I'm not your ex-husband, I'm your *son*.' Silas has always had a visceral reaction when being pulled into the narrative of his mother's life. How effortlessly she manages to do it. After all these years, he *still* didn't see it coming until he was once again a part of it all.

'Don't do that again.'

Lou Lou seems not to hear him. He knows she did, but her longstanding pathological lack of boundaries has caused the spectrum of behaviour that she deems normal to become so irreparably skewed that it trivialises other people's negative reactions to it. She could knock your teeth out with a brick, then call you melodramatic when you bent down to look for them.

'Last I heard, he was *marrying* that man. By now they're probably both dying of AIDS. *They* get that, you know.'

Silas doesn't take the bait. He has found the trick to surviving is to ignore most things. If you don't, you're likely to exhaust yourself in her whirlwind – which is what she wants: attention at any price.

'Wouldn't know. Last time I saw him, I was six years old, Mom. Remember?' He lets the rhetorical question linger for a while before remembering that that sort of subtlety never works on her. You have to trade bricks for bricks.

Goober trots up to Lou Lou and affably sniffs her foot. She bends down to stroke him. 'Who is this?'

'This is Goober,' Rose says as she kneels and scratches his furry rump. 'We've had him a couple of years now.'

'Wonderful! He's adorable. What breed is he?'

'Not sure,' Rose says, smiling down at the little guy. 'Just a mix from the shelter.'

'Oh.' Lou Lou slowly withdraws her hand. 'How nice.'

Rose looks a tad confused, unsure what the sudden frost is all about.

Silas knows – when he was a kid, the regional animal shelter had filled up and run an adoption drive. Silas had asked if he could get one of the puppies. He promised to take care of it and offered to pay the nominal adoption fee out of his own pocket money.

'We don't take other people's trash,' Lou Lou had said before offering to take him to the pet store in the city. As a small act of defiance, he had feigned total disinterest in having pets after that.

Lou Lou stands and wipes her petting hand on the back of her lime capris.

'Come say hello to your housemate!'

'Wait, what?' Silas stammers.

'Aunt Bunny,' Lou Lou replies as she turns, beckoning them to follow.

Silas steps ahead of her. 'Mom, Bunny better still be living in the lake cabin.'

'No, no, the cabin burned down last winter. I told you,' she says placidly.

'No, you didn't.'

'Of course I –'

'*No*. You didn't.'

The only reason Silas even considered coming to the house with Rose and Goober in tow was because Bunny was in the cabin on the lakeshore. Away from the house. Away from them. Away from him.

A few hundred yards from the house, the terrain begins a gentle decline to a lake, where a small cabin once huddled on the shore. The lake itself is appropriately named Long Lake, as it is not much wider than a football field in most parts. It stretches north and snakes its way up the valley for approximately ten miles before braiding into tributaries. The southern end is near the house and cabin, then it slowly widens to a teardrop surrounded by reed-covered wetlands. Although narrow, the lake is deep, reflective and remains cold all year; partly due to the pines surrounding its edges keeping it shaded for much of the day. The cabin started life as a boat shed, but was little used when Silas's father was there – and not at all after he left. Years ago, Lou Lou put an end to the small boat inside by filling it with all the belongings Silas's father had left behind, dousing it in gasoline, and pushing it out towards the middle of the lake before drunkenly screaming homophobic slurs at it. Then she fired roman candles at it until she finally managed to hit it. Silas's ol' dad received the first and probably only pre-humous hillbilly-Viking burial.

There are no other structures on the lakeshore as it is, frankly, not a very pleasant place to be. Fishermen and duck-hunters tend to frequent other lakes in the region as Long Lake is inexplicably devoid of the usual fauna – and the dense reeds mean mosquitoes in summer. In Silas's final year in high school, Bunny had abruptly insisted she move out to the cabin. Lou Lou indulged her, which, after viewing a segment on *Oprah* starring Nate Berkus, prompted new flooring and a mains power line that was run out to the boathouse by local tradesmen with an aversion to civil paperwork and permits. Silas had welcomed the move.

With Bunny ensconced in the ex-boathouse – now more Swiss chalet than cabin, thanks largely to Lou Lou's divorce settlement money that paid for the design challenge – Silas saw appreciably less of Bunny.

Lou Lou would sit most evenings with her in the new cabin and drink. Silas spent his final year before college blessed with bubbles of solitude in the main house. It was in one of those precious bubbles that he had decided he would leave home on his final day of high school. He took a rucksack of clothes to school with him and called Lou Lou from the bus stop, a one-way ticket to New York City safely secured in his front jeans pocket.

'I'm *sure* I told you about the fire,' Lou Lou says, with great concern.

Silas slowly shakes his head and holds her gaze.

'Well, last winter,' she begins, 'last winter there was a fire.'

'Where did it start?'

'We don't know what happened.'

'Well, what did the fire department say?'

'Oh no, we didn't call them, it burned out on its own,' Lou Lou says as if she's discussing whether she prefers peach or pecan pie. 'It happened at night. I didn't see it burning. I woke up in the morning and Bunny was out in the backyard; she was sitting in the snow, just staring at the smoke.

She'd been out there for hours, poor thing didn't want to wake me.'

Silas looks over at Rose. Silas can see she's willing him with her eyes to stay calm.

'She's living in the house again,' Silas says to himself.

Lou Lou mistakes it for a question. 'Yes, in her old room.'

'Across the hall from my room.'

At his sides, his hands are alternately balling into fists and opening wide like he's working two giant, invisible stress balls. *I'm gonna get Rose and Goober back in the car and drive in any direction away from this place until the gas runs out.*

The car keys are in his hand and he's drifting back to the driver's door when Lou Lou speaks again:

'She'll be quiet, darling. She spends most of her time gardening now.' Lou Lou blinks back tears – hard to tell if they're crocodile or not. 'She isn't the same as she was when you left us, Silas. She's had a problem with drink for a long time now.'

Silas's eyes flick down to the perspiring glass in Lou Lou's hand. She notes the glance and shifts self-consciously before continuing, 'You might get a shock when you see her. She won't be how you remember. The doctor says she has liver failure, but she won't stop drinking. She's in a bad way.'

'She must be thrilled,' Silas says. *She's been trying long enough.*

Bunny has casually threatened suicide for decades; at least annually, while Silas was still living there, a morning would start with a trail of congealed blood from the kitchen drawer where the carving knives were kept. The morbid trail would stain the wooden floor that led to her closed bedroom door. She would invariably be found in an alcoholic stupor with superficial vertical cuts up the inside of her arms. Pre-teen Silas had been horrified by these mornings. Late-teen Silas had stoically cleaned up the dried blood while Lou Lou wailed unintelligibly before retreating for a long walk through the pine trees.

'Son, it's a disease.'

Rose walks up to him and gently rubs calm into the small of his back before he moves the situation from awkward to unbearable. 'I'm sure it will be fine. I'm looking forward to meeting her,' Rose says diplomatically.

Lou Lou brightens at the olive branch. She wheels back around, beckoning them to follow as she trots ahead. 'Coo-ee! Bunny!'

Silas won't admit it, but deep under all the other feelings is a kernel of iron-taste-in-mouth fear of seeing the woman again. It has been almost thirteen years, almost as long as he lived in the house with her. Once he'd left, Lou Lou had had to come out to the city if she wanted to see him. He always had an excuse for not coming back.

They follow Lou Lou to the beginning of the gentle slope at the back of the house to find a terraced vegetable plot, roughly an acre in size.

Lou Lou respectfully stops a few feet from the rows. 'Best to stop, let her come to us. She's very particular about her garden,' she whispers reverently.

'Technically, it's not really *her* garden,' Silas mumbles. Rose stares him down before pinching his arm.

The garden's size is impressive, but what's more impactful

is the bizarre state of it, rows upon rows of spinach – it's the only crop planted. It grows tall, but looks unwell. The colour is green, but diffused, like the crop has been fed bleach instead of water. The earthen lanes between rows are a carcinogenic mulch of countless cigarette butts, all burned down to the charred filter. Empty gin bottles hang from the boughs above to chase away birds, like a crib mobile for adults who enjoy a tipple. The garden looks like an overgrown garbage heap with the gravity turned off. At the bottom of the slope stands a grimy, bald mannequin. *Fucking weird scarecrow.*

'Coo-ee!' Lou Lou crows again. The mannequin begins to move.

Silas's face falls in disbelief. The decades since her husband's death have turned a milky-skinned blonde woman (who looked like a young Farrah Fawcett impersonating Sharon Tate) into the person that now stalks through the rows of anaemic spinach towards them. Her head and shoulders slouch forward in a pre-arthritic tilt. The lack of muscle tone on her anorexic frame creates an effect where her movements seem to defy logic, like a life-sized puppet bobbing towards them on infernal strings. Her head is shaved; the once alabaster skin has, through years of solar abuse and dehydration, turned a pink hue. Sunspots blossom over the surface of her skin, which has the visual texture of crackling on an overdone pork roast. A burned-down cigarette butt hangs from her mouth, and her hand clings to the gold crucifix around her neck as she carries a mug in the other. A ragged pair of baggy shorts from the late nineties and a T-shirt with Huey, Dewey and Louie on it hang off her frame.

'Her clothes burned in the fire, so I gave her your old childhood ones,' Lou Lou whispers to Silas.

'I see that.'

Though still at a distance, Silas sees her striking green eyes boring into him. In them is a boiling violence at odds with the serene arrangement of her other facial features as she lopes towards them. Two rows of diseased spinach are a welcome moat between them and her. She bends down to relieve herself of the mug she's been carrying – it's a large white novelty cup with a sassy statement on it, but a chip over one letter means it now reads:

I ATE MONDAYS

'Welcome home, Silas.' Her voice scarred and dry like an animal carcass in a drought.

The old woman in the diner said the same thing. Coincidence? What else was she supposed to say?

Bunny's eyes flick to Rose as she cocks her head towards her like a bird of prey. 'You must be Rose.'

'Nice to finally meet you,' Rose says warmly.

Bunny's eyes crawl over her. 'Well, I could just eat you up.'

Without warning, Bunny is over the remaining rows of spinach, embracing Rose like a long-lost love. Rose freezes, arms pinned at her sides. A wiry arm shoots out, roughly pulling Silas into the embrace. It ends as suddenly as it began.

A smile breaks out on her face as she stares at Silas. He assumes she must be attempting a warm smile, when in actuality he feels as if he's looking at a rabid animal – repugnant to behold, but he dare not look away. It's safer to know what it's doing.

Bunny breaks the connection and turns back to retrieve *I ATE MONDAYS*.

She freezes.

Goober has crept into her rows of spinach. He snuffles the base of a plant, then cocks his leg without reservation.

Bunny belts towards him, letting loose a guttural shriek that sounds like it's tearing the smoke-stained leather of her throat apart. Goober bolts mid-stream, flying out of the dirt rows. Once he's out of the garden, Bunny stops chasing him. He wheels around, barking madly at her, hackles raised and ready to fight, piss dribbling out of him in fright.

'Goober!' Rose runs to him, scooping the little guy up in her arms protectively.

Bunny watches her before laughing. Something in the laugh is wrong.

'He won't be back in a hurry,' she purrs.

The look of amusement on her face is worse than the shriek. Silas stares at her. *There you are. There is the reason I ran.*

'Don't ever do that again,' Silas states in a tone more threatening than intended.

Bunny blinks, taken aback. She whips out a man's cut-throat razor from her pocket and flicks it open. For a mad instant Silas contemplates using himself as a human shield to protect Rose, but Bunny kneels, beheading a cluster of spinach with one swift stroke. She places the cut-throat back into her pocket, grabs her mug and spinach, and stalks away into the woods.

'Time for prayer, children. God bless,' she murmurs as she leaves.

Goober has quietened in Rose's arms. She lowers him to the ground. He sits facing the direction Bunny took, like a sentinel.

1994

MISSING TIME

Silent. Dark. Immovable. Solid. Smooth. She concentrates. She's not connected with her body yet; the nerves are still sparking up like Christmas lights on a weak current. She manages a small movement against it, but there's no give. *That means I can move, though. Okay . . . Now!*

Move, Bunny. Move! It works. She feels herself moving. Breathing. Can't open her eyes yet, lids heavy. But sensation is coming back. She feels a comforting warmth in her arms. Dead weight – but warm. And wet. Her arms are clamped around this thing. She must have held the thing for a long time. Her biceps and forearms ache. She relaxes her grip on the thing. As her arms drop, it shifts under its own weight like an off-balance sandbag. She becomes aware of the rise and fall of it – it's breathing. They are breathing.

God, what am I holding? Where am I? She draws her arms close to her and away from the breathing form in front of her. Her skin whispers tiny pockets of information to her as she moves. It tells her that she's on a level surface, she guesses a floor of some kind – probably indoors. It is wet and cold. The wet from the floor and the warm breathing thing has soaked her clothes. The being near her fades further into her consciousness as sound returns to her ears – no, not returns, it was always there, but it was turned down, *she* was turned down. A distinct knob is being twisted inside her, turning her back up to the right levels.

She concentrates on sounds now. She can hear the still being breathing fast and shallow breaths near her. *Open your eyes*, she thinks, and it happens. Her eyes flutter open, but vision isn't there yet. Her hand is numb and tickly-painful to move, after God knows how long it was stuck under the still, warm, breathing thing that lay on top of it. She lamely reaches for the gold chain around her neck. Her fingertips trace along the small looped coils until they discover the crucifix. She pinches it tight between index and thumb and raises it like a shield between the breathing thing and her. The dark slowly shifts, splintering into different shades of black, and then into muted colours as that internal knob turns her eyes back on. Focus sharpens the borders of colours and shades, and her eyes read them as a dark wooden leg, a piece of furniture. She raises her head, colliding with a hard surface above. Her mind tells her to look in the direction of the breathing thing in front of her. *I don't want to*, she thinks.

But she does . . .

Later, the paramedics who had been called would note that when they arrived at the home, every door and window was wide open. They would enter the house and record that Silas was found in a catatonic stupor.

When Bunny had opened her eyes, she saw that she was under the old family cabinet that resided in her nephew's bedroom: that they were under there together. That the warm, breathing thing she had been holding on to so tightly was a six-year-old boy, curled up in a fetal position, in a patch of his own cold urine. Eyes wide and unseeing, mouth stuck open, his pale face frozen in a silent scream.

2018

FATHER AND SON AND GHOSTS

Inside looks the same. A museum of late eighties and early nineties furnishings: white melamine plastics yellowing with age, and comfortable puffy couches with tired upholstery – all old but solid. Nothing from an IKEA kit here. Too new for hipster interior decorators and too old for everyone else.

Silas and Rose drag beaten suitcases behind Lou Lou, who escorts them up the stairs like a marching band leader, her highball glass acting as her baton.

Despite Lou Lou's disdain for him, Goober has taken a shine to her. He stands at the top of the stairs with her, wagging his tail as he watches MomDad ascend.

They enter Silas's old bedroom, originally designed as a guestroom with its own small en-suite. It's the same as he left it. The untouched artifacts give the room a shrine-like quality. Silas is secretly surprised that Lou Lou hasn't raked all his childhood keepsakes into boxes for Goodwill. He feels himself soften slightly.

'You two must be hungry. I'll make a snack,' Lou Lou says from their doorway.

They didn't manage to eat at the diner, what with all the vomit and weirdness. They also didn't bother to eat anything else on the drive after.

'No, Mom, don't –'

'That would be lovely, thank you, Lou Lou,' Rose interjects with a hungry Colgate smile.

Goober excitedly loiters around Lou Lou's feet. She glances down at the little black dog.

'When Silas was younger, he wanted a puppy. I'm glad he finally got one.'

'He likes you,' Rose says.

Lou Lou brightens. She smiles as her eyes moisten. 'I'll take him down with me to the kitchen. If you don't mind?'

Silas gives her a curt wave.

She smiles again at Rose. 'Well, we will see you downstairs when you're ready.' She closes the door and patters down the stairs, the sound of Goober's wagging tail thumping into walls as he follows her.

'Stop being so standoffish all the time,' Rose whispers savagely. 'You don't like them – growing up here was shit, I get it, but stop making it worse. We have to be here for a while and she's trying to be nice. If you're not going to make it less . . . I don't know, then stop making it awkward for me. It's uncomfortable.'

Silas nods.

'We can deal with your aunt, but we can't deal with *both* of them, okay?'

'I'm sorry. I'll cut it out.'

Rose searches his face, making sure he means it. Satisfied, she runs her hand through her hair and exhales loudly.

'Jesus Si, your aunt. Was she always like that?'

He tries to remember specifics, but a lot of her was less exact memory and more a recollection of dread, which one day he simply couldn't endure any longer. When Rose talked about her childhood, she could paint whole fluid scenes with her memory. His memory was more stroboscopic; there were gaps in the impressions that implied – rather than illuminated – the whole through the shadows it cast during his brief flashes of recollection.

'I think so. She used to have hair, but I don't really remember specifics. She turned on a dime a lot. Now it just feels like she's playing a game the whole time.'

'That whole thing with Goober in her garden . . .' Rose says, searching the room for an accurate description of what happened. There is none.

'As much as you can, just try not to engage,' Silas says.

'She comes near him again like that though – I'm cracking her.'

Rose could put up with a lot as long as Goober was fine. Rose and Silas both knew that she would be nothing but polite and jovial around everyone, no matter how uncomfortable things got, but someone becoming antagonistic towards her dog was the limit.

'I'll race ya to it,' Silas says with a grin.

The pact of violence soothes the tense mood.

'Come here,' Silas says, bringing Rose in for a hug. 'Three weeks,' he whispers into her ear.

'Three weeks,' she says into his chest. 'Where the fuck is the food? I'm starving.' Rose laughs.

'I got a box of Clif Bars in my case – you eat and I'll start on this place.' He hears her stomach gurgle while she's opening the suitcase and tearing through its contents before raising the box of bars triumphantly. She sits cross-legged on the floor as she tears open the box and pulls out a bar.

Silas turns back to his teenage bedroom and starts the task of rearranging their new office. They'll be sharing his single bed, so Goober will have to sleep in his own bed on the floor. He'll be unimpressed.

The quiet hours of afternoon light have given way to crepuscular rays.

Rose and Silas open the bedroom door to find themselves greeted by the smell of good food. Downstairs, Goober is barking – he has a way of doing it that is absolutely, adorably tone deaf: each bark, no matter the circumstance, is generally the same pitch. In order to figure out what's happening, you have to listen to the length between barks; far apart means he's playing, close together means something is amiss.

At present, the barks are a relaxed length apart – he is playing and all is well.

Rose walks downstairs. Silas shuts their door. As he turns, he sees the closed door to Bunny's bedroom, almost directly opposite theirs. He walks quickly past it to join Rose downstairs and is greeted in the kitchen by Goober dancing about on his hind legs, trying to get a scrap of roast chicken from Lou Lou's raised hand. Goob barks as he makes small hops to reach it and Lou Lou playfully drops it in his mouth. Then he plops back onto all four paws and contentedly inhales the morsel before looking back to her for more as he licks his chops.

'Dog tummies never fill,' says Rose.

Despite Lou Lou's frosty response on meeting him, she

seems now to have fallen under his little mutt spell. 'I hope you don't mind.'

'Oh no, just be careful he doesn't take a finger with it – he's badly trained.' Goober jumps up and patters Lou Lou's lap with his paws as if to illustrate the point.

'Thank you for cooking. We didn't get a chance to eat on the road,' Silas says. His voice still has a dull edge to it.

'Oh, I just whipped up some vegetables and reheated a roast chicken I picked up.'

'Well, thanks. We appreciate it.'

The image of cigarette butts and grey spinach flashes into his mind. 'Uh, are the vegetables from the garden?'

Lou Lou understands what is being asked.

'Bunny keeps her crops for herself. At least she used to while she was in the cabin. I'm not sure how she cooks it now without a stove. She's a bit of a night owl so maybe in here when I'm asleep. She's very private about things. But no, don't worry, I haven't used any of Bunny's vegetables. These are from the local market.'

Silas has forgotten how much Lou Lou shies away from confrontation; you could tell her that a wall was actually a door and she'd agree with you just to keep the peace. After decades in the woods with her sister, Silas isn't surprised that she assumed the submissive role.

'She doesn't want to cost me is all, wants to grow her own food to save money. I've told her it's fine, but she's, well, she's Bunny . . .' Lou Lou says with a practised smile. 'Oh, also, she won't be joining us. Please don't think it's you two,' she assures Rose. 'She never does. Let's sit, shall we?' She leads them around the corner of the open-plan, but sequestered, kitchen and into the lounge-cum-dining-room, and places a steaming clay pot on the table.

'Where is she?' Silas asks, pulling out a seat for Rose.

'Usually out walking at this time. Oh –' Lou Lou hesitates, measuring what she is about to say. 'And if you hear noises in the night, pay no heed. As I said – bit of a night owl.'

Midway through their meal, Goober comes and lies luxuriantly under Rose's chair; he's pestered everyone so frequently that his stomach is now generously lined with chicken. As Goober's body fills with sleep he closes his black-rimmed eyes. He is drifting off when his body feels it – something approaches. He rises, a low growl vibrating from deep in his chest.

'What's wrong, boy?' Rose asks, chewing an over-boiled potato.

The latch on the back door in the kitchen rattles, then the click of the catch releases and the door opens.

'Is that –' Silas hears the fridge's rubber door-seal peel away from its metal frame before it shuts again, then opens and shuts, opens and shuts.

A lull morphs into a long pause.

Lou Lou leans over. 'Bunny's home.'

Rose puts down her knife and fork and lowers her hand to soothe Goober as she tucks two fingers underneath his collar to ensure he stays, and doesn't bite anyone.

They can't see into the kitchen, but they can hear her at the cupboard as she opens and slams it shut three times just as she did with the fridge door.

'What's she doing?' Silas asks.

'Making a drink.'

'No, I mean all the banging.'

Lou Lou eyes him quizzically. 'Don't you remember?'

'Remember what?'

'The Trinity knocks.' Lou Lou's red-lacquered fingernail taps the table. 'Father – *tap*, Son – *tap*, Holy Ghost – *tap*.'

Silas sits back in his chair as a memory unwillingly surfaces. His body twitches with a sudden chill.

When he was small – before things went bad – he, Lou Lou and Bunny had a night-time ritual, a comforting exercise of familial reassurance and love. It was a ritual that allowed the three of them to know that they were always together. After Silas's father had disappeared, Silas had become pathologically afraid that everything and everyone would disappear, as if he were living on quicksand. It wasn't until therapy in his twenties that he could admit without embarrassment or sarcasm that being abandoned really fucking hurt.

It was in therapy that he realised that his child brain had been attempting to assuage and extrapolate a pattern from the chaos of this parental abandonment: *if one goes away, does that mean the others are going away too?* Bedtime became the hour that Silas's anxiety would raise its front hoofs and hammer him, causing a varied mix of insomnia, exhaustion and panic. The evenings had become a back and forth of the two sisters promising Silas they would never leave him (although Lou Lou frequently did).

After months of attempting to soothe Silas's unease, the family finally found a way to make things work, one that satisfied them all. Three knocks, like that of the Holy Trinity:

the Father, the Son and the Holy Ghost – *knock, knock, knock* – Silas, Lou Lou, Bunny – *knock, knock, knock*. All Silas had to do from his bed was knock on his wall, and two knocks would always answer back – one from Lou Lou and one from Bunny. Similarly, if they knocked, he had to answer. And so, every bedtime, the house filled with the sound of knuckles rapping on timber walls. Father, Son, Holy Ghost – Silas, Lou Lou, Bunny, until finally sleep would come.

Lou Lou's voice pulls Silas's mind back to the present. 'I mentioned the door-slamming to the doctor. He thinks it's obsessive compulsive disorder. He believes it's going to get worse if left untreated, but therapy and medication won't work if she keeps drinking. So . . . I don't know.'

Another cupboard slams shut three times.

Bunny drifts around the corner and into the lounge. Her dirty bare feet carry her noiselessly to behind Lou Lou's chair. She rests a hand on Lou Lou's shoulder, an implication of ownership in the gesture. Her eyes peep over the top of her *I ATE MONDAYS* mug as she drinks.

She lowers the mug, her green eyes catching the light as they roam. 'Tea.'

'I didn't hear the kettle,' Silas says.

Rose winces. She hates this part of his personality.

Bunny's face cracks into an unreadable smile as she gazes at him. Lou Lou gently pats the hand on her shoulder before pointedly returning to her meal.

'Good night, children,' Bunny quips as she leaves. 'God bless.'

Lou Lou walks a conversational tightrope between saying what she *thinks* they want to hear and what is actuality. *Such is life.* He notes that Rose is well engaged and even seems to be enjoying the conversation. It's not an act with her; she really is that sweet. With Silas's melancholic view of the world, he knows that Rose is his life raft in a sea of despondency. He only hopes that his problems won't rub off on her and dim her glow – recently he has felt that she's less hopeful than she was when they first met; more affected by the bumps and setbacks in their lives. *You'd better make this script work, boy. Not for me, for her.*

The night wears down to a nub; all retire to their bedrooms. Doors are locked and lights extinguished. Goober, somewhat begrudgingly, curls up in his corner bed on the floor. He briefly attempted an occupation of the main bed but quickly realised that MomDad were in fact truthful in their claims of limited real estate on the boy-sized mattress.

Three hours after the house goes dark, a shuffle in the hall alerts Goober. He raises his head and his ears prick up to catch the faint sound. The shuffling pauses outside the bedroom door. The silence grows heavy.

Goober isn't concerned with this shuffling thing, but there is *another* thing with it. His canine mind, unfettered by intellect and rich in instinct, senses the silence for what it is – a predator measuring prey.

I love MomDad, he warns it, as he lowers his head and creeps towards the door. A barely audible growl vibrates the pricked fur between his shoulders.

Bare feet pitter-patter away down the hall and down the stairs. Below, the kitchen door opens and slams shut three times, making a hollow, wooden sound that isn't enough to wake the people.

Even though he *felt* what was on the other side of the door, not *heard* it, Goober stands for a long while in the dark, listening. He swivels to face the window. The noises of the night animals come to him, but nothing else. Still, he listens, but not with his ears . . .

There.

Both things are outside now. One is close – the one that didn't bother him, although he disliked it. The Other – the one that was different – is far away. It creeps along the edges of his awareness like an animal around a campfire waiting for the flames to die.

I love MomDad . . .

1995

THE ROOTS IN THE ROCK

Dear God in heaven, what the golly gosh is happening to me? It's early. The cold grey air is as yet unkissed by morning rays as Bunny stumbles her way through the trees, like Gretel in that fairy tale about a lonely cannibalistic woman in the forest.

Silas loved that story. She voiced Gretel and he voiced Hansel. She even had the picture book that had ten different buttons for sounds down the right-hand side. Silas loved hearing the sounds for birds, wolves and the other forest creatures, but he especially liked pushing the button for the witch and hearing the actor's voice cackle through the minute speaker. Unfortunately, he would get carried away and Bunny was forced to hide the book until he was able to exert a little more self-control. She meant to give it back to him, but forgot.

She now finds her mornings are quite like that story, except instead of breadcrumbs, she's following small piles of darn pinecones . . .

The first time it happened, she thought it was just too much drink and a midnight walk gone wrong. But then it happened again a few weeks later. Then again, a week after that. And now it seems that every other day she finds herself waking in the forest, just before dawn, kneeling in front of a pile of pinecones. She assumes she gathers them when she's drunk, then afterwards doesn't remembering having done so.

Bunny shivers, holding herself in a hug as she makes her way back towards the house.

Maybe I'm cold when I gather the pinecones? Maybe I think I'm building a fire?

Travelling back to the house in the morning is becoming increasingly easy at least; she just follows the new path she's making. Luckily, her feet have begun to wear a faint dirt line that snakes through the dry pine needles and scrub of the forest floor. Every time she wakes up in front of a new pile of pinecones, all she has to do is look around until she spots the pile she made the last time, walk to it, and then spot the next, which gets even easier once the path begins to be increasingly worn down. The first time it was only a two-minute walk from the house; she was able to just see the top of the roof from where she first woke up. But now it probably takes a good forty-five minutes of walking to get back to the house.

But it's always the same time when she gets there, as if her brain knows it will take an extra few minutes to get back home from the new pinecone pile, and so she naturally wakes a few minutes earlier every time it happens. When she first moved out here, the dark woods creeped her out – all those dumb spooky movies like *Friday the 13th*, they all start in a house or a forest, or an abandoned cabin, or whatever, so you end up thinking you have to be scared of them. But you don't. Not really.

That whispering voice is never in the woods.

She has begun to hear the voice more and more, but only in the house. Day or night, it doesn't seem to matter, but it only speaks when things are quiet. Sometimes she's in the lounge with Lou or watching Silas – although he's getting older now, so that's less often. She finds it whispers to her from the hallway, or the bedroom, or from under the kitchen sink, but usually it happens when she's alone in the house.

'The roots in the rock wake me. I bite them. The land is dead.'

Or sometimes just a part of the sentence: *'the land'* or *'bite them'* or *'roots'*. Like it doesn't quite know what it's saying; speaking a language that is not its native tongue.

She finds herself staying out in the woods later and later, inventing reasons not to be in the house. The whispering voice doesn't scare her (well, apart from that time she walked into the pantry looking for sugar, and from the dark corner above her, so close to her ear she could have sworn she felt cold breath tickle her cheek, it whispered *'The-roots-in-the-rock-wake-me-I-bite-them-the-land-is-dead'*), but she feels uncomfortable in the house, always waiting for it to happen again.

The drinking makes it stop (or at least she doesn't remember if it doesn't). Mornings are hard. She often wakes with the cobwebs of the voice in her ear, as if it has been whispering to her as she drifts awake.

It definitely has its favourite phrase: *'The roots in the rock wake me.'*

The other selections fall in and out of favour, but that's the one she hears at least half of the time. And so, before she knows it, her days start to begin with a clandestine drink before Lou and Silas are awake, just to shut the thing up, or at least turn down its volume for a while. Her drink is still gin and tonic. A part of her clings on to the belief that you can't have a problem if it's just G & T. People who have problems drink out of jugs, boxes and cans. G & Ts are for people on yachts like the one she and Jonathan owned in what now feels like another lifetime. She doesn't bother with the slice of lemon anymore. Gin, tonic and ice (if she or Lou have remembered to refill the tray from the night before). Usually they haven't, so the morning drink usually consists of gin and just tonic water, gulped down as she refills the ice tray from the tap, reloading it for the coming evening.

Bunny finally returns home. Her legs feel a little wobbly, but her spirit is euphoric. She's really building up some stamina for this now. Her hand pats down the pockets of her cotton shorts and she finds what she's hoping for – a soft, half-full pack of Winstons, and tucked in next to it a small gold Zippo she took from an ashtray when she left Jonathan's house (her house) for the last time.

The first time she bought a pack of Winstons was because she hadn't been able to find her usual Chesterfields on the way back from shopping one day in her blessed past life as a Lady Who Lunched. When she returned home, plopped down next to Jonathan and lit one up, he saw the pack and growled, *'Those are nigger cigarettes. You're not a nigger,'* before taking it from her lips and extinguishing it. So now she always lights her Winstons with his lighter. *Fuck you very much.*

Bunny inhales the warm, toasted smoke and stares up at the tallest pine on the edge of the clearing in which the house stands. It's her sundial. She always arrives back just as the top turns a pale gold in the first rays of morning light over the horizon. *Yup, just in time for Jessica Rabbit to have a little drink.*

2018

PURE MORNING

A midge floats through the open window, then through the no man's land between the window and the drapes – where several fallen relatives lie drying on the wooden sill – until finally it continues through to the crack in the fabric and into the bedroom.

Goober watches the midge drift idiotically around the room. He stands to stretch. As his downward dog morphs into cobra pose, a short toot of air from behind causes him to peer around at his rump quizzically. He pads towards the door and sniffs it before testing it with a determined paw. It doesn't budge. He circles around to sit by the foot of the bed before deciding to expedite matters. He needs to pee, and he also wants to sniff new morning smells outside – not surprising, considering the air in the bedroom smells of old fire.

He hops onto the small nest where MomDad lie sleeping and licks their faces (making sure to ram his cold, wet nose into their cheeks, which he has found to be especially useful when getting them up). Dad's arm flies out of the blanket nest and wrestles him into a cuddle.

'Your son needs to go out,' Rose mumbles through her pillow.

'Ya,' Silas says, his face half buried in the fur at the back of Goober's muscular neck, as Goober's tail madly slaps his thigh.

Silas sniffs the air and grimaces. 'Why do I taste cigarettes?'

Rose raises her hair-covered face from the pillow and inhales. 'Ah, gross. Feels like I smoked a pack.'

Silas begrudgingly casts off the sleepy warmth of their comforter. He opens the drapes and shoves the window as wide as it will go, then coughs and rubs his chest. It has that hollow, sunburned feeling inside that virgin lungs get after cigarettes and cold air.

'Bunny's the only one who smokes. She probably does it in the house all night. I'll have a word with her.'

Rose shifts over to gently kiss Goober's ears.

'Si, leave it alone.'

'Why?'

'She's . . . Just ask your mom to speak to her maybe.'

Silas casually rubs his jawline with the back of his fingers – like Mickey Rourke might in a quiet bar scene before a fight. Silas isn't always aware of doing it, but it's a tell that he's considering doing the opposite of whatever he's agreeing to.

'Okay.'

'Si?'

'What?'

'Don't ever play poker,' Rose says, with a hint of a smile.

Silas knows he's been busted. 'Okay.' He lowers his hand with theatrical flair.

Rose presses him. 'Okay what?'

'Enough from you, okay?' He pounces on her and peers

into her dark eyes. There are tiny threads of gold in them in the early mornings (and when she laughs). 'Your son and I are going for a run, pretty brown eyes.'

'Poop-brown,' she purrs.

Never good at compliments, she always says that she has 'poop-brown eyes'. Silas has been fighting a cold war against her knee-jerk defensiveness to receiving compliments for years.

'I love your poop-brown eyes.'

'Don't leave me here alone. I'm serious,' she diverts.

'*Serious*, you say?' Silas says with a smile. 'Don't worry. You should have the place to yourself for a while. They're late risers. Coffee is above the toaster, mugs below. You'll see a Mr. Coffee in the corner by the window. I checked it was still there last night. It's an old friend, just don't leave it on. The warming plate goes nuclear and burns the coffee.'

'God forbid,' she chuckles.

'Listen, hon, I love ya more than Gabagool, but we ain't at a point in our relationship where you can burn the coffee yet,' Silas says in a terrible Jersey accent (he's been enamoured with Tony, Sil and Paulie for months now, following his recent discovery of *The Sopranos*). He pulls on running shorts and bends down to lace up his sneakers. 'We'll start work when I get back. Cool?'

'Cool.'

'You okay living off sandwiches and cereal for a few days?' he asks.

'Sandwiches are fine. Coffee'll be on for ya when you get back.'

'Thanks, my love. Come on, Goob! Time to go.'

Goober jumps off the bed. Sneakers mean W-A-L-K with Dad, or R-U-N at the P-A-R-K. They disappear through the door.

※

In the hall, Silas pauses at Bunny's closed bedroom door. *Nah, better not*, he decides and heads downstairs.

On their way out, Silas notes that the back kitchen door as well as the front door are already standing wide open – probably have been all night. He remembers how Bunny used to pull this same shit when he was still living here, leaving everything open on her nocturnal wanderings. They were miles from anything, but still. He locks the doors before heading out.

Goober sniffs the air outside.

Purple finches rest on the branches of a browning sugar maple.

A blur of purple feathers whisks through leaves and into the sky. Goober barks, excited for their journey. Silas looks down at Goober, who peers up at him as if to say, *what's the holdup?*

'Wanna go on a long one, buddy? Let's go!' And they're off.

※

Rose kicks the blankets off to stretch in the warm morning rays. After letting the sun wash over her face, she squints as she smells the air, then retreats to the en-suite to brush her teeth, hoping to lose the cloying burned tobacco taste at the back of her throat. *Wow, she really burned them at both ends*, she thinks as the blue fluoride paste froths on her tongue. Even the bedclothes have a faint smoky smell, like clothes after a big night out.

In the kitchen she discovers a box of Cheerios beside the coffee. She helps herself to a bowl and flips the switch for Silas's beloved brew. Then she quietly snoops around the lounge while the antebellum Mr. Coffee gurgles away lamely.

Dozens of miniature brown pinecones peep at her, their scales tightly bound to their core, still intent on protecting their fragile seeds. She didn't notice them before as they appeared tucked behind or beside things: not exactly hidden, but rather placed where your eyes wouldn't be drawn to look. Big ones seemed to be used as bookends on shelves or propped up in unused corners, similar to how people who own beach houses invariably litter them with seashells found on lazy walks.

Rose decides the room possesses a genuine rustic charm; a breath of fresh air from the plastic 'wooden' veneer that so often appears in newer homes.

Mr. Coffee begins making an ominous buzzing sound, and Rose discovers that the warming plate is indeed starting to boil the contents of the decanter. She switches it off before pouring a generous mug that will keep her happily caffeinated until early afternoon. Coffee and Cheerios in hand, she sighs as she recalls the quinoa avocado salad breakfasts (with a side of brick-dense, toasted seed-loaf slices) that she has become accustomed to in New York. She knows they can't quite afford the way she eats, but she isn't a drinker, is more of a stay indoors type, and if she didn't spend a little money on herself, she wouldn't be living an NYC life. Besides, she still manages to send money home. *Did* send money home. *Will* send money home.

Soon. Rose's family still thinks she's in NYC, doing well, but when she let slip that money was getting a little tight, her mom told her to stop sending money back (which she did), and she didn't want to make things worse by telling her that she was temporarily locating into the woods in the hope that a better paycheque was on the way. Rose is hoping that in a few weeks she can purchase organic ingredients without feeling bites of guilt. She is also hoping to send back a couple of thousand, and hell, even take a trip home with Si. It will happen, she's sure of it, and she's done harder things before – much harder than hammering out a few more pieces of paper. *Best to let them think everything's fine.* Which it is – she just needs to churn this script out, a few synopses, character breakdowns and boom, baby – you're back in NYC.

She gazes down at her bowl and wonders what her mom is eating, what her brother is eating. The thought stops her on the stairs. She misses them desperately. Pretending that she doesn't has become a full-time occupation, but she doesn't have the time (or financial backing) for melancholic mornings (although she writes these for her characters, it's an indulgence she would never allow to fester within herself).

Es mejor que lo hagas, vuelve al trabajo. Rose thinks and speaks mostly in English now, but when she's tired or on edge, her mother tongue comes out. *Three weeks. No más indulgencias del primer mundo. No more complaining.*

Get this done. Fuck Silas's puta familia! What about your own family?

Rose pushes her work desk up against the window. When Silas writes (swinging from the nooses in that gallows-humoured head of his), he prefers to look at a wall, but she prefers to be somewhere airy – a space where she can look at clouds. It's clichéd, but she does. Silas can draw the drapes on his side of the window so half the desk will be shaded, and Rose can look out the window on her side. She unpacks their laptops between mouthfuls of cereal. Songs about *working* and *girl bosses* and *getting it done* play in her head like a spring-cleaning Spotify playlist, all songs that she'd never share publicly. She places the bowl on the windowsill. She drops the power cables onto her desk and climbs underneath it to find somewhere to plug them in. She spots the face of the outlet, which always reminds her of a grieving marshmallow, and lifts a hand up to pull the cables down, but she yanks a little too hard and they flick up in an arc, slapping the side of the cereal bowl before sinking into an irritating gap between the desk and the window. There's a porcelain *dink!* as the bowl skips over the joinery and sails out the window. Rose hears a faint milky thud as the bowl lands; dead pine needles act as a sufficient cushion against any breakage. She grunts in frustration, plugs in the laptops and reverses herself out from under the desk. *Idiota!*

She pops her head out of the window. The air is still morning-damp and the smell of the pines washes through her nose. She looks out into the forest for a moment. The silence is good, but jarring after the city; it's as if the forest is holding its breath, waiting for her to introduce herself.

Hola maderas, soy Rosa, soy de Nueva York.

Pardon, Rosa, I don't mean to be rude but this is New England – I hope you don't mind . . .

Fine. Hi woods, I'm Rose, a writer from New York City.

Hi Rose, good ta meetcha. Say, you wouldn't perchance be a Nuevo-Beat Generation- Brooklyn-Writer, would you?

'Fraid not, woods. No trust fund. I'm a Queens writer – broke, and originally from Puerto Rico! Cue the violin, get out your tissues – which are both made from . . . woods! Okay, I'm here all day.

Oh jeez, Rose, thanks for the joke and sorry to hear about your current situation. Well, best of luck.

Gracias, bosque de madera!

Introductions over, a smile creeps along her lips. She looks down and spots the upside-down (but intact) white bowl below. Soggy Cheerios lie in a dripping Milky Way, orbiting the upturned bowl like flying saucers around a moon base. Her gaze travels to a disturbed patch of earth, a foot away from the bowl.

Her mind dissects what she sees. She would dismiss it as unimportant information, but the conspiracist part of her sees something that isn't right, and this part hijacks her mind and hastily sets to work connecting the dots.

Her breath catches in her throat. She pulls her head back into the room and quietly makes her way downstairs.

Goober is fast. He likes to sprint a dozen paces ahead of Silas, then cruise, head down, nose sniffing. Then he'll patiently wait for Silas to catch up before darting ahead again. Sometimes Silas sprints ahead to surprise him. Goober then takes off like a bullet, tongue lolling, running in tandem with him until Silas slows.

They have been running for three-quarters of an hour north on a rarely used mountain-bike trail that runs parallel to Long Lake, a hundred yards through the trees to their left. Silas doesn't bother with exact distances, just an hour or so running is usually enough for his head to reset. But today he requires an hour and a half minimum. Clean out the pipes, clean out the head before attacking the scri–

Woah, shit, Goober! is verbalised as 'Woash, Goob!' Silas skids before jumping over the dog just in time not to smash into him as he stands, frozen, peering into the forest. Silas stumbles to a stop, breathes and turns to see that despite the close call, Goober hasn't budged.

'Goober?' No response. A little more firmly. 'Goober!' Goober glances at Silas before sniffing the air and taking off into the scrub. *Shit, he's seen a rabbit or something.* Silas dives after him. 'Goober! Come 'ere!' A furry black butt weaves through the pines as if it's on rails. Silas struggles to keep up, jumping over a fallen bough like a baby giraffe on its first legs, in stark contrast to the black missile ahead of him.

He bursts through the trees and onto the narrow shore of the lake.

He had forgotten how unbelievably still its surface lies.

Ahead of him on the damp grey pebbles, Goober sits staring out over the water to the opposite side. The sun's rays haven't quite reached the lake yet, blocked by the height of the pines on either side. Silas watches delicate wisps of mist drift across the still, black surface as he catches his breath.

'Whatcha looking at, boy?' Silas asks, sitting down beside Goober. The water laps Goober's front paws and the tips of Silas's sneakers. 'Huh?' Goober doesn't budge. He's intently focused on the opposite shore. Silas peers across to the other side of the lake; it's darker, much darker, from the lack of sun, and a steep section of earth has slipped away, revealing muscular white roots that reach out towards them. He can't spot anything out of the ordinary, although he's not really looking. He picks up a pebble and casts it into the still water. Ripples glide across the surface before slowly fading back to stillness.

Did I ever swim here? He can't remember.

He *does* remember once, years ago as a boy, wading in up to his knees on an unbearably hot summer day. The flat rocks of the lake bed were slimy under foot as they descended steeply into the depths. His boyhood mind had imagined that he was standing on the edge of the large gaping mouth of a giant river monster that peered at him from just beyond the murk below.

A worried whine escapes Goober's lips as he shifts on his paws.

'It's okay, boy.'

Silas wonders if Goober has a similar feeling about the lake. In a cheesy, laugh-out-loud way that he would never admit (even to Rose), Silas has always had a quiet belief that he and ol' Goob share a psychic . . . well, not psychic . . . an *intuitive* bond.

Goober shifts his gaze further up the shore, seemingly torn between standing and sitting. 'Something there, huh?' Silas follows Goober's gaze, hoping to God it's not a bear, although he's never seen one this way before.

A figure drifts along, just inside the murk of the tree line. *Fuck.*

It leaves the trees and slowly moves towards the lake edge. 'Fuck,' he whispers aloud.

Rose creeps outside and rounds the house to the spot below her bedroom window. The cereal bowl lies in front of her, but she isn't interested in the bowl – she's interested in the disturbed patches of ground that lie three feet past it. The carpet of dry, brown pine needles tells a story – tells her that two feet have been there, clearing away pine needles to reveal the dark, rich soil below. Just ahead of the patches is a pile of what must be at least a hundred cigarette butts – all freshly burned down to their filters.

Something else – between the footprints, soaking into them – is evidence that whoever stood there (directly outside their window long enough to smoke that many cigarettes) emptied their bladder and bowels, and then stood in their own filth, kneading it into the ground with their bare feet.

Rose can see the outlines of the toes in the shit.

A fly crawling over the patch lifts up into the sky. Instantly Rose is aware of the sensation of a tiny brush on her lip as the insect zips along it. She squeals before wiping her mouth and spitting violently. She steps back, turning from the scene to collect herself. Her eyes sweep up the side of the house; a face stares down at her from the open window.

'Eeeahhh!' Rose recoils as Lou Lou looks down at her.

'Easy boy, shh,' Silas whispers as he caresses Goober's back with long, calming strokes to keep him quiet. *She hasn't seen us; just keep still, keep quiet, with any luck she'll keep moving.* She draws closer, now almost directly across from them. Through his hand, he feels a bark boiling up in Goober. He gently presses his hand into the dog's back to interrupt it.

Bunny's skeletal form looks even more alien from a distance; the legs seem too thin to support the body, let alone transport it over rocks. He notes she's barefoot and still wearing his childhood clothes from the day before.

As she draws perfectly opposite to them, she begins swerving back into the forest.

Thank fuck for small miracles. Another minute and she'll be off the shore and back in the trees. We'll wait a couple of minutes after that and then sneak away without her ever knowing we were here.

He watches her slowly, almost aimlessly, pick her way up the bank. *Keep going, keep going.*

Goober lets out a single bark.

No.

He squeezes the loose skin on Goober's shoulders. Goober shifts uneasily under his hand, but remains seated.

She doesn't break stride. He contemplates the chances that Goober's bark didn't carry across the water . . .

Her route slowly curves more sharply towards the trees, bringing her back opposite to them, but that's okay now, because she has her back to them and is heading away. He releases the tension in his hand and pats Goober with long strokes as he allows himself a deep breath. Goober lifts his nose to the air, sampling it the way dogs do when they smell impending rain.

As Bunny keeps moving away, she lifts her arm above her head. It looks as if she's stretching – no, waving. As if to something in the murk of the woods. Her stooped shoulders straighten to her full height as her legs slow, then stop walking altogether. Her arm still slowly tick-tocks at the shoulder and elbow.

Her head swivels on the corded rope of her neck, then her body follows until she's facing them. She walks back onto the lakeshore proper, never taking her eyes from Silas's, and her insect-like legs fold beneath her as she sits down opposite them on the stones, still waving.

Silas lifts his hand and raises it in greeting.

What should be a momentary greeting drags into an exhausted awkwardness. Silas slowly lowers his arm. Bunny follows suit. Goober lets out another yelp.

Silas replaces his hand on the dog's back, patting him reassuringly. *I don't like her either, buddy*, he says through the touch. He looks back to Bunny and notices she too is reaching out with her hand, stroking the empty space beside her. She turns her head to the space, stroking calm into nothing.

What's happening?

Her head turns back towards them.

Silas draws his hand away from Goober as her hand does the same. The realisation blooms in his head, crawls down his spine and into his limbs: *She's mimicking me.*

He becomes self-conscious, aware that every movement is being monitored. Recorded. He considers simply standing and (*running*) leaving with Goober, back into the woods and away from (*her*) the lake. His body is reacting as if he stumbled upon a rabid wolf in the path rather than a dirty scarecrow on the other side of a lake. He feels his lizard brain snap from flight to fight. *No. You ran from her once. You're never doing it again.*

So, fuck it – when in doubt, play chicken. He sits as still as he can manage.

Two statues face one another across the water. Silas feels the chill from the lake. The adrenaline and heat from the run are fading, he feels his ass becoming numb on the rocks, but still he refuses to move first. *If my ass is turning numb, I bet yours is about to implode.*

Goober is growing increasingly tired of this game; his senses feel assaulted by the one watching them and he doesn't know why. The fatigue of it drains him. He growls across the water, willing the one there to leave. He slowly edges into the water. His front paws stand in the shallows. He dares not go further. He doesn't know what this is, but Dad is nervous – the little dog feels this, and that in turn makes *him* nervous. He growls. Inside the growl is a question that vibrates invisibly across the lake like a skipping stone. *What you do?*

Quiet, boy, Silas wants to say, but he doesn't want to move, not even his mouth. He won't be the first to break – not until *she* does.

The tone of Goober's growl changes from low to high in his throat, like a buzz saw biting into a tree. His mouth opens, his lips peel back, exposing pink gums and quivering teeth.

Silas has heard a similar sound only once before, on the news. The segment showed footage from a Florida police body cam of a raid that went bad; the sound came from a police dog right before a meth head exploded from his house with a shovel. He took one step too far towards the officer, and the police dog subsequently tore into the junkie's throat instead of politely tearing into his arm as per protocol.

Bunny springs backwards as if frightened by something.

Silas doesn't have time to gloat.

The water in front of him boils with activity. 'Goob –'

A dark, serpentine monster erupts from the shivering water. It bites Goober's leg with a maw as wide as Silas's thigh as the thickly muscled pipe of its body wraps around behind Goober to draw him into deeper water. Teeth, muscle, skin twist around his small frame. Goober screams in pain and fright. Then he snarls and repays teeth with teeth. Entwined, the two animals skitter along the wet rocks of the shallows as scarlet blooms of blood appear in the water.

In the instant between fright and jumping to help Goober, Silas is dimly aware that he jumped exactly as Bunny did, as if she had *known* he would; he knew in some way that she had seen it coming.

But there isn't time to ruminate over this; Goober is a small, agile ball of muscles, but he's losing ground against the black thing, which is much larger and is successfully pulling him into the water. Another three or four seconds and the dog will be in too deep to stand. In the time it takes Silas to scramble towards his struggling friend (his *best* friend, apart from Rose), Silas's brain recognises the black firehose as an eel. *But eels aren't this big, are they?* His mind spins questions as instinct drives his body. *Jesus, this thing's the same girth as my thigh.*

The eel's flat, wide head is clamped onto the ankle joint of Goober's front leg. Small rivulets of blood run from its black skin where Goober has raked his teeth over it. One of its black eyes dangles on a white stem from the now empty socket. *Good boy, son.*

Silas feels as though he's moving in slow motion, hyper aware of every sensation, every breath, all his surroundings. He reaches out towards the eel and his fingers find oily black skin. It instantly releases Goober's leg, before whipping around and clamping down on Silas's right hand. The bite feels like sheets of coarse sandpaper wrapping around his hand with two tons of pressure behind them. To his horror, it begins pulling him into the water. He manages a mighty, panicked heave and pulls the eel up onto dry grey stones.

Goober quickly surveys where his jaw can close around its wide frame for optimal bloodletting. He lunges into the

bunny

eel's side, near its tail. The muscular tube of its body whips away from Goober, but just as the dog's jaw successfully locks, he skids along with it. Goober pulls at the eel as if he were playing a game of tug of war – shoulders low and planted, ears back, rump in the air.

It's true: when you travel from anger into rage, you really do see red.

The exact moment Silas flips into red is when he spots the loose flap of skin hanging from Goober's front leg as he fights to keep the eel's tail in his jaws. This thing, *this thing* that's latched onto his hand has hurt *his* dog. He drops to his knees, lowering his centre of gravity like a wrestler. His kneecaps collide with stone. He knows they'll hurt later, but not now. A jagged triangular rock is the largest thing he can see through the red mist of rage. His fingers close around its sharp edges as he raises it above his head. He brings it down, once, twice. *Die.* He hammers it into the eel's skull relentlessly. It sounds like a ball-peen hammer hitting waterlogged oak.

The stone's edge catches the remaining eye; Silas drives it deep into the socket, hammering until the sound morphs from a dull thud into a soft crunch. The jaws around his hand relax slightly. Silas feels the skin on his knuckles catch on the sandpaper teeth, then tear as he wrenches his hand free. The flat centre of the eel's skull shatters as he hurls the stone down onto it. Oily black skin gives way to white bone and red gore. He hits it again. And again. And again.

Rose holds one hand on her chest and another on her stomach as she exhales through pursed lips.

'Sorry, didn't mean to startle you, dear,' Lou Lou calls down cheerily from the window.

All Rose can manage in response is a faint hoot of accommodating laughter.

Rose watches as Lou Lou peers up at the sky, revealing deeply etched lines around her face.

'Ah, it's going to be a beautiful . . .' Lou Lou says as she looks down. Rose sees the glint in her eyes disappear as she spots the cigarettes and footprints. '. . . day.'

Rose hasn't noticed it before, but the way Lou Lou's face falls into a cold scowl is effortless.

'Wait there, please,' Lou Lou says before disappearing from the window.

'*Carajo*,' Rose whispers to the trees. She thinks about that fly walking along her lip; in her mind's eye she sees a trail of tan-coloured, watery shit behind it. She roughly wipes her lip on her sleeve and spits again.

When she turns around, Lou Lou is standing in front of her in a baby pink robe. The look on her face is a subtle mixture of strain and propriety. Fear, too, maybe.

'May I?' Lou Lou gestures towards the cigarettes.

Rose has no idea why Lou Lou is asking her permission, but she nods anyway.

Lou Lou kneels before inspecting the scene. It takes her a moment before she obviously sees, or smells, the more disturbing aspects. 'Oh my.' She stands, spinning around to face Rose. 'Um, well, that's something new.'

'I'm sorry?'

Lou Lou rests an affable hand on Rose's forearm. 'She does it outside my window too sometimes. The, uh . . . watching. It's perfectly harmless. I believe she thinks she's making sure we're safe. The, the other thing there is, ah . . .'

How does one diplomatically refer to shit, piss and bare feet? Rose watches Lou Lou try. 'Rose, Bunny's body is failing, and with it, I believe, her mind. I'm so sorry for all of this on your first day here.' Rose notes how every time Lou Lou speaks, it sounds like badly rehearsed dialogue from a forgettable old movie. It causes the moment to become even more surreal and uncomfortable.

'I'll just –' Lou Lou kneels again, and, unbelievably, begins scooping up the butts before stuffing them into the pockets of her pristine nightgown. Rose notes the bottom of the pile is still damp with urine. Lou Lou doesn't seem to notice as she shovels the butts into her pockets. She straightens and smiles radiantly before looking squarely at Rose. Something about her demeanour reminds Rose of a new display in a shop window: pre-arranged, 'spritzy' and ready for business.

'No need to worry Silas about this, don't you agree?'

Rose knows what she's supposed to say, but can't. This was too strange, too uncomfortable for her to sit with alone . . . Or worse, with Lou Lou.

'We try not to keep things from each other.'

Rose expects this to be the beginning of a conversation where they would discuss things: why they needed to be here, why this was important, what exactly was wrong with Bunny. Could she be of any help? How does Lou Lou feel about faecal contamination? Any thoughts on E. coli?

But Lou Lou frosts over before Rose can finish speaking. 'Do what you want,' she states flatly before marching away.

What was supposed to be a productive morning has collapsed into Rose being left outside with the smell of two different kinds of shit in her nose.

***

Silas slowly begins to feel as if he is back in his body. His senses return, but he's unsure of the amount of time he's spent by the river or how long the fight lasted. He swallows thick saliva and realises his throat is sore from screaming. Below him lie the remains of the eel. Its body now resembles a hellish black version of an exploding cigar: the front of its thick, corded body ends in a bloom of gore scattered across the shore and over Silas's face.

Goober is panting by the eel's twitching tail with his injured leg lamely raised in front of him. His furry black chest glistens with water and blood – mostly eel blood, but plenty of his own, too. A small volume of blood gathers on the end of his raised paw before dropping onto the stones. Goober is bleeding. Not a torrent, but enough to jog Silas into action. He tears off his shirt, turns it inside out and wraps it around Goober's lower leg. Goober allows this without struggle.

'It's okay, boy. It's okay,' Silas says, blinking away tears and eel guts. There's something about the way Goober calmly peers into his eyes as he works . . . it crushes his soul. He picks Goober up and cradles him before making for the tree line.

Wait.

He stops and looks back across the lake.

Bunny is naked and ankle deep in the water. She wades towards them from the opposite shore, a wide, cold grin on her face. She reaches a drop-off point and plunges below the surface. Silas wants to leave with Goober but he can't look away.

The top of her head emerges, followed by her unblinking eyes, as her body remains in the cold, deep water. Small circular ripples appear over the entirety of the lake surface, as if it has been disturbed by drops of rain. Silas lifts his head. The sky is clear. In the midst of the ripples, dark shapes rise to the surface. Black eels. They appear much smaller than the ruined one lying in pieces on the bank, but there are hundreds of them. *They're watching me.*

Bunny begins swimming among them in the icy water. Her bare, skeletal frame looks like the white unearthed roots of the pines on the shore behind her. She turns onto her back and laughs into the cloudless sky.

Silas checks he is holding on to Goober tightly. He turns from the lake and runs home.

COLD COFFEE

Rose picks up the white bowl and walks around to the side of the house. She's purposefully loitering around outside, not wanting to encounter Lou Lou again. She looks out at the fresh sun filtering through the green forest in warm, yellow-gold rays. It strikes her how anything can be made ugly by context; she knows that years from now, if she ever stands in a pine forest again (particularly on a perfectly golden morning) she will not find it beautiful.

She ventures inside after hearing the roar of an engine on the opposite side of the property. Lou Lou's leaving. *Gracias a Dios!*

She walks upstairs to their room/office and slumps down into her designated office chair – a cheap wooden fold-out that she knows will murder her back – as she waits for Silas. It's been well over an hour since he left, so they should be back soon – she was hoping to have a head start on the script by the time he got back, but that idea went out the window with her breakfast.

Her cup of coffee has turned cold. She can do without a proper breakfast, but she can't work without hot coffee, so she descends the stairs as quietly as possible, taking care not to wake Bunny. Her door is closed; she must still be sleeping (especially after her adventurous night outside their room).

As she reaches the kitchen (having discovered every creak in the old staircase), she greets her friend, Mr. Coffee. She flicks the switch and stands watching it, willing it to make that dangerous buzzing sound and nuke the coffee urn. *Venga venga!* All she wants is to get back upstairs to the relative security of their bedroom, as fast as possible, with a hot cup of coffee. Mr. Coffee indulges her, and she turns him off before the electric buzz starts sounding any angrier. She is just pouring a new cup when a wall of sound erupts from the adjoining lounge. She jerks in fright as an arc of steaming brew lashes her hand.

'Ow!' Rose spins around to the basin, running cold water over her injury.

The sound – it took a moment for her to recognise what it was: music turned up full blast. The twangy intro to Geoffrey Clare's 'Night Walk' blares out of the living-room speakers, evoking deerskin jackets and long hair. The smooth male voice croons:

When the day is swallowed by night,
Counting memory lost in moonlight,
Foreign hands reaching out to your shadow.

Rose lets the cold water linger on her inflamed skin before shutting the faucet off and walking through to the lounge. She approaches a wooden turntable which has 'Made in America' embossed on the side in small, gold-hemmed letters. Rose determines that it was bought in a time when stereo systems lasted for decades, not just one summer. She lifts the clear plastic lid –

Oh, the stars we can't count and can't see –

– and flicks the switch that lifts the needle.

The silence of the room is broken by a few mechanical clicks from the player as it lapses back into inaction. She's about to call out, 'Hello?' when three fast claps ring out behind her. A voice that sounds like a silk scarf tearing murmurs in a sing-song lilt, 'That's my song there. Good morning.'

Rose whirls around to see Bunny disappearing past her into the kitchen. Her clothes (Silas's clothes) are noticeably damp; soaking, even. Rose also notes that her feet are bare and dirty. Rose can hear her feet as her soles hit the wood; a repugnant *shlupping* noise that grates at Rose's patience. She winces as a cupboard slams three times – the ritual of Bunny's drink prep has begun. Rose edges towards the kitchen; her dogged politeness requires she initiate some form of polite interaction, if nothing else then to demonstrate that she isn't a foe. More trios of slamming and banging echo from around the corner before Bunny reappears around the kitchen counter and promptly walks back into the lounge nursing *I ATE MONDAYS* in her hands.

'Morning, Bunny,' Rose offers.

Bunny lifts the mug to her lips and tilts it to drink. Her eyes peep over the rim as she gives Rose a wink. Rose smiles politely as she tries to figure out the next move; in her own culture she would know what to do, although in her own culture interactions aren't this uncomfortable. She thought she understood American Caucasian culture, but these women are causing her to question her 'appropriate white interaction' knowledge. Bunny stands drinking and staring.

Diga algo, estúpida!

'Uh, are you planning on gardening today?' is the question

that comes out. What she wants to ask is, *Why on earth would you shit outside our window, you fucking weirdo?* But she keeps this question silent. Rose has learned that in white American culture you don't talk about a problem at hand, you talk around it until everyone forgets. Sometimes when her relationship with Silas is bad, she employs this tactic – forget until it's okay.

'Rose!' Silas calls outside the kitchen door.

'Coming!' She tears herself away from Bunny's gaze with a polite smile as she moves past her. *Wow, she is wet.* As she does, Bunny leans in towards her –

'Not yet.'

'Excuse me?'

But Bunny is already walking away, towards the front door.

'Now, Rose!' Silas cries.

'Sorry,' she stammers as she walks to the kitchen door. Before she passes into the kitchen, she looks back; through the open front door she sees Bunny scamper off into the woods.

ROSE IS RIGHT

Silas places a gin-soaked flannel over Goober's wound before applying a generous dollop of Neosporin to his injured leg. A round wet patch on the bed circles Goober like an antiseptic halo. He finishes by wrapping Goober's injured leg in a pink bandage.

'What happened?' Rose asks. She's on the phone as she paces.

'I'll explain later.'

'What's that crap all over you?'

Rose freezes as the phone stops ringing in her ear . . .

'*Hello!*' chirps the crackling, cheery voice that sounds like it was recorded fifty years ago. '*You have reached Hamner Veterinary Clinic. Please note our opening hours are 9 a.m. to 5 p.m. Monday to Friday. Thank you!*'

Rose looks at her phone:

07:34 Sun 11 August

'*Mierda.*'

She waits for the voice to list an after-hours number – there is none. She waits for a *beep* to leave a message – the call dies.

'They're closed weekends. I'll check where the nearest ASPCA is.'

'I think he'll be okay,' Silas says, scratching between

Goober's shoulders. The dog's ears perk up as his tail drums the comforter like a canine metronome.

'Well, I think we should take him in tomorrow.'

'Yeah, sure.'

'Si . . . Si . . . Silas.'

'Yes, Rose.'

'Can you tell me what happened, please?'

'What happened? Well, at the lake . . . at the fucking lake, an eel, it tried to pull him in.'

'What? Do they even do that?'

'I have no idea, Rose.'

'They eat plants and stuff at the bottom, don't they?'

'Again . . .'

'Don't get short with me.'

A headache licks the back of Silas's eyeballs. He rubs his temples to stave off the pulsing. 'I don't know. This one was big . . . I've seen small ones in the lake before, but this thing was way past that. And they're supposed to come out at night. I mean, it was ridiculous – the thing jumped out of the water to get Goob.'

'What?'

'Then tried to pull him in.'

'Christ.'

'How did you get that?' Rose points at his mangled knuckles, bathed in antiseptic.

'Thing bit me when I tried to get it off Goob. Smashed its head in with a rock . . . Bunny was there.' The last statement is tacked on; Silas doesn't know how to introduce the next part any other way than by objective reporting. 'She was across from us, on the opposite side of the lake, when it happened. When I looked up after killing the thing, she'd taken all her clothes off and was getting into the water.'

Rose's face looks like a baby tasting lemon juice for the first time. 'What the fuck?'

And then she floated in the water and watched me with all the eels that came up to the surface – like she had called them, he wants to say.

But instead, he says, 'Then I left.'

Rose cocks an eyebrow as she gazes out the window. 'Well, at least her feet got washed. I have my *own* little story for you.'

'Oh God, what?' He abandons rubbing his temple.

'First, promise me you won't do anything about it, because I think that'll just make it worse.'

Silas reluctantly nods.

'The cigarette smell this morning?'

'Yeah?'

'She was outside the window half the night. I found a mountain of butts out there.'

Silas feels himself winding up to punch something – the wall will do. He falters; bad idea. He slowly places one hand against the wall before trying to push it over.

'What are you doing?'

'I don't know, losing my mind?'

'Well, do you want to know something?'

'Sure, I'm listening.'

'Good, I'm glad you're listening, because your aunt went to the toilet out there and stood in it. Like, stamped it into the ground or something. I don't know what that means, or what you're supposed to do . . . Even your mom was surprised by that part – she didn't seem to mind the loitering outside the window part . . . She said that Bunny does that sometimes outside her window too, to check on us or something. Lou Lou seems to think it's all part of her mind going. She's sick, Silas.'

Silas laughs darkly.

'She doesn't want us here. Your mom isn't going to see it. She can't see it. If she does, then she has to see everything else. So we're on our own.'

'Always have been,' he mutters.

'Well, we have to stay here to finish work. We have the en-suite so we only have to leave this room to get food and let Goober out. Once we figure out when she's here and when she isn't, then, well . . . I don't know, we'll be around the house a bit more. It'll mean we don't antagonise the situation.'

Silas visualises the next three weeks before finally nodding in agreement.

'And Si?'

'Yeah?'

'It's *you* she has the problem with. You know what I mean – you have to control how you react.'

'Yip.'

'Before I opened the door, when you came back, she was in the house. As soon as you showed up, she was out the door again.'

'She doesn't like being around me? Great, I'll be around and she can fuck off.'

'Seriously. Please, watch your mouth and your temper. Have you noticed how she's hardly said a word to you since we got here?'

bunny

Silas thinks for a moment. Rose is right; even when they arrived, Bunny mainly addressed Rose. She only included Silas for a brief 'welcome home' and an awkward-as-hell hug.

'People do that when they're waiting for a fight to start. So, don't start one.'

'You're right, I'll take care of it. Make sure things are as calm as they can be.'

'Really?'

'Really. I promise.'

Rose gives him a quick peck on the lips and turns away. Goober sits up and makes a small *awp* sound as he yawns.

'The kid needs breakfast. Think the coast is still clear?' Silas asks.

'I could tie some rope around your waist and send you down to find out?' Rose suggests with a smile.

'Fried eggs?' he asks Goober.

'Continental, buster. That goes for both of you. We got work to do. I don't want to get off track.'

Silas opens the door, listening for anything downstairs. He lingers as an unpleasant thought stops him. 'She got back before me?'

'Yeah, I told you.'

'She was still in the water when I left, and I didn't spare the horses getting back.'

Rose shrugs. 'From what I hear, she spends most of her time in the woods. Maybe she knows a secret path.'

'The left-hand path?' Silas says dryly.

Rose responds in kind. 'Of course. She's a *bruja*.'

Silas grins at her.

The angry Rose has gone. They always find their way back to each other with lame jokes, crass humour and movie nights that involve pure escapism and shitty food.

'We're gonna have to burn the midnight oil today if we're driving Goob to the vet tomorrow. It'll eat up half the day. Town's 'bout ninety minutes' drive one way,' Silas tells her.

'If Goob's gotta see the vet, he's gotta see the vet.' She smiles.

Halfway down the stairs his smile falters. He wishes he had told her the truth. He wishes he had told her about the eels.

1995

THE SEAT OF THE OTHER

'*Come on, slowpoke!*' Bunny calls. Silas scampers along the shore behind her, his hooded ducky towel giving him the appearance of a small yellow elf.

Lately things have become better between them. Silas has started school and the time away with kids his own age seems to do him good. Whatever the episode was under the drawers, he has slowly bounced back from it.

On this warm summer afternoon, he even lets her walk him back from the lake without Lou Lou (who lies dozing on a towel by the boathouse with a belly full of cheap Chardonnay).

He's a curious child, and has every intention of exploring the shore further . . . Even if it is with her crazy old ass.

They walk along the natural cobbles of the shore together. Every dozen yards or so, Silas picks a spot and shuffles into the water. A look of fear and excitement washes over his face as the cold water tickles his knees. It's at these times that she loves being his aunt; it's at these times when she feels like his mother.

He stands in the shallows, shuffles in further, then squeals, '*Something touched my leg!*' before scrambling out. He repeats this process down the entire shoreline as Bunny smiles and shakes her head.

'*There's something here too! It touched my leg again!*' Silas yells before scrambling out for the umpteenth time. Bunny continues her stroll. She knows children are 'supposed' to be chaperoned around water, but honestly, *what kid can't swim? It's easy, it comes naturally, like breathing*, she thinks as she leaves him behind to play.

He eventually catches up with her. '*You didn't wait for me!*'

'*No, I didn't.*'

They fall into step with one another.

'*I'm cold.*'

'*I told you not to jump in with your ducky towel on.*'

'*It's only wet at the bottom.*' Silas pulls the yellow hood up conspiratorially so that the orange beak drops down and covers the majority of his face.

'*Wanna go home now, wizard boy?*' Bunny wiggles her fingers at him as if she's casting a spell.

He laughs and wiggles his fingers back as his eyes glint wickedly under the shade of his hood. '*Yeah.*'

'*How about we take a shortcut that your Aunt Bunny knows?*'

Bunny has gotten to know the lake and woods pretty well after all her early-morning wanderings. She's pretty sure that if they cut into the woods, they will run into her path . . . The last few months have quietened down; she is no longer waking up in the forest as much as she used to, and that whispering voice has largely gone silent. She still occasionally hears murmurings in the house, but she spends most of her time outside now, so it doesn't bother her as much. She has become used to just ignoring it. When she does wake outside now, she's stopped waking in new places. Now it's always the same spot – the furthest spot from the house, which annoys her. She has to walk for an hour and a bit to get back home. The novelty of where the path would lead her died when she ceased making new pinecone waypoints. The pile she now wakes at is much larger than the others; every time she wakes she seems to have added more cones to it, and the ground around it is trampled bare, like she walked around it in a slowly widening gyre a million times. *Oh well, who cares? Not this Jessica Rabbit.*

'*Where's the shortcut, Aunt Bunny?*'

Bunny turns into the cool, dappled shade of the forest. '*Just through here, kiddo.*' They duck under bushes and around branches and trek just long enough for the water to be lost through the trees. The path Bunny assumed was just through the trees fails to materialise, but she knows the general direction, so they press on.

'*Aunt Bunny, are we lost?*' Silas asks from behind her.

The question grates more than it should because in a little while, if no path appears, they might be.

'*Nope. Just taking a shortcut to the shortcut.*' She grins back at him tightly, hastening her pace in a silent caution to Silas that he need not bring it up again.

A few hundred yards later she can almost feel the same question silently bubbling up behind her when she steps onto the thin path of her nocturnal wanderings. *There you are.* Silas follows suit (with a few new nicks and scratches from the brush). He looks down the path.

'*What's that, Aunt Bunny?*'

Bunny turns, following Silas's gaze; the large pinecone 'mothership' pile lies at the end of the path. She's only ever seen it in the half-light of morning when she wakes there. The stark daylight shows the full extent of it. She hadn't realised it had gotten so big, and the circle her feet made is now more of a dirt clearing than a small bare patch.

'*That's weird,*' she says. '*I didn't realise we'd walked that far from the house.*' The shadow behind the thought is concerned with how long it will take to walk back, particularly with Silas slowing her down. Jessica Rabbit is getting thirsty. Her tongue rakes dry spit from the roof of her mouth and she swallows as she lights up a 'fuck you Jonathan' Winston. It won't help the cottonmouth, but it might dull the edge of the craving behind it.

'We're not going that way, kiddo. Come on.'

But Silas is locked on to the big pinecone pile like a retriever on a bird.

'Can I go see, please?' The little rascal's legs are already carrying him towards it as he asks.

'Quickly then,' she says, through a blue plume of smoke.

He bounds down the path, his little duck head bobbing up and down. As he gets closer, he seems filled with wonder by the giant cairn. To an adult, the five-foot pile is not especially noteworthy, but when Silas looks up at it, he probably sees a grand tower.

'Wooow,' he whispers.

Bunny stands at the edge of the circle, biting her nails – or what's left of them. It's strange being here in the naked light of day. It makes her uncomfortable for some reason. As does sharing it with someone else. *Get away, little ducky. Get the fuck away*, she thinks (or whispers?).

Silas half turns back towards her. *'What'd you say, Aunt Bunny?'*

Whoopsie, who said that? Jessica Rabbit? . . . Jessica Raaaaabiiiit? She smiles and bats her wrist in a 'don't mind me' gesture. He turns back and she watches his little body bobbing towards the pile. As he reaches it, something about him actually touching it makes her skin crawl.

'Don't do that!' she barks. The edge in her voice freezes his small hand. She doesn't want to scare him, so she adds, *'It might fall on you.'*

'*Okay.*' He lowers his hand a touch sulkily and walks around the small clearing, obscured from her view by the cairn. '*Aunt Bunny?*'

'*Yes?*'

'*Who made this?*'

'*I don't know.*' Sorry kid, this is Jessica Rabbit's little secret place and you shouldn't be here.

'*But how do you know about it?*'

'*I . . . found it.*'

'*Aunt Bunny?*'

I'm thirsty, kid, not now. '*Yes?*'

She feels it's time to go, before the questions turn more probing.

'*Where does this path go?*'

'*The way we came,*' she tells him, a touch of frustration crawling into her voice this time.

'*No . . . this one,*' Silas says.

Yep, all aboard for Kid Question Land. Next stop, Bullshit Town. Time to wrap this up. She enters the circle and walks around the cones. '*Sweetheart, there's only one path and that's the one –*'

Silas points down a path leading out of the circle that she has never seen before.

Because she didn't make it.

It gently curves away. She can't see where it leads. Pinecones lie along the edges like lights on a landing strip.

'*Uh, we're not going that way, kid. Come on.*'

'*But, I –*'

'*Next time. Didn't you say you were getting cold?*'

Silas looks at her, disappointed. He's a child in the grip of an adventure interrupted by the world of adults who know nothing of longing and wanderlust.

'*Come on.*' Sensing an upcoming standoff, she grabs his hand, then not so gently pulls him out of the circle and down her path, back towards home.

'Stop. Stop hurting me!'

She releases his hand.

'I'm not hurting you!'

'Please! I want to stay.'

'Stop giving me shit! Next time. I promise.'

The protestations continue for a spell before Silas gives in. He stomps behind her in a huff. The path is too narrow for anything but single file. Bunny's head swims with questions: *Did I make the path in my sleep? Maybe I didn't notice it the last time I woke up there? No, it's impossible. The pile of cones is seriously tall now, far too tall. Maybe in the morning I didn't see the new path before going home? Definitely not impossible. You've got it, Little Rabbit, you've got it! If it's not impossible, then it's possible, isn't it? Although, it looks well worn. So?* She made all the other waypoints without ever remembering doing it, so what's one more little weird thing she may (or may not) have done while sleepwalking?

'Aunt Bunny, look!' Silas's voice enters her thoughts like a loud fart in an empty church. They have walked straight back into the circle.

'Yay!' Silas crows as he runs around it. '*Thanks, Aunt Bunny.*'

Bunny is in disbelief. She looks at the soil; fresh footprints – but so many of them. '*How did we get turned around?*' she ponders aloud.

'*We didn't turn around, you took us to your secret place,*' Silas calls out as he dances around the cairn, swinging his ducky towel like a cape. 'Look! I'm doing a magic dance!'

Bunny ignores him and looks to the sky. Time to concentrate. The sun is past noon and heading west over her left shoulder.

She turns back towards the path leading home. But the sun has shifted; now it's on her right shoulder. *Or was it that before? Fuck I'm thirsty. Okay, home is south. Keep the sun on your right and you won't get turned around again. Come on, Jessica Rabbit, you know your left and right, dontcha?*

'Come on, kid, we really have to go now.'

Silas skids to a halt. 'But we just got here.'

'I know. We can come again tomorrow.'

'This isn't fair. Five more minutes. Please?'

Bunny's getting frazzled – they walked for about a quarter of an hour before ending back here again. That's a quarter of an hour longer until her late-afternoon G & T.

On the way back (for the second time), Silas is apoplectic.

Bunny thinks that the last time, somehow, Silas managed to steer her back while she was occupied with her own thoughts.

That's not happening again. *God, I'm thirsty.*

She watches him suspiciously, shepherding him along in front of her. He kicks at roots and waves his hands like a tiny Italian mobster chewing out his crew as he expresses displeasure.

'Why?! I don't understand!'

She doesn't respond, although she finds it funny. She nudges him along while keeping an eye on the sun. *Right shoulder. Right shoulder.* The staccato rhythm of the phrase matches the sun as it bobs and weaves behind tree trunks. *Right shoulder. Right shoulder.* It starts giving her a headache. Gone. Back. Gone. Back. Light. Dark. Light. Dark.

Cheeky little sun, playing tricks on Jessica Rabbit so she doesn't get her drinky-poo. The winding path ahead straightens out for a spell. She closes her eyes tightly for a second to try and let the sunspots fade. The round ghost circles of light dissolve, the darkness on her retinas is soothing. *Didn't I have sunglasses? Was I wearing them at the lake?* she thinks as she walks, eyes still closed. *Where the hell did, they go? They're fucking Versace!* She bumps into Silas. She's about to give him a light shove when he speaks.

'*Oh my gosh,*' he blurts. She –

Her eyes.

The sun is now back on her left – the circle stretches out in front of them like a place setting at the Hotel California.

'*What the fuck?*' she says.

'*Ha! You said the fuck word!*' Silas is in fine spirits again. '*And stop bringing me, taking me away, bringing me back here. I don't like you playing your tricks.*'

'*Okay.*' She doesn't know what else to say.

Silas picks up the tone in her voice. '*Are we lost? We should try that way.*' He points towards the unknown path. Bunny doesn't respond, so he gingerly crosses the circle, edging towards the path and periodically glancing back at her like a dog that has been told to stay but doesn't want to.

She follows.

The only way to describe the path is enchanting; it's beautiful, more beautiful than her original path behind them could ever be.

Her ankles are gently caressed by tall, soft grass. The soil darkens as they march along, filling the air with the pleasant smell of fertile green things. Occasionally, wild daisies line the path's edges, adding a dash of white and a faint smell of sweetness to the lush greenery. The unease of before melts away. *We've been going the wrong way, but the right way isn't leading anywhere, so what the hell – may as well see where the path leads.*

Silas is a yellow jet plane, *'Nyyyeaaaoooow!'* Arms flung out like wings, swooping from side to side as the path winds left and right in lazy zig-zags. The sun is on her left again, so they're definitely (probably) heading away from home, and have been for some time now. She forgets her thirst in the cool floral air.

Silas hangs another left as he streaks forward. Bunny jogs to keep up with him. *Hey, kid, I'm still the adult here.* But this turn doesn't relent like the previous one. It continues in a wide, lazy arc until she's sure of it. *We've turned around.* She glances up. Over the next few minutes, the sun slowly shifts to her right . . . then left . . . then right again.

They're travelling in a circle.

She doesn't recall seeing a crossroad junction in the path. *Shouldn't we have doubled back over my path by now if we're moving in circles?*

Silas disappears from view again. She still hears him making swooping plane noises up ahead, but it's farther away than she'd like.

'*Silas, slow down please.*'

She speeds up. The unease in her gut returns.

'*We're going in a circle, Aunt Bunny!*'

'*Sweetheart, slow down!*'

Silas doesn't answer. The plane noises have stopped. No bird noises either. Nothing.

'*Silas?*' A gentle descent into panic tightens her throat. Her arms pump at her sides as she muscles ahead. She ran track and swam at school – she was better at swimming, but had dropped it when her mother had warned her that '*it made girls' shoulders too broad*'.

Her Winston-kissed lungs rake up mucus in protest and she spits out a lung-loogie the consistency of oatmeal as she hurtles down the path.

'*Jesus . . . how fast . . . is . . . this kid?*' She wheezes. She runs and runs, unsure for how long; but the stitch tearing up her gut and into her ribs is telling her that it's been a while and that she should probably stop. She can no longer coordinate her gait as she tires beyond the point of control. She feels her head beginning to flop around on her neck like one of those bobble-head dogs in cab windows. She gulps air and tastes bile. Black and red shapes fray the edges of her vision. The thought of slowing forces itself into her mind like a flashing orange road sign. *Slow down, Jessica Rabbit. Jesus, slow down. I'm hurting, Rabbit, I can't breathe, Rabbit, I'm thirsty, Rabbit. Jessica Rabbit? Rabbit?! BUNNY, STOP!*

Her foot lands wrong on an exposed tree root and she flies forward in a bastard swan dive, landing belly first on the dark loam with an '*OOF!*' However, the landing is softer than she expects. Lying here isn't totally unpleasant; the ground is spongy, and the grass tickles her face with a thousand feathers as she lifts it up.

A small distance down the path, a flash of yellow towelling against a black background catches her eye. She pops to her feet.

'*Silas!*'

Silas spins around, wearing the look of a kid caught pilfering a candy bar from a Walgreens. The black background behind him is the entrance to a large cave that she has never seen before. '*You little shit!*' she says, walking towards him. '*I was calling you! Don't go in there.*'

'*Sorry,*' Silas offers.

Bunny's panic evaporates into a disquieting cocktail of awe and dread as she absorbs their new surroundings. The lush path ended abruptly, and they now find themselves standing in a clearing. Surrounding the clearing stand tall skeletons of long dead, but for the most part still upright, pines, their bark sloughed off long ago, exposing dry, white bones of wood beneath. The earth in the clearing is in total contrast to the path. That was dark, moist and aromatic, while this soil is coarse, dry and almost bleached. It reminds Bunny of pictures of Hiroshima from high school history. The living soil seems to have avoided this place; there's no gradual change from living to dead, simply living things, and then an invisible border after which everything is barren and dead.

Behind Silas a mammoth grey granite outcrop thrusts out of the ground like a primordial pulpit under the cathedral of dead pines. The outcrop is jagged and rough except for one large, flat side facing them. In it is the entrance to a cave, a beckoning four-foot-high hole in the rock. From where she stands, she can just make out the back of the cave through the murk. It is smooth and bare.

'Didn't you hear me telling you to slow down?'

Silas is confused. *'But you were right behind me. You told me to go faster.'*

Bunny raises an eyebrow in disbelief.

'You were,' he says. *'You told me to find the cave and go inside . . . but, I don't want to,'* Silas says, sounding scared, almost apologetic in his reluctance.

She looks at him a long while, hoping the answer will come, although she never asked a question.

'Silas, get away from the cave. You don't have to go in. And if we come here again then you must promise that you will never go in . . . even if . . . even if I tell you to.'

She doesn't know why she's saying these things, only that she knows she's right. Silas walks towards her, wraps his arms around her waist, and hugs her. She hugs him back. It is the first time he's let her since the episode under the drawers.

He pats his hand on the small of her back.

She smiles inwardly. *The Trinity knocks come to the rescue.*

She pats twice between his shoulders – pat, pat. *I'm here, kid. Always will be.*

SLAP . . . SLAP . . . SLAP. The sound echoes out of the darkness of the cave like a giant's hand slapping the smooth rock inside. Silas turns rigid in her embrace. '*Bunny?*' he whispers in a small voice as he buries his face in her cotton shirt.

She looks into the cave, and for an instant sees another depth to the darkness. In a blink it's gone.

'*Hello?*' Bunny calls. Not even the air answers. From where she's standing, she's almost positive she can see the entirety of the interior of the cave.

'*Silas, stay here,*' she says as she releases his small body. She approaches the cave. Silas watches her go, his shoulders hunched. He squeezes one hand's thumb with the other hand's fingers.

With only a few feet to go, Bunny confirms that the cave is indeed empty, no crazy people crouched inside watching them . . . No monsters.

Then she hears it. The muttering.

Like someone backstage in a theatre mouthing a soliloquy before stepping out under the stage lights. There's no air in the voice, no weight, it's barely audible. She would have missed it if it hadn't been for the otherwise total silence. It's so faint she can't make out what it's saying, which makes it sound more like quiet static on a radio. She edges forward until her head ducks into the cave entrance. She thinks she can make out the spot it's coming from, but she still can't actually hear the words – if they are words.

'*Bunny?*' Silas whispers from behind her. She dares not turn around; she has a feeling the muttering will stop if she does, and she wants to know, needs to know, what it's saying. Is it like her voice? The one at home that follows her round the house? The one that brings her to the woods? She makes a 'not now' gesture behind her to Silas. She bends down and crawls into the entrance of the cave.

This is where it's talking, this is where the voice lives. She makes sure there isn't some secret crevice or crack she has missed, a crack where the voice may be living. Satisfied that she has surveyed the interior and determined that it is intact, she returns to the back of the cave wall. It smells dry and unremarkable as she presses her ear to the rock . . .

Silas watches Bunny enter the cave.

'*Bunny?*' he whispers.

She shoots her hand out at him.

She creeps forward until she is right up against the back of the cave. First, he waits, afraid and quiet. After a while though, nothing has happened. Bunny has stayed in exactly the same spot.

Well, what now? He shifts his weight on his legs and rocks back and forth, tugging on the yellow cotton drawstring of his ducky hood (he likes listening to the zipping sound it makes as he pulls it one way, then the other, through the eyelets). His internal child-clock estimates that it has been approximately four million years since his aunt entered the cave and stayed hunched over in the back of it.

'*Bunny?*' The sound of his own voice is alien in his ears because the place is so quiet. She doesn't answer, or even move. There is no 'not now' hand this time, though, so he decides to try and push his luck.

'*Bunny?*'

Nothing.

'*Hey, Aunt Bunny!*'

Still nothing. Silas has had enough of this game; Bunny has somehow managed to make finding a secret cave boring. He waits a little longer for her to move, to come out before he gives up and begins exploring. He tugs back and forth on the drawstring until (inevitably) he pulls too hard one way – it slips, loses its equilibrium and slides out of its fabric tube. He immediately loses interest in his towel hoodie and decides to gather old, brown pinecones from the surrounding green bushes. There are no cones in the clearing itself as the dead white trees surrounding it are hundreds of years past their fruitful prime. Silas fashions a wreath-like crown out of his treasures, held together with his liberated bright yellow drawstring.

After securing the pinecones, he places the crown on his head. It feels heavy. He nods his head emphatically to ensure his crown is sturdy, then marches on. King of his imaginary kingdom. King of the dead trees . . .

Bunny presses the side of her head against the rock. Her ear seals itself against the smooth stone as the words come out:

'The roots in the rock wake me I bite them the land is dead the roots in the rock wake me I bite them the land is dead the roots in the rock wake me I bite them the land is dead.'

'Who are you?' she whispers.

The muttering stops.

Then answers.

'*I am old.*'

'Why are you here?'

'*I do not know.*'

'What do you want?'

'*I do not know.*' There's a pause. It's thinking; gathering words in its native tongue and translating them into things she will understand.

'*I visit you,*' it whispers.

She thinks she can hear it stir in the rock.

'Why?' Bunny asks.

'*You visit me,*' it replies.

Her mind whirls. '*I don't understand.*'

'*You visit me I visit you visit me I visit you visit me I visit you –*' it drones on and on.

Bunny lifts her ear away from the rock and stares at its bare, smooth surface. She expects to see the face of the voice inside it. She feels the cave whispering in the ancient air around her, pulsing into a crescendo: '– *me I visit you visit me I visit you visit me I visit –*'

The whisper grows into a dark, hard voice, becoming more insistent '– *YOU VISIT ME I VISIT YOU!*'

She's about to scream when the voice stops. She holds her breath in the silence.

'*The Little King.*' There's a corrupt purr of amusement in its voice.

It makes Bunny want to dig her nails into her face and tear it off so she would have something else to feel other than the amusement in that voice. *Maybe I should try?* she thinks madly before hearing Silas humming outside. She turns around and sees him marching along the perimeter of the dead clearing, humming and wearing a crown of pinecones on his head. '*The Little King?*' she asks, and realises that it's seen him too – and it is delighted.

'*No!*' she screams at the rock. '*No!*'

Outside, Silas spins around in fright. Bunny runs out of the cave towards him and half scoops him up as she runs. Her nails dig into the same rib that she hurt last time. He yelps as he feels the same red glow of pain singe his skin. He wriggles free as she puts him down, letting him regain his footing as she drags him along behind her.

'*RUN!*' she screams.

He obeys. As they hurtle towards the green path, he glances back towards the stone outcrop, but he sees only flat stone where the cave is supposed to be.

'*Aunt Bunny, where'd the cave go?!*'

Bunny doesn't hear him or turn around. The path stretches out ahead of her in one long, straight line. *Where the fuck are all the curves?* If they had taken another wrong path, that was fine – they would not be turning around. One foot in front of the other, heading away from this place.

Silas skitters along behind her like a stone skipping across water, half dragged, half sprinting. He travels three paces for every one that his feet touch the ground. As they enter the lush path, an overhanging branch sweeps over his head, catching his pinecone wreath – his self-proclaimed crown. He howls as the branch rakes through his hair, bending like a catapult as it holds him by his scalp. Bunny keeps going. Finally, the branch whips free of him, carrying the wreath with it. Silas steals a final glance behind him. In the grey dust of the dead clearing, directly in front of where the cave was, lies his wreath. An offering to the dead stone.

2018

AND PUPPY DOGS' TALES

A man who looks to be an accurate amalgamation of every extra in a Kid Rock music video stumbles out of the only consultation room at the Hamner Animal Control office, which also doubles as the local veterinary hospital.

'Fu . . . fuck you, Eugene. You'll be hearing from my lawyer!' Donovan bleats, as he pushes open the front door and half leaves.

'Ya, get that line from *Boston Legal*, ya fuckin' dong? Calm down, mate, it was only a backhand,' the veterinarian explains, stepping out of the consultation room. 'I warned ya. Keep running the puppy mill up there and I'm taking Nellie off you. Plain and simple, mate. You know – like you.'

Dr Eugene 'Euge' Demopoulos is a transplant from Australia; he moved from Melbourne to New York in the mid-eighties after winning the Green Card lottery. When quizzed about why he had moved, he would respond: 'Met many Aussies before, mate?'

Back then, the person he was talking to would usually shrug, indicating they had encountered none to one (which was usually him).

The Australia Euge had left in the eighties had been a very different place. He had not been a fan of its societal and political landscape at the time, particularly when it came to race relations, or how the country treated anyone that wasn't Hitler's idea of the 'perfect specimen'.

Being of Greek heritage, his folks had been the latest wave of immigrants (along with the Italians and a smattering of Eastern Europeans) to flock to Australia after the British, Irish and Scots. In school he had been called a nigger enough times by pink-skinned classmates for him to decide that the place would never be his home . . . Although it hadn't taken him long to figure out that America had similar issues. (It was, after all, also populated with human beings.) But he had stepped off the plane determined to make it work. And he had. The majority of his family had stayed in Melbourne, had families and bought up large chunks of real estate, while he had made the decision to live alone with dogs, and had purposefully become the self-described town asshole. He often found it peculiar that his Australian accent was as pronounced today as it had been the day he stepped off the plane almost four decades ago. He wondered why it hadn't softened, although at the back of his mind, he knew it was because it made him different – exotic even – and he realised it gave him a sort of jaundiced pleasure being the 'educated other' among his predominantly white-bread peers.

The constant 'fuck you' to the world was more satisfying than the blow jobs he infrequently received from his married veterinary nurse, Carolyn.

And, after all these years in this country, he'd realised that by moving here, he had acted no more superior than a disenchanted moth flying across a dark field to batter itself into the sweet release of a hot light bulb. He had gently come to the realisation that certain men came to as they wrestled through their enraged twenties, scowling thirties, bemused forties and beyond – he knew now that he didn't much like *anyone.*

Fuck, he didn't even really like Carolyn much. His dogs didn't like her and she was needy. When she acted cutesy at work, she either wanted sex or attention; she would ask him stupid questions, like, 'Do you think I have wrinkles?' She was fifty-six, married for over twenty years, had three children and one grandchild. *Fuck, Cazza, what do you think?*

Although, this didn't seem to bother her (or him), when on the occasional Friday night, they would wipe down the consultation table and perform oral sex on one another. Euge always thought that this base need to rut would have diminished by fifty (he had hoped it would), but he found himself sliding towards sixty with the same inflamed needs he'd had at fifteen. If he had one goal in life, it was to be beholden to nothing and nobody for *anything* – apart from Kayle, Birdy, Choo-Choo and Tripes (his three rescue dogs and one three-legged cat).

But today, his mind is on another, soon-to-be rescue dog.

Donovan stands in the doorway rubbing the side of his pubic-bearded face, which is now flushed bright pink from the verbal and physical slap Euge inflicted on it. 'Nellie is my property!' Donovan yells.

'So's your life.'

Confusion washes over Donovan's face. 'So?'

'So, I can take that away too.'

Euge lunges forward, grabs the handle and shuts the door behind Donovan before he can leave. His other hand shoots out, wraps itself around Donovan's wiry neck and slams his body against the shut door.

※

Carolyn sits at the reception desk aghast, prickling with anticipation. Her thoughts run from the situation into her make-believe world, a world with very different possibilities: *I could ask Keith for a divorce. He's nearing seventy, in a wheelchair from the stroke and losing control of his bowels . . . But he knows how to use the microwave and could always get a helper – a nice Mexican girl. Oh! Or that Indian girl that Barbara used for her mother? Then I'd be free and me and Euge could retire to . . . Bali? Oh my God, just like in* Eat Pray Love!

Watching Eugene, she's (almost) ashamed at how aroused she feels. She's menopausal, her oestrogen rapidly decreasing, and theoretically, shouldn't she be *losing* interest in sex? *I knit, for God's sake. I'm a grandmother. Christ, Carolyn, you should be thinking about how you're going to be seeing your grandchild in a week.*

Carolyn's only daughter, Brenda, moved to Florida with her only grandchild two years ago. There she sold Avon products and lived a perfectly peaceful domestic life with her husband, Owen, who sold holiday packages. Carolyn often felt a sense of anger towards Brenda for 'having it so easy', while Carolyn cared solely for Keith. The upcoming trip to see her daughter and grandbaby would be for a month, and Carolyn knew that Brenda and Owen would foot the bill, which she (of course) was grateful for. Carolyn had spent her long evenings knitting two jumpers for her beloved grandbaby, Cora (one SpongeBob SquarePants knitted print and one striped pink and white cardigan). She just hoped that Cora would still fit in them by the time she arrived. She was leaving in just a few days. She *should* be making a list, checking her bus itinerary (she agreed to take the bus as it was cheaper for Brenda and Owen, although she'd been hoping that they would surprise her with a plane ticket) and she tries to make a list in her head of the mounting to-do's that have not been done (like ensuring that the live-in nurse *really* will be a live-in nurse for Keith while she's gone).

But instead, she's getting horny.

She always fought the urges, but sometimes she just couldn't and that's where Euge came in. It was mostly on the odd Friday night, but lately they've been using the *'Back in 15'* sign during midday lulls. Although, they really only need eight.

She'll be gone for a month (maybe a little more if Brenda needs help). Brenda and Owen are hiring a new landscape gardener and Carolyn feels her knowledge of American perennial flowers could be of great use for her and Owen's expansive garden. The point is, she will be gone a while, and nobody could reasonably judge her if she needed a small glass of water before the drought set in. Besides, she has never seen him like this before, so *threatening* with someone. Carolyn wonders if she should intervene as Eugene presses Donovan's throat harder into the shut door. She decides against it. *Best not get involved*, she thinks, before fantasising about the mid-afternoon lull and that *'Back in 15'* sign . . .

Eugene feels Donovan's neck becoming greasy with sweat under his hand. He notes the mixture of nicotine and the sharp cat-piss-vinegar scent of meth sweat.

'I know what you do with those pups, ya cunt. You supply dog-fighting rings. The big ones, like your Nellie, are pumped full of steroids and coke and made to tear each other apart in backwater shitholes all over the fucking country. I know runts have their mouths taped shut – get thrown to the big ones to train 'em to kill.'

'You've got no proof. I, I got raided and they got no proof!' Donovan stammers.

'Who do you think I am, fuckwit? The police? I don't need evidence cos this isn't gonna go to court. I'll just put you down, you insignificunt,' Euge growls.

Carolyn summarises in her head how best to explain to her children that *Mom and Dad still love each other very much, but not in that way anymore.* She also mentally prepares herself for having sex with Dr Demo when the meth head leaves. Carolyn has never been able to say Eugene's last name without making a mistake, so she has abbreviated it.

'I have to drive along the interstate and see discarded dog carcasses with no throats because some micro-penis had them fighting and they've lost. A lot of them look just like Nellie, don't they?' Euge squeezes Donovan's throat and nods his head for him. ''Cos she's your champion, isn't she? *Lots* of pups from Nellie.'

A whimpering sigh escapes Donovan's lips. Euge moves

in closer, cheek to cheek now – it's a strange intimacy. Euge only lets his dogs and people he doesn't like get this close to his face. He whispers into Donovan's ear so Carolyn can't hear what he's saying, 'I've put up with four years of this shit from you. But no more, mate. Any more nonsense and I'll sneak into your house one night and overdose you with the ketamine I use for Nate Sullivan's horses. Then I'll run you a nice hot bath. Your mates, or the cops, will find ya in the bathtub and assume you smoked something, assumed ya nodded off and drowned, ya junkie fuck.'

Euge simultaneously twists the doorknob and releases Donovan's neck. The door swings open against the weight of Donovan pushing against it and he tumbles onto the sidewalk. The street is empty; it's that mid-morning quiet when everyone is already where they need to be for the day. Euge glowers at him, purses his lips and blows him a kiss. *Just to show him he didn't imagine the last twenty seconds*, he thinks, before closing the door.

He's silent for a moment before a single amused hoot bursts out of him. This is the first time he has ever *truly* threatened a man's life, and it doesn't feel as terrible as popular morality suggests it should. In fact, he feels great.

'Shouldn't'a watched *The Equalizer* last night, Euge,' he says to himself, as he walks past the reception desk.

'Doctor, should I get the room ready?' Carolyn purrs as he walks past.

'No,' is the reply.

That was far better than any thrill he's had with Carolyn.

Carolyn feigns a smile and returns to her administrative work, the potential divorce and soul-searching pilgrimage to Southeast Asia now a discarded daydream.

⸙

Euge walks into the back room and opens the door to a cage that holds the biggest pit bull he has ever seen. The hulking old bitch is white with brown spots. Tired, sagging nipples hang down from her belly in tattered rows, like deflated speed bags in an old boxing gym. Her face is covered in knotted pink scars that peek out between the fur from past fights – a hint of her life before she was turned into nothing more than a breeding commodity. Her one and only eye shines brilliant blue, and fills with love when she sees him. Her tail wags as her enormous mouth opens in a friendly smile, displaying large, battle-chipped canines. From behind them lolls a tongue that resembles a tattered red necktie, the left side torn off in a past fight.

'Hello, Nellie, come here baby,' Euge says in his deep, baby-talking voice he reserves only for the purest creatures of the world. He kneels and gives Nellie the first cuddle that she has had in a very long time.

ARTISAN BAKERIES & PRETTIER TOWNS

Silas, Rose and Goober climb out of the car. 'Welcome to Hamner,' says Silas as he twirls the car keys around his index finger. Rose looks up and down Emerson Blvd. She decides that whoever anointed the street with the title of 'boulevard' must have had a sense of humour.

Emerson comprises two narrow lanes with parking spaces on either side, making it feel significantly wider than it is. It's lined with a jarring mixture of quaint old storefronts and prefab-looking strip mall cubes. If the town's story were a song, it would be the industrial Northeast's greatest hits. Whatever commercial undertaking precipitated the town's creation dissolved sometime in the previous century, leaving behind a sadder, emptier, poorer place as a eulogy; a Springsteen song with the barrel of Gramps's American-made Colt 1911 waiting between gritted teeth for the final chorus. A scattering of nearby regional towns have been (or are in the process of being) resurrected by wealthy out-of-towners buying up homes and businesses to accommodate their leisure activities on long weekends. Artisan bakeries with overpriced 'deconstructed' sandwiches (meaning you pay a premium to butter the rustic sourdough slices yourself) breathe life into old towns that offer pretty views; those by the sea, or with a view over the valleys. These towns are the first in line to get a new lease of life.

If Hamner is even in the line, it's definitely at the back.

'Where's the vet?' Rose asks.

'Down here somewhere, if I recall. Google Maps shit the bed when I asked, so I'm going off memory now,' Silas says as he scoops Goober up from the sidewalk. 'Come on, kid, you'll get your bandage wet.'

A light drizzle in the early hours slicked the ground, and it's jacket weather.

The street is quiet as they walk along the sidewalk. They pass by shopfronts: a diner, a boarded window, a drugstore, a clinic, a boarded window, an empty lot, a bar and much the same on the other side. The rudiments of the town remain (services and a handful of eateries), but as they pass the window of the local realtor's office it shows faded property listings curling with age.

Silas's eyes fall on their destination: a squat, grey building across the road, on the corner, resembling a Russian Cold War–era bunker. 'There it is.'

On the facade painted block letters read:

**HAMNER ANIMAL CONTROL AND
VETERINARY SERVICES**

A weedy-looking man wearing a sleeveless Pantera shirt loiters outside. He jerkily paces up and down as if deciding whether or not to enter the premises. He hovers by the entrance door, talks to himself angrily and scuffs away down the road in unlaced combat boots.

'Friend of yours?' Rose inquires jokingly.

'He might be the mayor,' Silas replies as they cross the road.

🌰

A young couple with a dog enters the stark reception area. Carolyn gives her biggest 'I'm accommodating!' smile. It's clear that while they aren't wealthy long-weekenders, they at least appear not to be on crystal meth – and they're new clients who look like they can afford their bill.

The amount of free work Eugene takes on means that Carolyn often has to put her best 'It's fine, honey! Honestly! Don't worry about it!' voice on when Eugene asks if he can pay her at the end of the month instead of weekly. They both know he often doesn't have the cash until after he visits the horsey people's stables in the third week of every month.

Carolyn is on the verge of greeting them when Euge's voice booms from the back of the building. 'Donovan, mate, take a fuckin' hint!' Euge says as he shoves the door open and sees new clientele gawking at him. The unwarranted aggression causes the young man and Euge to size each other up instinctively, but the awkward switch of Euge's body language from aggressive to 'whoopsie' means that the young woman and herself see two men who look more like co-workers bumping into each other in a brothel at lunch hour, rather than two potential alpha males preparing to battle.

🌰

Euge sees a cute couple. The woman is black-haired, honey-coloured and striking; the man is shaggy, pale and possesses a forehead that says he frowns too much. In his arms is a medium-sized black dog – a mixed-breed rescue that looks just like his baby, Choo-Choo.

🌰

Silas sees (to quote the Antipodean vernacular) a brick shithouse of a man, mid-to-late fifties, with hard but benevolent eyes.

🌰

Carolyn shoots Eugene daggers for scaring the potential paying customers.

I'm not going to have it, especially when he can hardly keep the doors open as is. Am I the only one here who knows how to run a business? The afternoon rendezvous is definitely off. How could I ever think of leaving my husband for this ogre? Keith was – well, back in his day – a pillar. Everyone in this town loves and respects him. That means something. The thoughts rattle off in her head until she rearranges the world back into a manageable form.

'Whoops, sorry about that. Thought you were someone else.' Euge tries to smile. He and Carolyn both do. Like a bad ventriloquist act.

'There was a guy outside,' Silas says, 'but he went down the road. Looked like God made him when he was drunk.'

'Inappropriate as always,' Rose says under her breath.

bunny

Eugene's eyes warm and crinkle at the corners. 'Yip, that'd be him.'

'Jesus!' Silas says.

Nellie's colossal head is peeping out around Eugene's thigh. Goober spots her and wags his tail. 'Good thing you carried Goob in,' Rose says.

'Took this one off of him. He came to, uh, voice his objections.' A deep growl vibrates the room. 'Shush, girlie,' Euge says as he returns Nellie securely to the back room, but not before giving the dog's head a gentle stroke. 'She isn't good with other dogs. Well, not yet. Let's go in here.' He gestures for them to enter the examination room.

'Eugene . . . Forms?' Carolyn holds up the clipboard and necessary paperwork for new clients and not so subtly taps the *'How would you like to pay?'* section at the bottom of the page. She looks pissed. Euge knows the fact that he runs his business like he runs his life pisses her off, which is understandable. He walks over, takes the clipboard and points to the examination room.

'Ah, yip. Great, so I'm Euge Demopoulos – vet and dogcatcher.'

Euge extends a hand to Silas, but both are full of dog.

Silas wriggles one free to do the formal greeting thing. 'Silas.'

Euge is about to turn when Rose sticks her hand out.

Whoops, Euge thinks before extending the greeting to her.

'Rose,' she says, making sure to squeeze his giant mitt firmly. 'And *this* is Goober,' she adds in the high-pitched tone that only besotted parents use. Goober squirms, eager to make Euge's acquaintance.

Silas lowers Goober onto the steel examination table, which Goober seems to think is *very* exciting. Euge gives him a good firm pat. 'Alright, mate, what have you managed to do to your leg?'

'He got bitten by an eel at Long Lake,' Silas says.

Euge cocks an eyebrow. Silas assumes the facial expression is scepticism. He's about to launch into assurances when Euge speaks first.

'That's not the first time I've heard of it. Last season a couple of duck-hunters downed a bird in the water there. Their retriever launched out to grab it and got pulled under by something. They reckon they saw a large eel. One waded in to try to get to the dog – but they were chased out of the water by the fish, eels . . .'

'They aren't supposed to do that, right? Don't they eat crap at the bottom – little bugs and stuff like that?' Rose asks.

'Yeah. My veterinarian's opinion is: it's a bit fuckin' weird.' Rose and Silas laugh at Eugene's glib response. He seems not to notice. 'Might head up there sometime and have a look-see. Maybe something's mucking around with their normal food source or pushing 'em out. Too cold for alligators, so might take a dip with a mask and snorkel.'

'I wouldn't advise it, Dr Dimpal–'

'He wouldn't advise that, Dr Demopoulos,' Rose chirps in.

Euge instantly finds Rose appealing. She's the first person in the town who has ever said his last name correctly. But what isn't to like? Rose has an accent, dark skin and a rescue dog. He looks at her dark eyes and hopes he doesn't come off as creepy.

Silas holds up his mangled hand. 'The thing latched onto me when I tried to get it off him. Damn near pulled *me* into the lake.'

'How'd ya get it off?'

'Smashed its head in with a rock.'

Euge digests what he's heard. 'I'll bring my dive knife when I go.'

Rose unwraps Goober's pink bandage.

'Ta. Now let's have a look, little fella.' He begins cleaning the wound, warm water at first and then iodine. He takes time to clean, inspecting to determine if stitches are necessary. Goober is placid as ever, enjoying *three* people giving him attention. Euge is always thorough, but he purposefully takes his time with this appointment; it's the first time in a long time that he's been able to enjoy the company and frank conversation that can be had with a certain type of stranger.

'Well, that's about as long as I can keep ya,' Euge says a few minutes later as he replaces Goober's bandage. He reuses the pink tape from the old one, as he has misplaced his roll – or used the last one on Nellie. Carolyn is supposed to keep on top of that, but he's not going to bring that up with her right now. It's fine, he'll order it himself. Goober looks untroubled as Eugene lifts him off the table and onto the peeling lino floor.

'What do we owe you?' Rose asks.

'Aw hell, make a donation to the ASPCA if ya get a chance. Little guy just needed a bit of a clean-up, but you guys did a real good job on it though,' Euge says, knowing that Carolyn might actually yell at him this time. He's smiling at them. He never smiles. He catches a glimpse of himself in the bubble dome convex mirror that Carolyn made him install after a client (probably Donovan) stole one too many over-the-counter deworming tablets. He frowns as he sees his own reflection and then catches sight of Carolyn behind the reception desk – standing. She's livid, and mouthing words that he thinks he can make out. It's either 'fuck you' or 'I'll fuck you'. He hopes it's the latter – it's better when they argue. He contemplates bringing up the fact that she hasn't sent off an inventory list to their wholesale supplier for at least six weeks. Now that would *really* piss her off.

Polite exchanges are made as Euge walks them to the door, then one final pat for Goober and a final smile, nod and laugh for Rose and Silas. *Dear Lord, this town needs more young people.*

A dejected little whine beckons to him from the back room.

'Coming, girlie.' He turns back to them. 'Pop by in a few weeks. You can buy me a beer at Surley's, and I'll tell ya what's going on in Long Lake.'

Silas offers to tag along on the lake trip, but Euge kindly tells him that he prefers to be in the woods alone.

'Thanks, Euge. Pleasure talking to you.' Silas shakes his hand.

'No worries, mate. Likewise.' And to Rose, 'See ya, love.' He takes her hand and kisses it, completely immune to the hokeyness of the gesture (and Carolyn's raised eyebrow).

WORK DAYS

Silas's childhood bedroom transforms into a dissolving barrier between days and weeks. His sense of time evaporates into a porous slush. Sleep and wake cycles are battered into strange shapes as the work of writing rudely unfurls itself over the room and their lives. Sometimes they write with clear-eyed energy and focus like pistons in a two-stroke engine – one bursting out work as the other recovers. Sometimes they finish each other's sentences and lines of dialogue with the speed of a South Korean game of ping-pong. Sometimes the notes from producers don't make sense, so they pace, curse, lie on the bed in defeat, or squabble over seemingly insignificant details, which (through squabbling) invariably become significant. Sometimes the notes *do* make sense, which is worse, because then they are forced to wonder how they could have missed such glaring issues. Sometimes the work is dry and so are they, numbly pulling every word out of the ether like exhausted commoners tugging on Excalibur.

When the black and white replicated prints of Hemingway fishing and Kerouac in repose fade from memory or slip off their tack on the wall, the writing becomes what it has always been – mostly work with brief moments of pleasure, like everything else in life.

*

Flat surfaces are populated with empty cups and plates that stare up at the ceiling. Crusty breadcrumbs tack onto the bottom of overworn socks. As Goober scratches, dog hair drifts into the air and falls onto several different cups and plates. He tests different spots to snooze in, his daily work consisting of watching midges and tracking sunbeams across the floorboards.

The script sees new scenes replace old ones. Characters leave the story, unneeded as others are born. Like a toddler about to stand, each day it pulls itself up more, gaining strength until it can walk all the way to Uncle Jerry and happily into the producers' hands, where they will then write a huge check instead of the tidbit notes that Silas is still adamant 'make no fucking sense'.

Food and sleep get in the way of productivity. Silas is sure they can survive purely off caffeinated adrenaline and snarky comments, but Rose talks of iron absorption and lactobacillus acidophilus. The food prep, though, is a bit of a juggling act. They have to make meals at certain times and in batches to avoid Bunny and Lou Lou. Bunny is out of the house most of the time, seemingly day and night, and Lou Lou can be managed with an outward smile and an inward grimace when circumstances demand. Sleep is stolen in fits and starts when their minds turn fluffy. This is determined when one of them struggles to find a word, or has that overbaked, detached look that can only be cured by sleep or a wellness retreat. The one that is holding on to sanity best will then instruct the other to take a power nap – the secret weapon of success and defender of reason. Sometimes, afterwards, they make love. It's a sleepy afterthought and more affectionate than erotic; pyjama-top-stays-on sex, while Goober politely looks away.

Occasionally, as they drift off to sleep, they hear the front or back door slam three times. 'You lock the door?' Rose will ask.

'Yep.'

'Closed the window?'

'And curtains. Every night.'

If there is cigarette smoke outside, it can't get through the closed window . . .

One morning Silas rises early to rid himself of a percolating idea. Rose wakes to find him wrapped in a blanket and typing at the desk. He hears her stir and looks over to see her smiling eyes. He quietly holds a finger to his lips and opens the blanket to reveal Goober asleep on his lap. 'I heart you,' Rose whispers. 'We heart you too,' he whispers back, as he closes the blanket.

The plan to finish the script and stay sane around Bunny was a simple one:

Keep distraction to a minimum by not engaging.

Some things they see, and some things they don't.

What they see:

Silas sees that over the years, Lou Lou's brand of suburban high-functioning alcoholism has been melded to fit life in the country. Her days are filled with ever-increasing minutiae to make them go faster; errands and visits into town propel the day into that sacred time when she can begin fixing herself a drink. During occasional evening encounters, if asked how her day was or what has she got up to, a vague confusion clouds her searching face; often she just doesn't seem to know. Her day? The tasks themselves were unimportant, as long as they got her to the evening.

They see Bunny come in and out of the house at all hours like an omnipresent wraith, sometimes leaving for mere minutes at a time, and sometimes for hours.

One day, Rose sees a tremor in Bunny's hands and overhears a small sob escape her as she prepares a drink – presumably having left it too long between doses. It is just past 9 a.m.

They see the true extent of alcoholic co-dependence that has overrun the house: the sisters' uneasy, decaying orbits, like twin black holes slowly swallowing each other.

Silas sees the subtle acts of dominance that Bunny exerts over himself and Lou Lou. One day, Lou Lou plants a rose near the kitchen door; the next morning the rose is surrounded by a halo of spinach. Lou Lou sees it, then unsees it, then fixes a drink. He remembers it being like this between them when he was younger, but not this bad. Previously it left him with a general feeling of unease that later splintered into dark rays of diagnosable anxiety disorders. Now it's worse – something he had not thought possible.

What they don't see:

They don't see Bunny in the secret folds of the night, standing for hours outside in the woods, watching the moon crawl through the tree branches as if she's waiting for permission.

They don't see Lou Lou gnawing her thumbnail in the town market as she buys ingredients in order to cook a nice meal for Rose and Silas, trying to coax them out of their room for an evening, because she desperately wants to mend her relationship with him. Gnawing and gnawing – only halting when she tastes iron... She worries that the frayed cord between them will disappear forever. She has only one son, one child and somehow, he got older.

They don't see her later that day, unpacking cartons of Winstons and bottles and bottles and bottles of rotgut gin, leaving them behind the shed among the cordwood before walking inside with only two, just in case her guests (her son) is keeping count.

They don't see Bunny outside the house that night, watching Silas, Rose and Lou Lou together at the dinner table eating a meal. And they certainly don't feel the swirling emotions inside Bunny, or how aspects of her former self still appear, contained within an inner cloud, like a time capsule of who she was. *You'd like me*, she thinks as she watches Silas pick up a glass of water. *You'd still like me.*

And then she's gone again.

Silas doesn't see her one afternoon, standing behind a tree, as she watches him take Goober out to snuffle around and pee after a long stretch cooped up in the bedroom. He doesn't see her watching him as he also relieves himself against the same tree. He doesn't see her waiting for him to leave before creeping out of the trees. He doesn't see her approach the same tree. And he doesn't see her squat in the same spot as she urinates over the ground like an animal marking territory.

He doesn't see how she is now being more careful than she was that first night... And so is The Other, the one that watches from within her, all too aware now of the small creature in the bedroom that can feel them (if they aren't hidden).

Rose and Silas don't see Bunny and The Other, outside their window watching them sleeping, working and making love.

They don't see how, even though it's dark outside and the drapes are closed, Bunny's head is still able to track them as they pace in the small room, as if the walls do not exist.

They don't see.

THE LAKE

Eugene is sitting at the bar in Surley's when he decides it'd be best to see about this eel problem before tourist season sees a bunch of complaints coming in. That's if there *is* something going on and *if* the tourists actually go to Long Lake, which he thinks is unlikely. He hasn't been up there for years and can't remember anything particularly noteworthy about it, other than the suffocating pine trees.

He once had (years ago, when he drank and didn't mind socialising as much) a boozy one-night stand out there with Louise Burbridge in a boathouse on the lakeside. He knew she lived in a rambling house nearby, and to his knowledge, still does. That name and her face have returned to his memory frequently over the past few weeks.

He thinks of her as he picks a salted cashew from a bowl and tosses it into his mouth, remembering his younger years. Lou Lou Burbridge was one of the few women that Eugene had actually (sort of) attempted to have a relationship with. After their tryst, he had become enamoured and tried calling her – but never heard back. When he had spotted her in town a few weeks later purchasing large show candles, he'd waved. She pretended she hadn't seen him before quickly driving off. In the years since, he had occasionally seen her from afar and walked the other way.

He prefers to dine alone, but enjoys keeping distanced company and listening to the old bastards who keep Surley's in business with their perennial stewardship. Even after decades of him living here, they still know more than him about the local terrain.

'Ayuh, that lake, *thaaat fuckin' lake is . . . dead*,' Dennis 'the menace' Garbrandt proclaims like a plaid-draped seer, to the nods and grunts of the others.

Euge tries some gentle coaxing but elicits nothing further that is useful from the old-timers – just a long-held consensus that the place just isn't very pleasant, that the fishing is bad and that the trout seem to prefer neighbouring bodies of water. There are ducks, apparently, but much fewer than there *should* be, and so, unless you're an out-of-towner doing some exploring, there isn't much reason to remember that the place even exists.

Dennis conspiratorially leans his white whiskers over Euge's ginger ale. Perhaps some useful nugget of information is about to be shared –

'*The gays* have been known to *frequent* the parking lot at the north end, if you catch what I'm drifting,' Dennis murmurs with sour-mash breath.

Euge sighs inwardly as he nods at Dennis's not-so-subtle eyebrow lifts and jerky head nods.

'How would you know?' squawks a butter bean of a man who's tightly packed into oil-stained Carhartt overalls with the name *NORMAN* embroidered on the bosom-like chest. The hooting that follows signals a definitive end to useful discourse.

*

Two hours later, Euge parks at the north end parking lot.

He sees no gays.

He opens the back door, hauls out a backpack and slings it over his shoulder. The canine mountain that is Nellie hops onto the ground with more grace than her size would suggest she is capable of. (He's not exactly sure how she'll behave if they come across other people or animals; he knows he's being irresponsible taking her out so soon, but he's doing it anyhow.) He gently places a lead over her head, which she watches with mistrust. When it is securely on, she immediately tests it with a tug. It's not a harness, but at least it's not the steel choker chains with inward-facing teeth that she's used to. Nellie watches his face, making herself available for kindness.

'It's okay, girlie, it'll be fun,' Euge croons.

The two make their way a few hundred yards down to the edge of Long Lake, ready for adventure and maybe, later, eel pie.

Somehow the lake looks colder in the afternoon sun than if it were cloudy. His ancestors ruled the Greek isles, and were known for being the best fishermen in the world – but that was in warm Mediterranean water.

He ties Nellie to the branch of a downed pine, and offers her a handful of Tasty Chewz. He knows it is crucial for her to learn trust, and to distinguish between life with a meth-head dog-fighting fuckwit and life with him. He fishes his snorkelling gear out of his backpack: wetsuit, gloves, fins, mask, snorkel, knife. He kits up next to Nellie, who has become attached to him over the last few weeks and now whines anytime he goes away.

'There there, love, won't be long. Just going to have a look and see what I can see,' he says, scratching her gnarled, pointy ears.

In spite of years of regular sessions of garage-gym weightlifting while listening to Chet Baker records, Eugene's wetsuit hardly fits; yes, his shoulders have broadened into mature, middle-aged brawn, but the pot belly now encased in black neoprene is the primary issue. *Well, ya can't listen to jazz while ya run, can ya, mate?* he thinks to himself as he tries to remember the last time he actually *saw* his running shoes.

He picks a spot, wades in and sits down in the thigh-deep water to put on his fins. Before he does, he slips his mask on and peeps into the water. The lake bed consists of a flat blanket of bottle-top-sized stones before giving way to a steep slope that disappears into the cold, tannin-coloured depths.

Nellie begins to whine.

'It's okay, girlie, it's okay!' He pushes his mask up on his forehead. The clear rubber sucks at his skin and he jams his left foot into the fin when Nellie stops whining and starts barking. He turns to reassure her. 'Hush now, girlie –'

He feels a tug on his ankle – small, like a toddler who wants your attention. A much harder tug jolts him so hard he hears his hip socket creak as a vice snaps shut on his ankle. By the time he realises he's being pulled into the water, he's already under. His mask loses its hold on his skin. It pops off the top of his head and floats to the surface for Nellie to bark at.

As he slips deeper, the sun's rays battle to penetrate the

murk and he begins to lose the light. His eardrums scream as he descends too fast. He feels surprisingly little pain as the bones in his ankle grind against one another and then give way in a series of crackling pops. *A new species? Newly introduced predator?* Eugene looks down before the light fades completely, expecting to see the black eyes of some Lovecraftian eel. Before the light flees altogether, he could swear he sees a hand below him.

In the dark he feels rock on both sides pinch shut against his belly as he's pulled into a crevice. A deep, heavy *crack* comes from somewhere inside him as his hip wrenches at an impossible angle and suddenly feels as if it's floating high up in his chest.

Shit, the dog's still tied to the tree.

He hears Chet Baker's trumpet sighing in his ears as blood wells up his throat, warming the cold water in his mouth as he closes his eyes . . .

Nellie strains against the branch. Her enormous chest rises as she stands on her hind legs, trying to tear herself free from the collar around her neck. She falls back, recovers and punches forward again. The leash snaps taut, she falls back, recovers and punches forward again. The branch splinters and breaks, freeing her. Nellie tucks her tail between her legs in terror and skitters away from the lake, her flanks dripping urine as she goes.

NOT YET

They wake on their bedroom floor; Silas first, which rouses Goober, who's using his outstretched arm as a pillow. Silas looks into Rose's sleeping face, her head resting on his other arm. A thin trail of drool has crept out of her mouth and dried on his skin. She looks happier when she's asleep. Her face is betrayingly expressive, so every thought is punctuated by small twitches around her mouth, or a frown dancing over her brow. Sleeping seems to be the only time she's at peace, the only time when she isn't trying to right the world.

'Rosie, Rooosiiiiiiiie.'

Goober assists Dad by gently nuzzling her cheek.

'Hello, boys,' she says.

She leans over Silas's shoulder at the laptop on the floor beside them, groggily attempting to read some of the section they were working on before their midday nap. Goober grows excited as she stirs.

'Hello, good sir,' she says into his playful eyes as his tail whips Silas madly.

'Fuck, Goob, careful of Dad's face,' Silas says, trying to keep black dog hair out of his mouth. As Rose reads over their pre-nap writing, she feels a gentle clinch around her sternum, which descends into a wrestling match between all three of them. Laughter bursts out of her, causing Goober to bark in excitement. 'Shh, Mom and Dad are trying to be inconspicuous!' she says before laughing again. Rose has a laugh that can shake a room. It comes from her gut and sprinkles others with happiness.

'How long did we sleep?' she asks as she stretches out, her body sputtering with vibrations as she lengthens.

'Dunno. Hour, maybe? I'm just spitballing here, but maybe it has something to do with the eighteen-hour days?' Silas says, giving her his best cockeyed grin.

'Almost done. It'll be worse if we slow down.'

'But sanity . . .'

'We're in so deep now, let's not give ourselves any excuse to slow down or we'll crash out and stop altogether.' Rose knows she's the marching girl with the baton; she knows she's got to keep up the pace or things could go sideways fast.

Goober hops onto the bed. He either wants to be tucked in properly, or is waiting for the latest wrestling match to commence. He waits expectantly above them like a patient priest waiting for his rowdy congregation to quieten down. As he does so, he sits on his haunches, kneading the blanket with his paws.

'Your son has something to say,' Rose says, knowing how to read her kid. His ears fold back. He looks *very* serious and achingly adorable.

'What say you, sir?' Silas inquires from the floor.

Goober pauses melodramatically, and they wait for what they know is coming. A small *ruff* noise rumbles out of his partially opened mouth, then another, and another. If they let him, the *ruffs* will build into growling *yarps*, before erupting into mad, full-throated barks. Then he'll tear around the room, his furry butt tucked under him, in the way that terriers do when they play. Before the second *yarp* erupts, Silas springs to life, pouncing up and descending onto Goober before pulling him back to the floor, pinning him down and tickling his undercarriage. Goober smiles, wriggles and makes small growling sounds, enjoying the pure magic of playing with Dad.

🌲

Rose watches them play. She was the one who proclaimed four years ago, in their Queens apartment, that they *would* be adopting a rescue dog. One week later, they sat in their minuscule bathroom with their tiny, eight-week-old shivering mongrel Goober-pup, taking turns cleaning him up before manoeuvring his small body into his first NYC winter puppy jacket. For months, Rose observed Silas gently caring for their furry child; the two of them had tag-teamed to crack her maternal nature wide open.

She coos at him on the floor as if he were a baby. He *is* their baby. His mouth lies cracked open in a canine grin and he lets loose another *yarp* as he struggles under Dad.

'Be quiet or you'll summon Bunny!' Silas says into Goober's fleshy tummy.

'Si! Shh.' The dreamy look on Rose's face vanishes as the potential of that happening plays in her mind.

'Buuunnnyyy!' Silas screeches into the air.

'Shut up. She'll hear you!'

'Preciousss. Where is Bun-Bun's aperitif, precious?' Silas squawks in his best Gollum impression.

The last one is too much. Rose cracks up, while trying not to, which makes it even harder. She jumps into the pile of mandog. 'Buuunnnyyy!'

Fuck the ghouls, let them come . . .

Outside in the darkening evening, a figure crouches on its haunches and watches them. The eyes gleam orange in the waxing glow of a cigarette being drawn on.

Had only Bunny been listening, the heavy drapes and shut window would not have allowed her to hear their mockery. But The Other listened for them, and they both heard the mocking call of her name. She sucks the cigarette down to the blackened filter and allows it to fall from her lips and bounce off her knee, where it hits the soft pine-needle ground. She hears her name called into the air and she walks back to the house.

Silas is drifting off again and Goober is fast returning to chasing squirrels in his dreams.

'Go make sandwiches. We have to finish working,' Rose says. She brings her knee up and grinds it into his side.

'Ah! Okay, I'm going, boss-lady. Whaddya want on yours? The usual?'

The usual is cheese and tomato on depressed-looking freezer-preserved seed loaf from their last visit to town.

'Yeah, sure.' She jumps up and makes her way to the

en-suite, raising her arms and removing her T-shirt as she steps into the bathroom. Silas hurriedly follows. His eyes trace her lithe back and waist. A freckle here, a mole there, and tiny hairs that prickle in the cold air. She doesn't get far before he wraps his arms around her, burying his face into the patch of neck between her collarbone and throat. 'But it looks more fun in here.'

'No. You smell like a mixture of Goober-breath and anxiety.'

She's expecting more resistance, but Silas cocks his head and mumbles, 'Actually, I'm hungry too.'

She laughs, pushing him out the door. 'I've been dumped for a bologna sandwich, haven't I?'

Silas shrugs. 'It just happened, babe. I'm sorry. I'm hungry and your bra strap is confusing.'

She reaches behind her to free herself. Silas looks down to see Rose's breasts smiling back at him. 'Not that confusing. You're just dumb . . . *Idiota*,' she says, tapping the side of her temple.

'*Idiota*?! Madam, may I remind you that I am a *marginally accomplished writer*!' He dives in and kisses both nipples, before flying out the door to make sandwiches.

Goober, now alert and eager to tag along, follows Silas to find out more about this bologna sandwich business.

The bedroom door closes behind them.

Rose turns on the shower tap, and cold water warms under her hand.

As he and Goob descend the stairs, Silas is in the best mood he's been in since the incident at the lake. That comes to an abrupt halt when he sees downstairs washed in gloom; the only light source is a weak orange glow from the corner of the kitchen counter where Lou Lou sits, moribund in its halo.

Hmm, she must have got the memo about my influx of positivity. Silas can read the scene from the way her shoulders hunch and how her elbows rest on the table. The shoe box of old pictures and the large wine glass with multiple lipstick imprints around the rim, act as sufficient supporting evidence. The shoe box is a sarcophagus for her wedding pictures and (after the divorce) any picture that contained his father. She visited the box two or three times a year to tear the healing scabs off and make the wounds bleed again. From what he figured, in her eyes, if the wounds were still bleeding, then the drinking was justified. And so, over the years, out came the box periodically like a masochist boomerang.

No chance of any drama-free sandwich-making now.

Her watery eyes drift to his feet, then climb to his face. 'Hello, son.'

Silas tries to maintain the pretence of ignorance as he slips past her into the kitchen. 'Hi, Mom. Uh, Bunny home?'

'I *don't* know.' Lou Lou always sprinkles strange and unnecessary inflections into her speech when she drinks. 'I haven't seen her this evening. I *think* I saw her this *morning* but it's hard to tell *sometimes*. She's so *quiet*. Poor thing. She's *waiting* for God now, my son.'

Silas notices that both doors are ajar – usually a telltale sign that Bunny is out. He gathers sandwich accoutrements in an attempt to multi-task as the well-worn drinking conversation topic unfolds with the familiarity of a used summer chair unpacked after a hard winter.

'Yup. She leaves the doors open all the time. Given up trying to close 'em,' Silas says without any attempt to hide his exhaustion with the dilemma.

'You know I tried to help her, don't you, son?'

'With what?' *Feign ignorance. Ask questions. Keep her talking till you can finish the food and leave.* He drops a slice of bologna to a waiting Goober – who has strategically manoeuvred himself below the counter.

'The *drink*. She *was* okay for a while. I think. But *over* the years, it just got worse and . . . *worse*,' Lou Lou says as she pushes herself up off her elbows and stands haughtily.

Oh Jesus, strap yourself in. 'Uh-huh. Yeah.'

'It *was* harder to . . . *support* her after she moved out to the boathouse.' Lou Lou drifts closer, leaning on the edge of the counter. 'You *know*, I had *hoped* the solitude was *helping* her, but I think it made it *worse*. She needed the structure of *being* together in the house. Together . . .'

Lady, structure with you is like the structure of a burned-out building after a fucking fire guts it; you two are the Twin Towers *of sisterhood*, he thinks. But what he actually says are the well-rehearsed words and tone of a person who's grown up around drinking. The '*I will be the voice of reason and middle ground, so that you can stumble, but still stand*' voice. It was the voice that children of alcoholics learned so that they could cope. Or pretend to.

'Yes, I think you're right. But, as I recall, it was her choice to move to the boathouse, so what could you have done?'

Whoops, I just used the last of Rose's fancy French wholegrain mustard. Time to switch back to synthetic yellow American.

Lou Lou shakes her head at nothing in particular before sipping the last of her wine. 'I *should've* been *there* for *her*. I should have . . . but *I* was in no state to be *anyone's* saviour.'

The pneumatic pressure of words unspoken is slowly starting to push a needle on a gauge in Silas's head. 'Well, you know, you tried your best,' he says, slicing a tomato with more force than is necessary.

Lou Lou swallows the appeasing comment, but finds it too small a morsel. 'Well, *my* best wasn't good *enough*, was *it*? If *I* wasn't such a mess *all* the time, then *I could* have *saved* her, you know. But *your father* –'

As Silas slams down the knife and opens his mouth to speak, he already knows he's making a mistake, but he's stepped out of his body and watches himself make it regardless. *Why can't you just shut your mouth for two more minutes while you finish the fucking sandwiches and go back upstairs? This is what she wants – attention. And now she's got it. AGAIN!*

'Okay, first of all,' he begins, 'Bunny married a dude a lot older than her who died *kinda* expectedly. She had plenty of time to figure out what to do with her life after that, and chose to do nothing but live here, rent free, and pretend to be a fucking forest sprite.'

'She *paid* rent,' Lou Lou stammers incredulously. 'She *paid* a lump *sum* when she arrived. Helped me out a *great* deal after *I was abandoned*. It was, it *was* quite *a lot* of money, Silas –'

'Yeah. A quarter-century ago.'

'That's not *fair*, I hope you *never* have to see how it *feels* to be *abandoned* by *someone you love*.'

'Secondly, quit dragging everything back to you and Dad getting divorced – not last week, but *also* a quarter-century ago!'

Cat's out of the bag and shitting on the radiator now.

Lou Lou looks at him a moment. Silas hopes against hope that something may have clicked, but he watches that promise shut away under old defences, like a steel roller pulled over a storefront window.

'*That bastard broke me*,' she hisses.

Silas sags against the counter as the weight and repetition of the conversation bear down on him. Goober sits by his feet, his face bouncing like that of a tennis spectator from one to the other as they speak.

'Ma, I love you. But cut the shit.'

Lou Lou's eyes widen and then narrow. '*I beg your pardon?*'

'You kept the paid-off house, got half a stock portfolio that pays every month, and retired pretty fucking early, not too bad, huh? The old man fell off the face of the earth, so you didn't even have to share custody either – or really raise me, 'cos let's face it, you had a live-in babysitter. An alcoholic one that scared the shit out of your kid, but hey! Good for *you*, right? Think of it like this, Mom – if the end of your marriage really was the horrific battle that you make it out to be, in the end, you won.'

Lou Lou's face is blank marble.

In the gloom of the lounge, it has been watching Lou Lou and Silas argue from behind the armrest of the couch. There is a gap between the wall and the couch, deep in the corner, where a neglected side table used to be. It moved the table and has been using the spot to watch them for weeks. Nobody has ever seen it. The lounge is rarely lit or used. Even the little black creature doesn't sense it; it has learned, with some effort, to block itself from it – as long as it isn't alerted. If alerted, the hateful thing looks straight at it – sees it in a way that it can't recall happening before, unless it had chosen to show itself.

There are other viewing spots in the trees, on the roof, even in the earth, but this one inside the house is the closest and the most dangerous for it. But here, it sees the most. Feels them most. Tonight is a thrill; he usually doesn't come down here, nor does the little black creature – but tonight he has.

The Little King has become much larger, and that is something to behold.

It reads the unfamiliar passage of time on his soul. Because it dances outside of time, it does not understand time – like the still depths of the ocean do not understand the flow of the river – but finds it curious.

When it first saw the Little King, the soul had been smooth, pure white and pale yellow swirls. Now the soul resembled the other lives here – rumpled and worn. They always seemed to turn this way. All their kind are brilliant flashes of light and noise that quickly become dim and silent, then disappear back into the dark stillness. And soon enough it is alone again, left to sleep without dreaming.

It walks out of its dark corner, brushing along the soft cushions of the couch as the two continue fighting. The little black creature still watches them, which is good – it will not see.

bunny

'*Are* you *suggesting what he did was* good?' the old woman says to the Little King.

Its closeness to them arouses it as it traces around the corner and up the stairs, quietly now, so that the little black creature doesn't feel it pass. Down below, it hears the Little King speaking loudly.

'*I don't know if what happened was good or not! I don't know if he was any good. All I know is that he wasn't around long enough for me to find out. I just remember he was there, and then he was gone. And those long weekend getaways to New York – once every, what, four, five years, so he didn't feel too guilty about it. I haven't spoken to Dad in fucking years. I don't know, maybe that's good . . . not everyone is cut out to be a parent or a husband. But do you know what? Maybe you weren't either. Maybe you'd both be stuck in the carcass of a marriage with no way out, both secretly hoping the other would hurry up and die so you could have some peace!*'

What is he saying?

It doesn't hear their language the way they use it; the specificity of their phrases is hard to translate, but it sees the complex multitude of colours, of their feelings, thoughts, vibrations – it sees everything behind the words and more; like reflections of the colours of the cosmos that it has watched being born. They remind it of that period where all was nothing – and then all was born. They are part of the shards of creation that it has watched burn out, like it has watched all creation burn out over and over and over again – mindlessly forever. They make such bright colours in the blackness . . . But not yet.

It slides down the hall and opens the door to the Little King's room. It slips inside and gently shuts the door; the one it is riding knows what a door is, and so it knows what a door is. The relationship within this being is symbiotic, but skewed in its favour. It is here in this room now because the one it is riding has heard a mocking call with its ears. It reaches out with her hand, and together, they lock the bedroom door.

Rose drops her shampoo-foamed head forward, letting the shower stream massage the back of her neck and shoulders while she daydreams. She hears the click of the bedroom door being locked. 'Si?' She sways gently in the warm stream of water, letting it wash the tension away. She watches soap suds congregate in a thin line before trickling down her stomach in a bubbly white procession as the bathroom turns black. She sighs in the dark. *He'll turn it back on in a sec when he doesn't get a rise from me.* She is used to Silas's pranks, so she disregards the darkness and continues gently rolling her head from side to side, loosening the wound steel cables that are her neck muscles. The bathroom light bulb starts flashing on and off like a strobe light. It has a nauseating effect. She listens and then hears, over the hissing water, the sound of the light switch being rapidly flipped back and forth.

'Silas!'

The light stops and remains off. She stands in the darkness, warm water washing over her shoulders – which regain all their previous tension. A wave of sudsy water slithers over her forehead and into her eyes. The shampoo stings, and the act of rubbing only makes it worse.

'Thank you!' she calls. 'Now I got shampoo in my eyes.'

She hears the bathroom door crack open, then shut. She looks over her shoulder and watches the door, exasperated. When Silas is bored and on a sugar rush, he is the most irritating person in the world – especially when he thinks he's funny. The door opens again – a sliver of light reaches into the dark bathroom, then disappears. The door latch clicks home again. It opens a third time.

'Are you serious?' She turns off the shower and watches the wooden door through the water-beaded glass of the shower cubicle. She doesn't even think she's rinsed properly. *There goes my relaxing shower.*

'Si? . . . Si!' The door swings open, revealing the lit bedroom beyond.

The light in the bedroom switches off with an assertive *click*. Rose stands in total darkness except for a minute amount of light seeping under the locked bedroom door from the hallway. She hears the water dripping off her naked body in staccato plops and the murmur of voices somewhere in the house. She notes the bass tones of Silas's muffled voice downstairs. He wasn't the one who locked the bedroom door, and he isn't the one who's in their bedroom. She knows who it is, but calling her name would make it so, so she says nothing and watches. Her eyes gradually adjust to the darkness. Shapes take form in the gloom – the vanity, towels hanging, their unmade bed in the room beyond, her body moisturiser standing tall beside the porcelain bathroom sink.

It's fine, just put on a towel and turn the light on. It's fine. You're fine.

She would see more if she wiped the mist from the glass

door, but she doesn't want to see more, doesn't want to deflate her courage, doesn't want to see that maybe it isn't fine.

'Not yet,' whispers a voice from the darkness.

'What do you want?' She meant to sound menacing but the words come out in a squeezed shudder.

'Not yet . . . Not yet. Not yet! Not yet! Not Yet! Not Yet! NOT YET! NOT YET!'

Bunny crawls on hands and feet into the bathroom. Her limbs bend at acute angles as her writhing jaw juts forward as she speaks. Rose wipes the mist from the glass. *Oh Jesus.* Bunny crawls closer. Rose can just make out her form in the near-darkness. Bunny's jaw snaps as if dislocating. Rose's eyes trace the prominent bumps on Bunny's back – vertebrae, which look disturbingly close to slicing through her anorexic form.

She's naked.

'Not yet not yet not yet not yet not yet – not yet.'

Bunny stands and runs the final few feet, throwing the glass door open and forcing herself into the small tiled cubicle. Rose gasps; her throat tightens as Bunny repeats the words over and over like an incantation. Rose flinches into the corner of the shower. Smashing her heels into the wet tiles, she grabs at anything to avoid falling. Bunny reaches out, closing her hands around Rose's arms. As Rose rights herself, or something rights her, she feels the stealthy grip of flesh as Bunny's cold, bony body wraps itself around her with incredible strength. Her throat purges a scream into the whites of Bunny's rolled-back eyes.

Goober is the first to react to the screaming. In the second it takes for Silas to hear the noise, figure out where it came from, and register it as Rose, Goober has already launched himself up the stairs.

Lou Lou looks confused as Silas runs to the staircase. He tops them and catches up to Goober, who's frantically barking at the bedroom door.

'Rosie?!' He tries opening the door but finds it locked. Rose screams again – high and animal-like – before the noise is cut short. The only sound now is Goober frantically clawing at the door as he barks. Silas's mind turns cold; panic screams through his veins like Arctic lightning. His body shudders as he shoulder-charges the door. It rattles in the jamb, but holds fast. He catches flashes in his mind – Rose cut and bleeding from the neck, wrestling a man in a dirty hoodie with a knife in his hand, needle tracks crawling up his arm. Or worse, Rose naked – held down on the bed, tears streaming as dirty hoodie man squeezes her throat as he pushes himself into her –

Silas's words come out as half-syllabled gibberish as he batters his shoulder into the heavy door again and again until a loud crack is followed by a wooden tearing sound.

The lock snaps and the hardwood frame splinters like green sugar cane. Goober shoots through the shattered doorway as the hall light shines into the room and washes away Silas's imagined dirty hoodie man.

Rose huddles on the bed, wet, naked and panting. She stares into the bathroom. Her eyes flick to Silas as he enters, before quickly returning to the bathroom. Goober's crouched on his front legs like a growling, coiled spring between Rose and the dark bathroom doorway. If something moves, he'll kill it. Goober looks twice his usual size – his hackles have occasionally risen when encountering other dogs in the city, but now every hair is prickling as if electrified, twitching with his growl – the same primal growl from the lake.

Silas opens his mouth but Rose speaks first. 'I'm okay – in there – Bunny.' It comes out in three short, hyperventilated breaths.

A burst of movement rattles objects in the dark bathroom. The bathroom window latch clicks open as Goober darts into the darkness, followed by Silas, who smashes the light switch on with sweaty hands. The bathroom instantly illuminates. Empty.

The open window hangs laughing into the dark night. Goober jumps. His body lands halfway out the window. He see-saws on the bottom edge as his forelegs strain to pull him through. Silas grabs him before he tumbles out, his best friend still barking madly, ready to kill whoever hurt Mom. Silas pulls him back in, and his small muscular body squirms in Silas's arms.

'Shh, boy, shh.' Goober gives Silas a reproachful look as he's lowered to the floor. He scampers out of the bathroom and hops onto the bed, licking Rose's knee protectively, soothing calm back into her. She picks him up and hugs him close. Goober makes sure she feels loved and protected. A sob escapes her as he does so.

Silas looks out the window and into the darkness. The dark, silent woods stare back at him as he scans them. Nietzsche worms into his innermost thoughts: *And if you gaze into the abyss, the abyss gazes also into you.*

He pulls his head back inside, shuts the window and tightens the latch until his knuckles creak. His hands are shaking with unspent adrenaline. His stomach feels upside down and hollow. The bathroom is a mess of water and toppled plastic containers. He catches his reflection in the medicine-cabinet mirror and tears it off the wall without exactly knowing why. He raises it above his head, with every intention of obliterating it on the floor, but instead lowers it, leans it against the wall and walks out of the bathroom.

Rose has pulled a blanket around herself. Goober is still fussing over her with licks and nuzzles, making sure she's alright.

'Are you okay?' Silas asks, his voice husky from panic.

She looks up at him as his arms reach out towards her. The shimmering fright in her eyes has burned down to heavy-lidded embers.

'I got the spare keys. Is everything okay?' Lou Lou asks, swaying in the broken doorway. 'Was it Bunny? Is Bunny okay?'

'Get out.' Silas tries to push the broken door closed. He waits until he hears Lou Lou's tipsy steps shuffle away before turning back to Rose. 'What happened?'

Rose stares into the middle distance. 'She just grabbed hold of me and . . . hugged me to her chest. It was fucking weird, Si.' She points to a spot beside the bathroom door. Silas notices the pile of grimy children's clothes for the first time.

'She took her clothes off before she came in. She kept saying *"not yet"* over and over again . . .' Rose expects Silas to say something. He doesn't. Instead he turns pale, holds his hand up to his mouth and chews at the palm.

'Si?'

He wakes from whatever place he's just visited. 'She used to do shit like that to me when I was a kid – catch hold of me and not let me go for hours, saying things into my ear. I didn't like to think of it. Sometimes, I think I don't remember – or, I don't think I remember it properly, because it was insane. I hoped it wasn't as bad as I remembered, but maybe it was. I didn't like to dwell on it, so I refused to . . . And then I forgot.'

'Did your mom know?'

'No. No, she only did it when Lou Lou was out. She went on a lot of dates when I was a kid – left Bunny to look after me.' He slumps onto the edge of the bed, unconsciously edging away from the dirty mound of clothes on the floor, his childhood clothes.

'I'm so sorry. I'm so sorry I brought you here.' Their hands meet and say things their voices can't.

Once breaths are caught and fists unclenched, Rose re-showers, washing away Bunny's desperately haunting embrace. Silas cleans the bedroom, his exhausted body lumbering from one side of the room to the other. He throws Bunny's clothes out the bedroom window and latches it, fussing at its lock, testing its strength. He washes his hands then washes them again. Rose climbs into bed, her limbs jelly-like and warm. She drifts off to a sleep full of dreams bathed in sickly colours. Silas rechecks the bathroom and bedroom windows, and then rechecks them again.

Before settling into his office chair, he grabs the backrest and drags it, squealing, to face the broken door. Goober sits on his haunches next to Silas. Sleep will not come to them tonight. They will keep watch over the shattered threshold.

🌰

At the same moment that Silas reaches down to rest his hand on Goober's back, a hand outside in the darkness reaches out towards the clothes that lie rumpled and stained on the pine-needled ground. It picks them up and retreats back into the black woods.

1995

THE JOINING

Bunny's hands feel like they're covered in oven mitts. She slugs a dry mouthful of gin from the bottle in the pantry as she grabs peanut butter for Silas's dinner sandwich, but it takes a minute for the gin-warmth in her belly to spread to her arms, legs and head, and calm her jitters. She tries to twist open the peanut butter jar, but it slips out of her hands and sails onto the floor – cracking open with a dull thud as the peanut butter absorbs the shock of the breaking glass. '*Fuck!*'

Silas gives her a 'jeez Louise' kinda look. He is well used to Bunny and Lou Lou dropping things, or accidentally knocking things over, or accidentally leaving flammable kitchen towels by hot stove elements.

Bunny pulls her soft-pack out and extracts a cigarette.

Of course it's the last fucking one. She perches it on her lip to light it, and notices it's snapped in half. *Jesus, Joseph and motherfuckin' Mary.* She tears off the hanging end and lights the remaining inch.

Silas stands in the kitchen, still in his yellow ducky towel. It's streaked with dirt and he has lost the drawstring somewhere, so the hood hangs over his forehead in a defeated slump as he looks up at her. She regards him as she exhales a halting lungful of Winston.

'Ice cream?'

Silas's face cracks into an affirmative grin.

The cigarette quickens the spread of gin-warmth and grinds the edge off her jitters – which were partly caused by lateness getting her drink, and partly by the weirdness in the woods and the retreat back to the house.

The whole ordeal gradually faded as they scrambled further from the clearing and closer to home. *Thank fuckin' Christ*, she thinks, rubbing her crucifix. It isn't that she's forgotten the clearing, the cave, or the voice inside it, but it makes so little sense that her mind classifies the whole experience as closer to being an odd dream than an actual waking occurrence.

She cracks open the mint-choc ice cream and silently thanks the gods that there's still half a tub for the kid to devour. Tonight, she'll let him have it all.

Lou Lou had already left by the time they got back to the house, away on one of her 'dates' with some seasonal logger-trucker type fella with small conversations, big arms and (under his faded Levi's) a dick with a two-month expiry printed along the shaft, counting down the time it has left in town.

Because of the long drive back home, Lou Lou almost always spends the night in the Hamner Hotel Motel (*why the two names?* Bunny always wonders). The Hotel Motel is also conveniently only a short stumble across the road from Surley's Bar & Grill. So, stumble back and forth Lou Lou does. Most of her dates pay for weekly lodging at the Hotel Motel, and if that isn't the case, there is usually an available room for the night – or the cab of the truck.

'*Don't tell your mom I let you eat it all,*' Bunny says.

'*What if she asks?*'

'Tell her I ate half, okay?'

Silas holds out a spoonful. *'Want some?'*

'No thanks,' she says as she dives towards the spoon and eats the scoop perched on top of it. Silas laughs and taps the empty spoon twice on the counter – *tap, tap*. Bunny claps once to finish the Trinity knocks – *clap*. Silas taps again – *tap, tap*, and she raises her hands above her head like a Spanish dancer – *clap*.

She walks back to the pantry to fetch the gin. The day's events have really unlocked that thirst, the one that sings a *'one more'* lullaby in her head until she obeys it several times and finally feels light and relaxed, as if the universe is gently cradling her in its loving hands.

She's thinking about wrapping her hand around a cold glass filled with tonic, gin and ice, when Silas chortles through a mouthful of ice cream and brings down his spoon again – *tap, tap*

– *THUD*.

Bunny looks down at her hands, poised to finish the trio with a clap, but they haven't touched yet. She turns to look at Silas; his head is tilted up towards the ceiling. The noise came from somewhere upstairs. The spoon in his hand rests on the counter. He tests it again – *tap, tap*

– *THUD*.

He drops the spoon, which jangles impossibly loud in the silence. They stand frozen, like animals in the instant between recognising the presence of a predator and breaking into a run.

Bunny's hands are still poised in front of her. Her eyes find Silas's and a short, unspoken conversation ricochets between them; he shakes his head as she pulls her hands apart from each other.

'Bunny, don't!' he hisses.

She brings her hands together – *clap*

– *THUD – THUD,* comes the answer from upstairs, shaking the house's timber bones like a heavy couch being dropped on a carpeted floor.

Bunny grabs Silas. They kneel behind the kitchen counter.

He's pale and frightened. '*Why did you do that? Why did you clap?*'

'*It's okay, it's okay. It's probably . . . it's probably an opossum. Remember last year we saw those, ah, little babies under the house?*'

'Yeah.'

'*Well . . . Your mama must have left a window open, and it's probably the opossum mama up there looking for food, just bumping things over, 'cos she's in the wrong place.*' She tries to sell the lie, but it doesn't take. She stands and pulls a kitchen knife from the block on the counter, comforted by its weight in her hands. '*Stay put,*' she says as she creeps towards the stairs. She doesn't look at Silas; she knows he'll disapprove. *If I can just go up and find a fat opossum up there then this will all stop.* She tentatively walks up the stairs, willing courage to come.

She stops on the landing and listens. Thankfully all the lights upstairs are on – she's not sure if she could have done this if they were off – 'cos that opossum will scare her when it bolts for an open window. This way, she'll be able to see it from the outset and not give herself a heart attack. She feels better as she edges forward. *Just a mama opossum. Just a mama, who's lost her way.*

Ahead of her are four doors. On the right is Silas's room, on the left, her room and a bathroom next to it, and at the end is Lou Lou's master bedroom. All the doors are open with the lights inside also on. *Relax, this isn't a horror movie – otherwise all the lights would be off.* A forced smile shimmers over her face like the reflection of a passing cloud on the surface of a cold ocean full of twisting monsters in the depths below.

Any moment now, that fat fucking opossum is gonna waddle round the corner into the hallway and I'll chase her out of the house. Five minutes after that, Silas will be complaining that his ice cream has melted and I'll have a fresh, cool drink in my –

The light switch in her bedroom clicks OFF – ON – OFF. Bunny's hand shoots up to her throat; her fingers fumble around the small gold crucifix. *Fat opossums can't reach light switches.*

'Get out!'

ON – OFF – ON, clicks the light switch in defiance. '*Whoever you are, you better get the fuck out of here, NOW!*'

She rushes forward, knife held out in front of her, while the other hand is firmly clamped around the crucifix. She's determined to reach the room before the light clicks off again. Whoever is in there is going to turn it off again. Whoever is in there is playing her game – the Trinity knocks. If she can't catch them before the light goes out, then she'll sure as hell make sure that her knife finds their gut and buys her time to get herself and Silas out of the house. She reaches the open door and whips the knife around in sweeping thrusts.

The knife finds nothing. It cuts through the air, glinting and utterly useless.

Bunny stands in the doorway. The room looks empty, but an electric twinge in the bottom of her spine sends a nauseous shudder up into her diaphragm and down into her guts, causing her sphincter to squeeze into itself; screaming at her legs to run.

Her eyes are lying. She can feel it. Something is so close that her own exhaled breath hits it and washes back into her face.

There's a sudden pressure on her breastbone. For an instant her mind flicks to the night that Silas had his episode.

The stairs . . . She had been at the top of the stairs and felt that same pressure tip her backwards and then –

'*Visit me I visit you visit me I visit you,*' the whispering pulls her mind back as she feels the pressure increase. It's pushing her back, cracking her ribcage. It crushes through her and into her, colliding with a part of her that was in her chest – not organ, meat or bone, but some more vital part of her is pushed past her spine and out of her back.

She falls out of herself and onto the floor.

She looks up at herself still standing in the doorway. She can still feel her body as it stands above her, but now, she sees through two sets of eyes: the one in her standing body, and the one that has been pushed out.

Her body feels heavy now. Whatever has pushed her out is filling this body up, tucking itself into her corporeal topography. She remembers once as a child finding a giant earthworm as thick as her finger. When prodded, it wound around itself in a tight, shuddering ball of wet, slithering muscle. This memory allows her mind to understand what is happening to her – inside her body, the giant earthworm shudders, filling all of her with an alien weight.

Her knees begin to buckle, but still it continues; it continues until it has stretched itself out and down into her legs, holding them up.

It uses her mouth: '*I visit you I visit you I visit you I visit you –*'

'Aunt Bunny?'

Her head snaps to look at him standing at the top of the stairs. Through both sets of eyes she sees him; as herself, and also as the visitor sees him: Silas. Beloved nephew. Child. The Little King. She screams at him from her place on the floor to run, but no voice comes out. She looks up from the floor at her other self, standing tall in the doorway. The worm looks at Silas through her eyes; the face (*her face*) is impassive, like an unplugged television, the eyes (*her eyes*) gaze at him, unblinking.

Because they are joined now, she can feel its longing for him; she sees his being like it did, colours and fizzes of light dancing out of his small body. She feels like a formerly blind woman seeing the sunrise for the first time.

The worm gently wraps itself around her, pulling her from the floor and back inside herself, tucking its body into impossible arrangements to accommodate the two of them inside one form. Upon feeling her face press into its fleshy folds and feeling the surface of the thing, she realises it's only a worm because she decided to see it as a worm. Almost in answer to her thoughts, it becomes soft, cool, silk fabric – she feels herself accept it.

She lets go, allowing herself to sink into the deep place inside her that it has made for her there.

2018

PLASTIC HEARTS & FRAGILE CENTRES

Early-morning sunshine weeps into the bedroom like clear fluid from a wound.

A few hours before dawn, Silas was listening to the jarring ramblings of birds and felt the world preparing to wake. He remembered walking back home from his mid-week job as a barback in his poorly attended college years. How utterly hopeless and free he had always felt hearing that sound. The birds had seemed to berate him for not being asleep, but there was a freedom in being so diametrically opposed to the rest of humanity's circadian expectations. At that time of day, the only other people out were drunks and joggers. Both parties would paint him with puzzled glances as he passed.

Goober had curled up beside his chair. Even in slumber, his ears remained raised and aware as he dozed, still listening for noises outside the window and door.

Silas lifts his tired body out of the chair to stretch. If there were any more visits from Bunny, he was fairly sure that they would have been in the preceding dark hours. His watch is now over. He leaves Goober in the room and heads downstairs for coffee (and to hunt around for a deadbolt he can use to fasten the broken bedroom door). He doesn't expect to run into Bunny. Not in the daylight. The thought still unnerves him, however, so he pushes it off a cliff in his mind. He makes his coffee and finds his deadbolt in a little-used corner of the garage that was once his father's woodworking table. The space is now just bits and pieces of hardware, and rusty tools strewn about on a dusty pine counter. Some ancient boyhood memory suggested he'd seen the deadbolt there years before – and being his father's, it would by now either be gone, or ignored and untouched by Lou Lou.

After finding it, he lingers, caught in a whirl of boyhood memories. Behind an ancient box of mismatched screws lies a heart-shaped fridge magnet with the message '*I love Dad*' in plastic bubble calligraphy. The plastic heart holds a fragile centre – a picture of Silas as a baby with his dad on his first Christmas, laughing beside obese Uncle John (Rest in Pork Rinds), who'd dressed up as Santa. Silas leans over the image, but doesn't touch the magnet. He sees the dust blanketing it and leaves it to collect more.

He carries the deadbolt back upstairs with a handful of self-tapping wood screws, a screwdriver in his back pocket, and a fresh cup of coffee for Rose.

'Where'd you find that?' Rose asks from the bed, sipping her hot coffee and watching Silas fix the bolt to the door frame.

'Just around. It'll do till I get another real lock in town.'

'Pretty long drive just for a new lock, isn't it? Besides, that chunky old thing looks sturdier.'

Silas shakes his head as he leans into the last turn of the last screw, tightening it into the wood. 'I'm going in anyway. See if I can get a doctor to put Bunny in rehab, or a psych ward, or a pig pen . . . I know that made you smile.'

'No, it didn't!' Rose snorts. 'I think she'd have to agree to that.'

'She will,' he says, fixing her with a reassuring look. 'She doesn't have to go for good, I just want her out of the house while we're here.'

'How?'

He winks at her. 'Don't worry about it.'

'Your eyes are especially green this morning,' Rose says over the steam of the coffee mug.

'Optical illusion. The dark circles and puffy red skin make the green pop.'

He stares loftily into the distance and strikes a Washingtonian pose. 'Writers always look their best when they look like they've been thrown off a cliff in a tumble dryer. Apparently, it's part of our charm.' Now *that* makes her smile. He shuffles over and kisses her forehead, but the moment is interrupted by a tentative knock on their ramshackle door. Silas stiffens, sighs and walks over to greet his mother, or the apocalypse.

Lou Lou stands in the doorway, readied words on her tongue.

'Yeah?' he says with as little stomach acid in his voice as he can muster (last night wasn't her fault, but in familial matters, logic and emotion could be strange bedfellows).

Lou Lou shuffles her feet like a little girl scolded.

'Um, well, I just wanted to say good morning and –'

'What do you want?'

Lou Lou leans around Silas so that she can address Rose as well. Despite the tension, Goober stands, affably wagging his tail at Lou Lou.

'I had a talk with Bunny and she feels terrible that she scared you.'

Rose manages a wan smile and a nod, but her eyes show that her mind is running a million miles per second.

'She made you something.' Lou Lou pulls out her hand from behind her back. She extends a wreath made from archaic brown pinecones. She attempts to pass it to Rose, but Silas takes it instead. He looks at it. Something about the faded yellow cord holding the wreath together rings a faint bell in a room in his head that he could never get to.

'Mom, can I talk to you outside, please?'

He shepherds her out of the room. Goober hops off the bed, expecting an invitation. 'Not this time, pal.'

'Bolt the door,' he says to Rose before closing it.

Silas doesn't know why the talk needs to happen outside, but it feels better in the cool, fresh air. The wreath is still in his hands. He swings it against his thigh, letting it bump up against him. Lou Lou stands in front of him, arms folded grimly, prepared for sober confrontation.

'Where is Bunny?'

'She wanted to give you two your space.'

'Bullshit, Mom. Stop it.'

'Out walking, I think,' Lou Lou says, pursing her lips and avoiding eye contact.

Silas stares up into the boughs above them and nods at nothing in particular.

'This is what's going to happen. You are going to get the doctor's number and I am going to call him. We are then driving Bunny to town to see him. She is going to go into a sober program or fifty-one fifty hold, and stay there until she's dead or sober.'

Lou Lou blinks as if English isn't her first language.

He ploughs on. 'Now, whatever co-dependent dog and fuckin' pony show you two have had going on, is going to stop. *Now*. And when she's away, I think it would be a good idea for you to have a think about how much *you* are drinking, okay? Find some AA meetings. In two weeks, Rose and I are gone, and you need to find a better way to live than this.'

Lou Lou's folded arms tighten against her body. It makes her bathrobe look more like a straitjacket.

'I suggest you sell this place. Move into Hamner. Or maybe one of the other towns where there aren't memories. Somewhere you can have some normal, healthy interactions with other people. If, after a while' – *as in when Rosie and I are very far away* – 'Bunny comes back, then she could live with you there and, God forbid, maybe get a job.'

Lou Lou sways slightly, doggedly attempting to keep her eyes on the ground.

He takes a more empathetic tone. 'I know this will be a big change for you, but you two have been left to your own devices for far too long up here. It's not healthy. For anyone.'

He waits for an answer, half expecting a shouting match, or tears, or some mixture of the two.

'Okay,' she says, still looking at the ground.

Silas blinks, nods. 'Good . . . Good.'

She looks smaller and older than she did a minute ago, in a way similar to what happens when children see their parents as fallible for the first time. As she blinks away the first non-histrionic tears he has ever seen in her eyes, he gently places his hand on her shoulder. *I do love you, Mom,* he thinks but doesn't say.

'How about you go get that number and we'll call them later on?'

She nods numbly and retreats back to the front door, only partially lifting her feet.

Great, now I feel like shit.

'If you feel embarrassed, you don't need to,' he offers up.

As she's about to step inside, she turns, straightens up and puts the mask back on. He's not sure how she's done it, but Lou Lou has regained that Blanche Dubois air about her; it enhances her to the point where you'd swear she had managed to put on makeup and grown a foot taller while her back was turned.

'Embarrassed? Whatever for?'

She swivels back and glides through the doorway, as if on the verge of delivering a grand public announcement.

Silas walks the short distance to the boathouse-cum-cabin-cum-burnt ruin. The lake feels as eldritch as ever. The last wisps of morning mist are fast burning away into the tree-lined banks.

All that is left of the cabin is a foot-deep rectangle of detritus-ridden, charred mulch where the structure once was. Metallic skeletons of a small fridge and hotplate stand to attention at one end, while half the house is quickly fading into the tea-coloured water's edge.

Silas feels foolish. He doesn't know why he's looking at the ruin; there would be no answer or explanation for his aunt here. At each corner of the burned rectangle stands a small pile of pinecones. *Some bullshit from Bunny, no doubt.* With nothing else to do, he strides up to each one and boots it over. With each kick a 'fuck you' hisses out of his gritted teeth.

He stands and faces the lake. He looks at the wreath in his hands. Her wreath. Something about that yellow cord holding it all together aggravates him.

Holding it all fucking together.

'Fuck you.' He hurls it into the lake like a discus. It lands and floats on top of the still water, its hollow centre agape at the cloudless sky.

2017

NOT YET

It rode Bunny's corporeal husk like a thrilled child on a new toboggan in the first snow of winter. To it, lifetimes were short, brilliant flashes in the infinite stillness that it came from, and so the years it had spent joined with her were akin to a short, hurtling ride on the burning missile from a Roman candle.

It had joined with other ones before, but because of the brevity of their lives, it rarely managed to catch a ride before they sparked out. When it did succeed, its joining with the brittle creatures prolonged their lives somewhat. But even then, eventually they simply faded away into the ether, like smoke disappearing from a clenched hand.

But for reasons it did not fully understand, this time – this joining – was different from the others. Bunny had taken to the symbiosis in a way that no others had before. She had welcomed the relinquishment of control and not struggled during the process of their joining, which had made it deeper and more profound.

It and Bunny had melded into a single tree made of two different woods, and soon a blossom would come.

Because it had existed outside of time, it could look over time and travel around it like a bird above railway tracks. But it had seen an event and an opportunity for something new and strange to happen between itself and the brittle ones it lived inside of . . . But not yet.

Not yet.

Bunny still cared for Silas as he grew from a small boy into a teenager, and some part of her understood that she was now dangerous for him to be around; the one within her was excitable when he was near, and like a child with a new hamster, was liable to squeeze him to death in its manically loving hands.

So, one day, she had moved out to the boathouse.

She spent very little time in the house anyway, preferring the woods, the earth, the stone.

She would return sometimes to its old nest – the stone in the clearing – where the deepest part of it still remained among the earth and the rock. Where it had chosen to sleep so long ago, falling so deeply into aeonic slumber that part of it would never leave there, and never fully awaken.

There, near the stone, they would wait together for what it was waiting for. Inside her, it would talk to her. '*Not yet,*' it would whisper, as lovers whisper in secret moonlit moments.

Years went by.

One day Silas left.

There was pain.

It had read the tracks of his life, though, and knew (and told her) that he would come back one final time before the blossom opened on their tree.

But not yet.

Lou Lou stopped asking questions. She had started hearing a voice in the house. If it could have, the one inside Bunny would have inhabited both of them, which would have been exciting, but it could only make a nest with one brittle one at a time.

As it waited, it grew restless; the husk it rode was tied inextricably to the tracks of time, and so, while they remained entwined, so was it. The depth of their joining meant that for the first time it experienced the passage of time in a similar way to the brittle ones: slowly. Until one day, on a horizon that the brittle ones could never see, its ageless eyes saw the moment it had waited for approaching.

The fire in the boathouse was lit to herald the end of the waiting and the beginning of Silas's return. The wood of her dwelling burned on the shore, and so Bunny moved back into the house. Lou Lou welcomed her, eyes downcast and silent, feeling in the very air the weight of the one that came with her sister.

2018

A MEETING IN THE DARK – PART I

A knock on the door interrupts Rose's work and Goober's nap.

'Who is it?'

'It's me,' Silas says.

She rises from the desk and unbolts the door. The action of the bolt works as a darkly comedic reminder of how ridiculous things have become in Silas's childhood home.

'Thanks,' he says, rebolting it behind him. 'Just got off the phone with the doctor in town. He's going to see Bunny tomorrow. I'm gonna drive her. I think it might be best if you stayed here for that –'

'Fuck, yeah. Absolutely,' Rose says. (Her patience with the familial situation is fraying at both ends.) 'I can't sit in a car with her. I'm just sorry *you* have to.'

'Mom is coming too, so you and Goob will have the place to yourselves for the day.'

Rose smiles momentarily before another thought clouds her face. 'How did Bunny take it?'

'Haven't found her yet.' Silas sighs. 'Mom is going to talk to her.'

'What does Lou Lou think of the whole thing?'

Silas ponders before answering, 'It wasn't much of a discussion. But she *seemed* to understand. Maybe not agree, but understand.'

He leans over her shoulder at the computer. 'Whatcha doing here?'

'Jerry emailed,' Rose says in a tone that suggests further sleep deprivation in their near future. 'He wants to see what we've got so far with the notes. Just pulling it all together to send it off to him.'

Silas scans the multiple PDF and Word pages that litter Rose's screen. 'Wow, didn't realise we were this far through already.' He turns and kisses her forehead. 'Listen, I'm baked from last night – gonna take a nap for a few hours.'

'Want some help?' She scoops Goober up from the floor. 'Best nap buddy ever!' Goober wags his tail in agreement.

'Indeed.' Silas ruffles Goober's ears and pulls a pillow over his head as he collapses into bed, falling instantly asleep.

For a handful of slow, deep breaths, Silas's closed eyes are still and calm. His breathing hitches momentarily and a jerking ripple runs below his eyelids. His pupils begin swirling with dreams as a tear of blood squeezes out of his left eye. It rests there like a small red warning light.

Silas walks towards the lake edge. It's the same spot he and Goober sat at on their run. The same spot where the *incident* occurred. The light is unusually dull, even though the sky is cloudless. Above his head the orb of the noontime sun, the stars and a full moon all crowd the sky, but they seem far away – too far, their lights muted, as if the eons have finally exhausted them.

Just like in the *incident*, Goober sits, looking across the lake for something not yet seen.

Why are we here again? he thinks to himself. Goober turns, as if Silas's thought has been spoken aloud. The little dog's eyes seem somewhat different to Silas. *Not different*, he thinks; *clearer, stronger, truer, like the same lamp light, but after the shade is removed.*

Goober slowly stands and walks towards him, his gait calm and composed. He licks Silas's hand and from inside himself, speaks.

Here, am real me, MomDad.

Silas's hand gently cradles Goober's head under his wide, muscled jaw. The voice that came from the dog was a thought, like his.

No talking in this place.

The voice from Goober sounds like the voice that (many

years ago) had told him to hide under a dresser; not exactly the *same* voice, but a voice from the same *place*. They look into each other's eyes, and find love there.

In this dream place, Silas is more aware of the selves that exist within, the selves that have no part of the fleshy, time-rasped messes of their fragile bodies but instead bounce inside their exquisite prison until the imperfection of life allows them to soar – *up, up, out*. With a transient sense of loss, he and Goober recognise that that time to soar is soon to come.

He feels a painful, burning itch in the corner of his left eye.

Goober blinks as if irritated by a dust particle and lifts a paw to rub it. Silas rubs the corner of his own eye with the tip of his finger. He looks at his finger and it is smeared with blood. He looks down – Goober scans the opposite lakeshore and the dark, still water.

It comes now, Goober's mind-speak states, calm but firm. *I fight it with MomDad. It comes.* Goober turns his face up towards Silas and a small tear of blood pearls in the corner of Goober's left eye. It slides down the short black fur of his cheek and lands on the stony ground between his paws. *I love. Be strong, MomDad. It comes.*

I will, boy. I love you too, Silas communicates back.

Together they face the water. Goober's hackles rise in anticipation but he does not bark or move, he simply watches the far bank. The water's edge laps the shore but makes no sound. No birds in this place. The trees stand still. Every branch, leaf and pine needle, absolutely still. Silas realises he hasn't taken a breath since arriving here. His hand finds his chest and rests on it. No rise and fall. No heartbeat. He looks down. Goober's ribcage sits perfectly still; the bellows of his lungs are suspended – unnecessary in this place. Silas's face feels strangely unburdened as he notices that he does not have to blink here – his eyes don't need to, because there is no air here to dry them. He feels his skin as he moves his hand through space. The tiny currents of air that would normally wash over it and between his fingers are absent. The world in this place is paused, frozen in a moment that extends in every direction beyond the horizon.

It comes, Goober says again, as if to snap Silas's wandering mind back to the task at hand.

They remain like this, watching for a long time. Silas's gaze softens as he loses concentration again. He's struggling to focus, struggling to keep his eyes open. The twinge in his eyes has slowly grown into a persistent sting that begins to scream, demanding that he close his eyes. It demands he lie on the cold, stony beach and sleep. He rubs the stinging eye and sees Goober falter, his hind legs slowly lowering his backside to the ground as he shakes himself, as if he were wet.

It wants you sleep, MomDad. Don't sleep. Not here. Goober's mind-speak sounds strained, like he's splitting his energy between too many tasks. Silas shakes his head to clear his mind. He takes a step towards the water's edge. The anaemic, circular glare of the sun's reflection on the lake surface shifts with him, revealing a blind spot in the water in front of them. In it, under the surface, two eyes, robed in the white flesh of his aunt's weathered face, stare back at him. The right eye is her own, the left, a darkly iridescent red orb that stretches the socket to twice its normal size, distorting her face in the process. The red orb is locked on to Goober. The other eye traces Silas as he moves. She sees him and he sees her. She erupts out of the water, clawing at Goober; she catches his front leg and yanks him towards her. Goober snarls like an unoiled buzz saw.

I SEE YOU!

Goober bites her hand. She recoils with a dry, reptilian scream, but her hand remains latched onto Goober's leg. She twists the joint and the little dog expels a jagged yelp, flipping heavily onto the stony ground as he's forced to follow the motion before it finally breaks his joint.

Just as before – at the *incident*, Silas feels as though he's moving through molasses as he reaches for her. His hand closes on her shoulder. Her face whips around. Tobacco-yellowed teeth sink into his hand. He feels a vice-like crunch as a knuckle pops. He winds up, and swings his fist into that pupil-less red orb. It feels as if he's punching a tennis ball. Bunny releases his hand and Goober's leg, freeing them.

Silas picks up a rock and raises it above his head. Bunny lifts her hand to counter the blow. Goober springs back up and pounces on her arm, clearing the path for him. Silas hammers the rock into her upturned face and the red orb bursts with a *pop*, releasing a tight, black, writhing ball of baby eels that cascade over Bunny's face. The acute edge of the stone rakes through flesh like a blunt snowplough, and half of her face is now hanging off. Below the peeled flesh, where there should be bone, are instead rudimentary traces of another skin, another face unearthed; oily black flesh like that of an eel. Amphibian. Predatory. Ancient.

Silas screams, terrified. His mind wills his body to make the face disappear before it cracks his sanity. He hammers the stone down again and again, until the other face is unrecognisable. Under the black skin of her second face, the bone is also black; polished obsidian enmeshed with white bone, like the interlaced fingers of two hands.

Silas's hands are raw and bleeding. He looks at her ruined head. Jagged shards of black bone and white bone lie among the stones. Most of the baby eels have slithered into the water, leaving faint trails of blood as they sink into the depths. Several remain, their small jaws attached to one another, mindlessly devouring themselves among grey brain tissue, blood and scalp. He looks at Goober, who sits as if he has been waiting for Silas.

Goober stands and approaches the mess. His snout gingerly snuffles a piece of brain tissue, before he takes it in his mouth and eats it. He snuffles another and gently nudges it towards Silas, looking at him expectantly. *Eat. You must.*

Silas's jaw muscles tighten in protest as he picks up the harrowing mess. It feels slick in his fingers, like the inside of a passion fruit. He scoops it into his mouth and chews as fast as he can. He doesn't swallow – but allows it to slide down his throat. His breath tastes salty as he does so. He stands, not knowing what to do next. Goober looks at him, then looks back across the lake as the screaming starts.

On the opposite shore, a figure emerges from the water. Black-skinned like the eel, but the geometry is vaguely human. It is malformed – the trunk of its body too long and thick for the withered arms and legs that slowly drag it out of the water and along the rocky shore, up towards the tree line.

A primordial tail hangs, palsied and inert, from the base of its spine. The hydrocephalic head is human and monstrously large, the mouth (her mouth) open in a whistling, idiotic screech that drifts across the water. It makes him feel like vomiting, crying and screaming. Its neck struggles to hold its head up, which tick-tocks from side to side as it drags itself into the tree line, before finally losing itself in the crowded murk of the pines. As the wailing shrinks away into the distant trees, it fades into a distant recess of Silas's mind – a cursed gift to be unwrapped over and over again in his nightmares.

THUNK.

A pinecone hits the ground behind him and skitters down into the water. He turns to the forest behind. Another cone sails out of the forest, landing on the stony shore. THUNK. The pinecone slips over the rocks, hitting the toe of his shoe before coming to rest in front of him. A third sails out from high up in the trees, as if thrown by a giant. It sails over the shore, above his head, and lands in the water with a hollow splash.

A sound like wind grows in the perfectly still trees. The sound travels closer. He hears twigs snap and a deep *whoosh* as a wall of thousands of pinecones hurtles out of the trees towards him, darkening the sky. The swirling wall moves faster as it screams towards the shore, and towards him and Goober. He squeezes his eyes shut and hears Goober's mind-speak in his head. *Hold, MomDad! You must hold!*

'Silas, wake up.' The voice smashes him back into the world like an axe-head burying itself in a tree stump. In the millisecond before he fully wakes, he still feels the uneven stones of the lakeshore under his feet.

'Wha–!' Silas thrashes upright.

Rose's face is lined with worry. 'Baby, are you okay?'

He blinks until his eyes find her. 'Yeah. Dreams.'

She nods, half assured. 'You slept all through yesterday and last night.' She speaks slowly, letting the information linger and then seep into his sleep-clouded wakefulness. 'It's six in the morning. I would have let you sleep a bit more, but your mom said to wake you so you guys make Bunny's appointment. They're downstairs, ready to go.'

He climbs out of bed. 'Okay, okay, okay.' He begins to stagger into some half-clean clothes from a pile on a chair.

'*Mi amor?*' A halo of worry and puzzlement shimmers at the edges of her voice.

He turns to her – she looks at the bed, then at his boxers. He looks at the bed, then at his boxers . . .

The last time he wet the bed was four months after his eighteenth birthday. He had read somewhere that kids who were chronic bed-wetters (especially when they're fucking *eighteen*) were often disturbed or traumatised.

And now he's done it again. In his thirties.

Shame moves like fear, except it's hot, not cold, and instead of creeping up his spine and through his guts, it radiates from the top of his throat and out of his face and through the top of his head. He can't look at her.

She pulls the blanket over the wet sheet. 'It's okay. I'll wash it. Just, go shower. I'll tell them you'll be down in a minute.' She rubs his forearm as she passes to leave the room.

For the first time Silas feels a transient revulsion towards Rose. Although it's through no fault of her own, she has now been absorbed into the humiliating dysfunction of his family and behaviour. It's a difficult stain to remove. The feeling fades as fast as it came, replaced by self-loathing for it ever being there in the first place.

A cold, wet nose nudges his leg. Goober looks up at him in that way that dogs do when they know something is wrong. To a dog, any problem can be solved with a wide blast of love through the tip of their nose. He strokes him, watching stray black hairs drift into the air and onto the floor. He walks into the bathroom to shower, in an empty attempt at removing the stain.

HAMNER – BY DAY

The sterile strip lights hurt Silas's eyes. He rubs the bony ridge above them with his thumb and forefinger, then tries blinking away the dull ache that still pulses behind his left eye. He scans the room for the umpteenth time as he waits.

Brown plastic chairs hug the walls of the clinic reception. In one corner, faded rainbow-coloured floor squares delineate the kiddies play area. A Fisher-Price–style scuffed plastic playhouse-cum-castle squats in its designated area – no doubt lacquered in clear smears of dry mucus from little noses. A prehistoric radio perches atop a wicker coffee table in the middle of the room, mewling banal, middle-of-the-road-horseshit country music. An assortment of mind-numbing magazines gathers around the radio like congregants, their covers festooned with the faces of the British royals in their latest *look-at-me-don't-look-at-me* flirtations with the American Tabloid Machine. Silas knows that if he chases his imagination down its current path, in about a minute's time he will have the royal family re-enacting *The 120 Days of Sodom* in his head, so he stops. His imagination always turns blue and yellow when he's in a bad mood. And he's in a bad mood.

The drive to town was about as uncomfortable as expected. Between Lou Lou's nervous stream-of-consciousness ramblings, and Bunny's eyes boring into him from the rearview mirror, he'd been casually tempted to pick an approaching roadside pine to wrap the car around.

But his suicidal fancies fled as quickly as they arose; he knew Rose and Goob would miss him too much, so he put the fantasy aside. We couldn't all be Yukio Mishima.

The opening gambit that morning had been Lou Lou's car not starting. He had come downstairs after showering, dressing and stripping the bed to find Bunny sitting in the backseat like a kid on a field trip. Lou Lou had stood over the open hood, looking at the engine as if she could fix it telekinetically. Silas probably knew less about engines than she did, so he had asked Rose to go and grab their car keys while he unloaded Lou Lou's trunk – *apparently, one psychotic drunk going to rehab requires three suitcases of stuff.* Bunny had remained in the car, watching proceedings while she rubbed her crucifix. Goober kept his distance, pacing back and forth, watching the back passenger window that Bunny peeped out of. Rose had returned with the keys, and had had to shepherd Goober inside. He started barking as soon as Bunny cracked her car door. Silas had invented a reason to go back inside, and stole a moment of privacy with Rose.

'I'll be back late afternoon,' he had said before kissing her. She had smiled, reassuring him that they would be fine, and that she'd enjoy the morning sun by taking Goober for a much-needed 'W-A-L-K'.

Everything was fine. Rose told him that she'd also finished putting the script together, and that she had already sent it off to Jerry while he slept.

He was grateful that she hadn't mentioned the bed-wetting

again. He hugged her goodbye and scratched Goober's ears as he walked out the door.

We rarely know which goodbye will be the last one, he thought, for no reason at all, as he walked to the car. He hastily dismissed the thought as quickly as it had arrived; there were myriad reasons to explain it away: anxiety, the stress of the current situation, overactive imagination, the fact that he sometimes had the temperament of a maudlin man-child . . .

The most precious moment in the drive had to have been when he'd parked in the gas station, waiting for Lou Lou to come back with two strong coffees – he had offered to buy Bunny one, and she had simply said, 'Bless you, no,' as she continued to sip from a thermos, ice blocks dully thunking against the plastic interior.

He had needed a shunt of caffeine, but the real reason he stopped was to grab a few minutes alone with Bunny.

He had waited until he saw Lou Lou saunter through the glass convenience-store door before turning to the eyes boring into him from the backseat.

'Rose and I are staying until the end of next week. If you do what I ask, you'll never see me again. I know you don't want me around; you've made that clear my whole life. Do as I ask and you'll get your wish.' It sounded ridiculously dramatic, but he said it as reasonably as he could. Bunny had continued rubbing her gold crucifix as he spoke.

She cocked her head as if to say, '*Go on.*'

'When you see the doctor, I want you to agree to go to treatment. Even if it's just for the time that Rose and I are here. When we go, you can do what you want. Come back if you want to, I don't care.'

Her lips peeled back in a saccharine smile.

'Sound fair?' he asked.

'But I *like* seeing you, I *like* having you around, we all do,' she purred, sounding like dry, creaking leather.

'You have a funny way of showing it.'

'You're funny,' she said, staring at him.

Silas knew he was about to lose his temper and he knew it would not help the situation. Impulse and reason ricocheted inside him like opposing pinballs.

'Listen to me, you cunt.' Her eyes widened in surprise as he lunged towards her from the front seat, stopping just short of grabbing her. 'That scared little boy hiding under his bed is dead. I killed him.' His voice was a swirling whirlwind of gravel and iron. 'If you touch Rose again, I'll kill you and hide your body in the fucking woods.'

There. It was out. He hadn't known what he would say until he said it, but the words had felt good coming out and he meant them.

Bunny stared back at him, unreadable. He held her gaze. Unfiltered hate washed out of his eyes and onto her, clear and pure like a snow-melt river in spring. The social niceties of passive aggression and appeasement had been replaced with bald truth.

'Agree to the treatment.' He held her gaze a moment longer, then turned back to the cracked steering wheel as Lou Lou exited the convenience store. A local man around his age held the door for her. She walked through coquettishly and looked mildly confused when he didn't respond to the advance.

Back in the car, Lou Lou felt the echoes of an unpleasant exchange, like the ozone after a lightning strike. She had heartily launched into nervous verbal diarrhoea as the car's tyres spat gravel behind them and Silas hurriedly accelerated back onto the road towards Hamner.

🌲

Silas shifts in his waiting-room seat, trying to wake up his ass. He decides to stretch and peruse the pamphlets on the wall: *Your Weight and Diabetes* and *Heart Health: A guide* stare back at him. He picks them up as if interested.

The prehistoric receptionist clears her throat. 'Y'all c'n go through to Dr Singh, please,' she yells deafly, pronouncing the doctor's name as *Zing*.

He and Lou Lou shuffle down the hallway into Dr *Zing*'s office. It has the unremarkable hallmarks of every doctor's office: a large white desk with a prominent desktop PC in one corner, a plastic elbow joint, and a hodgepodge of knick-knacks with pharmaceutical branding strewn across the front of the desk – a stealthy breakwater between patient and doctor. The patient side has the obligatory three chairs – on one of which Bunny now sits, trying to face away from them.

Silas imagines a typical Hamner family consisting of Mom, Dad and Timmy sitting on these fake leather chairs as they discuss (as is common in these parts nowadays) Timmy's burgeoning Oxy habit.

Dr Singh is standing by the door to greet them. They make small-talk introductions before sitting – the pleather chairs farting as they adjust themselves. Dr Singh leans back slightly in her chair, lacing her fingers together in a false, but reassuring, show of ease and relaxation. *This'll be a near-facsimile of a conversation – she's probably done this once a week since opening up shop.*

'Now,' she begins, 'Bunny has expressed an interest in seeking help for her issues.' Dr Singh speaks in a soft, eloquent voice with just a hint of an accent. *Probably second generation American – the light accent a gift from her parents, like a cultural fingerprint, fading in the bleach-bath of Americana,* Silas thinks, before pondering if the thought is unintentionally racist. He can't tell, but he hopes not. He's made comments several times in the past that made Rose cock an eyebrow. All he knows is that when people repeatedly refer to Rose as 'exotic' it makes him wince; these people are sometimes their friends, and (like him) are white.

'That's wonderful,' Lou Lou says, casting a small, panicked look at Bunny, who sits beside her, poker-faced. The sisters have been each other's gin-soaked rocks (but rocks all the same) in the great twin-timed storms of their lives. A parting, even if temporary, will be painful.

Dr Singh continues. Her words, though sincere, are slightly too well rehearsed, like those of an actor who has played a part in a play for a few too many performances. 'Bunny has also said that she would like to start as soon as possible and I agree that that would be best.' Dr Singh switches on her best friendly smile. 'The nearest facility is in Clearidge – one of the only no-cost centres in the state. It's not flashy, but it's a very fine place, so with Bunny's permission, I'll make arrangements for her to check in today. As I explained to her though, the demand for care far surpasses available supply, so it would need to be today.'

'We're happy to drive her,' Silas says enthusiastically.

Dr Singh's eyes flick to Silas. A shadow of reproach in them says: *Careful, fella, we're on a knife edge here. Let me do the driving.*

'Actually, that won't be necessary. The centre runs an outpatient service that makes rounds to neighbouring towns. They drive through here on their way back, so they could pick Bunny up, say, a little bit after midday?'

'Fantastic,' he says.

Dr Singh gives Silas another one of those looks. *Empathetic, active listening; firm answers; caring delivery.* 'Why don't you folks go get something to eat, and I'll get the receptionist to call you around then, when the van is here. It's half-price burger day at Surley's, I believe.'

'Never had a doctor suggest a burger before,' Silas says as they stand.

Bunny and Lou Lou walk down the corridor ahead of him.

Lou Lou's hand finds Bunny's, gripping it until her knuckles turn white. Bunny leads her like a mother leading a timid little girl through a mall.

They walk through the clinic door, hand in hand, and turn left on their way to Surley's. Silas opens the door and watches them walking away. Lou Lou leans into Bunny as the two speak quietly. *Something tells me the ride home will be a quiet one.*

'S'cuse me, chief,' a voice says from behind him.

Silas has been standing in the doorway, blocking it as he watched them go. He hops aside. 'Sorry about tha–'

Shit.

By the look on the other man's face, he's just thought the same, but has the courage to say it aloud, 'Well shit . . . *You.*'

'Me,' answers Silas.

The mechanic from the world's shittiest diner stares back at him, eyebrows raised, in a cloudy mix of surprise and amusement.

What feels like an awfully long time is actually only three seconds. Silas hasn't shifted into a different stance, but the tension in his body is ready to do so quickly. *I cold-cocked him last time. This time he isn't going to be taken by surprise, and he's a lot bigger than me. I'm fucked.*

Mechanic turns his head to the side and spits out a toothpick, never taking his eyes off Silas. *Here we go.* But instead of swinging, the big man's eyes flick to Bunny's bald, emaciated figure down the road and out of earshot.

'That *your* anchor, huh?' he says as he jerks his jaw at her.

Silas chews the question over. Your anchor? *Oh shit . . . Scary mechanic . . . alcoholic granma . . . anchor . . . equals . . . Anchor equals projectile-vomiting Granma! Gotcha, buddy – olive branch accepted. Sweet Jesus, please be an olive branch.*

It amazed him how people who had lived with a drunk could so easily spot other drunks in a crowd, just from their gait or body language. He had experienced it himself while working as a bar-back, or when he saw a homeless person. He could always tell if the forty-something working stiff at Thursday night happy hour, who seemed just to be blowing off steam, had a genuine problem with the bottle by the way they edged past him on the way to take a piss; it was the way that after two beers they cleared up, rather than fuzzed down. Or the way, if you watched for it, their hands never *quite* came to rest, fluttering from one surface or texture to another like bees on spring blossoms. Same with the homeless person; he couldn't tell you if they were crazy or just plain down on their luck, but he could tell you whether or not alcohol was a patch in that quilt.

Silas steals a glance at Bunny. 'It is.'

'Looks a beaut,' Mechanic grunts sardonically.

'Yeah.'

And just like that, they run out of things to say. Given their history, Silas isn't sure how to disengage without making the conversation uncomfortable, so he continues, slowly nodding as if he's still digesting the remark.

This is when he punches me.

Mechanic shifts from one foot to the other, and for the first time, Silas notices that he is holding two prosthetic legs.

Anchor Granma . . . and her fucking legs. And I thought Bunny was bad, he thinks, staring at Granma's legs, which Silas guesses are supposed to resemble some sort of Caucasian skin tone, but appear more off-yellow.

'I shouldn't have tried to grab your lady like that,' Mechanic says. 'Deserved what I got for it. No hard feelings?' He extends his free mitt towards Silas. The legs chatter as they hit one another. Silas shakes his hand, making a gallant attempt to match how hard Mechanic is squeezing – which is extraordinarily firmly. *No moisturised city-boy handshakes round here, folks.*

'Morgan.'

'Silas.'

Silas releases Morgan's hand. 'So, uh, how is your grandmother, Morgan?'

'*My* anchor?' He holds up the legs and looks at them as if they're a cage containing a rare bird. 'Sunk,' he says with a hint of both weary relief and grief.

'I'm sorry,' Silas says diplomatically.

Morgan's heavy-lidded eyes drift over to his. 'Don't be. It was time for the urn. The drinking . . .' His eyes flick back over to the back of Bunny again, more distant now. 'Well, I don't have to tell you.'

'Takes its toll,' Silas offers.

Silas knows the thing with alcoholic relations is that they often drown everyone around them before they drown themselves. They don't mean to, they just can't help it. And the fact that they can't help it makes the guilt much worse when you begin to hate them, and then hate yourself, and then *Mary Lou and do-si-do, grab a partner, here we go!*

Morgan snorts and raises a thick eyebrow like Dwayne 'The Rock' Johnson right before he defeats John Cena in front of eighty thousand screaming fans. 'Was gonna say that it makes 'em all fuckin' assholes.'

Silas laughs out loud and his body is grateful for it. There's a tenuous bond of common experience between the two men, like returning soldiers from different fronts in the same war, who agree that the whole business is bullshit.

Morgan continues, 'Granma insisted she needed to go for walks in the woods, made me get these expensive fuckin' things fitted for her and then the first goddamn day she has 'em, she gets loaded, sneaks out in the middle of the night on 'em, and gets lost.'

He shakes his head and snorts with a bitter but amused grimace. 'All the search party found were these things' – he jangles the legs at him (Silas *really* wishes he wouldn't) – 'and an empty bottle of her favourite on the riverbank . . . Figure she went for a swim and never came back up. No point looking anymore either. She would have died from exposure by now, even if she didn't drown . . . Ayuh, by now she's definitely coyote shit.'

'Jesus Christ,' Silas says, more out of shock from the 'coyote shit' comment than from the disappearance/death of projectile-vomiting Granma.

Morgan's eyes crinkle against the sunlight as his gaze drifts to the green-forested hills in the distance. 'Nah. He ain't got naught to do with it. Not here.'

'I don't understand,' Silas says.

Morgan seems to be deciding whether or not to tell Silas a secret. As the big man leans closer, Silas worries that he's about to be told about aliens doing 'butt exams' by the local crackpot, or maybe Morgan hasn't really gotten over the fact that Silas punched him and this has all been a 'don't worry, we're cool, bro' ruse so he can head-butt him through the clinic window.

'Out back of the diner, me and Granma live in a couple of old worker's cottages right up against the pines. It's not much, but the bank hasn't owned it since before fuckin' Reagan.'

The left-handed pride seems to be masking something, like he's working up to saying what he's actually wanting to share.

'When she was *real* liquored . . . y'know . . .' Morgan is choosing his words carefully, with a level of reticence that convinces Silas he isn't talking to the local crackpot, or at least not the garden variety one – those ones had a well-rehearsed presentation memorised and would often deliver it enthusiastically, invited to or not. Morgan, on the other hand, is not enjoying talking about this.

'She'd just sit out back, facing the woods, and talk into the trees.' His eyes turn to Silas, then back to the wooded hills in the distance as if pulled there. 'This wilderness. It's never been kind to the white man. And we sure ain't never been kind to *it*. Maybe we should've been, 'cos there are older things than Jesus and God out in those woods. And if you sit on the edge of them when the sun goes down and the world gets quiet . . . sometimes, you feel 'em in there.'

He looks back at Silas. 'Right before the end, it felt like, maybe, maybe she was talkin' with those older things . . . and maybe they were talkin' back . . .' Morgan blinks away the thought and stares at the ground where Granma's feet cast an unpleasant shadow.

Still frames from his nightmare shutter over the back of Silas's head. Morgan's words have reached inside him and clamped a cold, white hand around his heart. It slowly tightens until he has to remind himself to inhale.

It's too uncomfortable. He changes the subject.

'Back in the diner, your granma knew my name.'

'You grow up round here?'

'Uh-huh.'

Morgan's face connects the dots, then lights up. 'Little

ducks, little ducks,' he says, pointing his finger into Silas's chest.

Silas considers flip-flopping on his previous crackpot judgement.

'You went to Little Ducks Aftercare, didn't you?' Morgan asks.

Silas pages through his memory: *ah, nope, nope, nope – found it!* He nods.

'Granma used to work there. Probably read you stories at nap time.' He looses a crooked laugh before continuing, 'Got fired when they found her one morning, asleep in one of the kids' bathroom stalls. They had those weenie kiddie-sized toilets . . . Well, she had her pants round her ankles, ass stuck in the bowl and an empty bottle of Stoli in her lap. Her skinny ass was so jammed in there, the fire department had to shatter the fuckin' bowl with a sledgehammer to get her out!' Morgan howls with infectious laughter. Silas grins, then snorts, then laughs with him. The laughter dissolves the remnants of the cold cramp in his chest like warm air on a snowflake.

Morgan wipes his eyes as he recovers. 'Fuckin' Granma,' he says with sad fondness. 'Listen, I got a long drive back.' He nods at the legs. 'Gotta see if I can get a refund on these or donate 'em or something.'

'Good luck,' Silas says.

They shake hands again. Silas oddly ponders whether he has just made friends with the guy he sucker-punched in the face. *Anything is possible*, he thinks with an amused grin – fuck, maybe one day even he and Bunny could hang by the lake with a bourbon and Coke, recalling stories of inflicted childhood terror?

Silas can only imagine how his facial expressions are coming across, skittering about between sheer panic, smiles, fear and unease. *He probably thinks I'm constipated.*

Morgan disappears through the clinic door and calls behind him, 'Stop by the diner sometime!'

'Will do!'

Will I? Silas thinks before realising that he's dripping with sweat.

A MEETING IN THE DARK – PART II

Rose hasn't really been into the woods since they arrived. Between fixing the script and avoiding Bunny, there hasn't been much of an opportunity. She's gone for little jaunts around the garden with Silas a handful of times, but mostly for Goober's ablutions – or for them to get their leg-blood flowing again and snatch a lungful of fresh air before returning to their self-inflicted body-odour cave.

Today is gloriously different; so far, the few hours she and Goob have spent walking in the woods have been wonderful. *Freedom*, she thinks as she watches the little dog trot along ahead. Goober's pink bandage (periodically unpeeled to apply more antiseptic) is looking worn and just about ready to come off. His leg has healed well. Silas, being Silas, demanded that the bandage stay on for another four days, 'just in case'.

Goober glances back at her with a copacetic grin as he trundles down the path. Rose stops and kneels to examine a small, intricately painted white and purple flower in the shape of a miniature trumpet.

Goober stops to watch a butterfly drift overhead. He tracks it with his face as it flutters back and forth, no clear destination fixed in its flight path. He wonders if he can eat it before he loses sight of it behind a bush. Then he pounces on a patch of earth and begins to dig.

Rose notices the spraying brown earth behind him.

'Goob, come here, boy.' The dog's small, muscular shoulders pop out of the fresh divot as he scampers over. 'Good boy,' Rose says as she massages his head, letting all sense of time evaporate into the trees. She tilts her face up into the dappled sunshine and inhales the peace.

The feeling radiates off her. A glint in the brush catches in her peripheral vision. She approaches the speckled light with little thought and no intention other than simple curiosity.

'Oh,' she says to Goober, as if expecting treasure. An empty old gin bottle, its once clear glass now frosted in places by rain and seasonal moss, stands neck down in the earth. Goober follows her through the brush and sniffs it, mildly disappointed. From the tone of her 'Oh' he was expecting something a little more interesting – something edible, perhaps.

Rose spots a path running past the bottle, narrow but well trod – more deer track than path. Her eyes catch three more bottles periodically stuck neck first in the soft earth beside the track before it winds out of sight. She walks down the path, following the bottles.

As she walks, she notices more objects and trinkets: occasional cigarette butts – many are frayed and green from past seasons in the rain, while others look freshly smoked. She spots small animal bones like the ribs of a mouse, or the filament-like bones of birds. The bones lie white and dry on the dark loam of the path in small arrangements. It all appears too ornate to be random. She takes care not to step on them as she passes, knowing they have been placed for a purpose, and she feels as if she has inexplicably come across a secret.

Goober, uninterested, stops to sniff a frayed tobacco butt, and snorts as if smelling something unsavoury before continuing.

Rose feels the path gradually rising in a subtle incline. Tree-growth thickens around them, and the air grows cooler as it lies tangled around thick trunks. A dew of sweat appears on her forehead and back as her legs work harder, but she feels cold as the air carries the moisture off her skin as fast as it appears. She steps over the occasional dead trunk and gnarled root. Her calves ache pleasantly as she walks, and she looks down and picks a spot for her foot to land as she steps over another bundle of roots. The forest feels wilder and more unkempt here, as if Mother Nature hasn't bothered brushing her hair.

Rose feels a rush of contentment. When she was deep in a writing project, life risked being described or explained away using dollar-store similes. She examined too much, observed too much, became easily irritable and cynical. But not here; here her thoughts . . . drift . . . away . . .

Rose stops just before she walks into the pile of pinecones in front of her. The air is no longer just cooler – it's cold. The day feels worn and old even though it should only be late morning.

She looks behind for the knot of roots she just stepped over and finds nothing but her own footprints on the flat ground.

A small whimper floats up from below. She looks down to see Goober beside her. He nudges her leg with his nose.

'Hey, boy,' she says quietly, testing her voice. Goober's tongue lolls as he nuzzles her leg again. He's behaving as if he's been ignored for far too long, and now he's *finally* won a response from her.

The pile of pinecones is taller than her by at least three feet, which isn't necessarily that hard when you're barely five foot three. Around the tower appears to be a beautiful clearing, the perfect place for Goober to warm his tummy and for Rose to enjoy the Monet clouds floating in the endless New England sky. This place is beautiful, but although she sees how beautiful it is, how warm it looks (but doesn't feel), she doesn't like it.

Shadows slide into the deep part of her brain.

'I don't like this, kiddo. Come on, *vamos*,' she whispers

to Goober, not knowing why she's whispering. She turns and follows her footprints back down the path . . .

A small squeal escapes her when she almost walks into the pinecone pile again. *Que demonios?*

She leaves several more times with the same result – as if she has been turned around without her knowing – a goldfish rediscovering the alien curvature of its bowl as it swims an eternal circuit.

'*Está bien, está bien, está bien*,' she says to self-soothe. Goober sits, ears unhappily flattened against his head as he watches her become increasingly frazzled. She walks around the clearing, trying to figure out what's happening when she sees *another* path – green and pretty. She calls Goober. Time to try the alternate path and get the hell home. They walk swiftly, almost running as the path winds in gentle curves left and right. She's relieved every time they round a corner and don't see that fucking pile of pinecones. The path starts to make a long, lazy curve to the left, which she dutifully follows.

Goober has slowed; he seems to have lost his sense of adventure. She notes that the sunlight is still clear and strong, but its wattage is slowly waning; it's well past noon and creeping towards late afternoon. *Mierda.*

The path winds around and around until Rose's internal compass objects – they're circling back on themselves. *Mierda, mierda, mierda. Fuck!* She debates stopping but feels as if something behind them would then catch up – and that she would then, somehow, wind up at the pinecones again. 'Fuck it, onward. Come on, Goob.'

Goober becomes increasingly agitated as she coaxes him along now.

Wrong way.

Words in her head. It doesn't feel like her voice, but it's hard to tell – it feels far away and muted.

Stop.

No. Onward.

Her thoughts throw juxtaposing stones at her feet. Minutes pass like blood through the chambers of a failing heart. The sensation of moving in circles joins panic and stalks the edges of her resolve. She's close to giving in to the feeling of outright panic when they round a curve – and finally meet with a straight path ahead. Goober howls; a long, low sound that he's never made before.

She stops and comforts him; he's shivering. 'Hey, kiddo, it's okay. It's okay, Goob.' It doesn't help. She breathes and walks along the path. Goober presses against her leg, still shivering.

The relief of not seeing the pinecone pile again turns to wonder as a clearing opens up in front of her. Dead white trees rise out of the bleached, chalky ground. The thought of a flaking, malevolent skin tumour surrounded by healthy flesh flashes in her mind. She attempts to reconcile these unusual features with the living forest surrounding it. The clearing feels dead and numb. But within the numbness is a vibration, the kind that bypasses ears and plucks at the gel between vertebrae. Around the clearing are more gin bottles, all upended in the dirt. She sees that living earth begins just outside the dead, grey dirt edges of the clearing, as if living organisms were afraid to cross an unmarked border.

In the centre of the clearing looms a rock outcrop like an elemental pulpit in a church that, as she looks up at it, feels *old*. The outcrop is jagged and uneven, except for a section of flat rock face that leans over her like a giant closed door. Halfway up the face, a horizontal crevice, roughly a hand's width wide, but black and deep, mars the otherwise featureless face of the rock.

At the base of the flat rock face lies a bunch of cut spinach heads, wilted and days old like flowers at a grave. They rest on a mound of progressively older bunches that turn from brown to black at the base of the pile. The chalky white soil seems to refuse the offering. 'Where are the bugs?' she asks herself quietly. There are no gnats hovering above it. Nothing. It looks as though instead of properly decaying and receding back into the soil, it lingers, as if the natural order hesitates to interfere. Goober's cold nose nudges her calf. 'Shit. You scared me, baba.'

He pads towards the pile, head down and distrustful. He sniffs it. He growls low and deep before cocking his leg and loosing a stream of yellow urine onto it. Then he looks up at Rose, looks back to the edge of the clearing, whines and takes a tentative step towards the path.

Rose considers leaving, but she wants to see inside the crevice.

Out of the rock, the vibration crawls towards her. She can feel it as she turns back to it, like an exhalation from a winter tomb.

Don't.

No. Yes . . . yes, it's fine.

Shoes off – she knows the soft rubber won't find purchase on the rock. She climbs up a few feet, her hands curling over the edge of the crevice. She pulls herself up and finds a tenuous foothold. She lifts her face and peers into the darkness, half expecting a snake to be coiled in front of her.

Don't.

She ignores the voice in her head, convinced that it's just some part of her overactive imagination, run amok after long days of storytelling.

The crevice opens to a shallow, circular, hollow space, like an empty womb. Its internal surface is smooth, nearly polished. A hint of colour in the dim blackness catches her eye. *What's that?* She wants to swing an arm inside and grab it, but she hesitates, again envisioning that big, coiled snake that could be waiting for her. She fishes her phone out of her back pocket and fumbles as she holds on like a rapidly tiring monkey. One hand turns on the camera app while the other grips the lip of the crevice, which is becoming slick with sweat under her fingers. Her finger taps the phone screen and the flash of light illuminates the rock's interior womb in flat white light. *What the hell?*

She releases her grip on the lip, landing on the ground like a cat. Goober vies for her attention, but it's on the picture on her phone; the hint of colour in the darkness was a faded yellow – not unlike the colour of Goober's pee. Inside the rock is a yellow cotton cord – like a drawstring from a piece of clothing – holding together a wreath of pinecones. She only saw it for a moment before Silas took it away, but the wreath on her screen looks remarkably similar to the one Lou Lou tried to pass her. Bunny's gift.

Rose suddenly feels like a kid snooping around in an adult's office. The bottles, the butts, the spinach – all part of the private madness of Silas's aunt. An aunt that, she notes with relief, is on her way to somewhere (*anywhere*) other than the same house she has to stay in for another week.

I'll show Si, she thinks, as she walks the perimeter of the clearing, snapping pictures. She even considers uploading one to Instagram later – a much-needed addition to her increasingly neglected private account @RosieRosaNYC. It could sit on her feed, beside her last photo (now six months old) of her and her friend Maria's foster kitten, Cumberbatch.

Once she has finished a circuit of the juxtaposing landscape (during which Goober keeps butting into her and whining), she stops in front of the crevice.

One last thing to get.

She climbs up the face again and holds onto the stone lip. She pulls herself up, reaches inside, takes hold of the wreath, and pulls. It follows and stops. She gazes back into the gloom; her arm trembles with fatigue.

She spots that one end of the yellow cord hangs taut from a small gap in the smooth surface, at the back of the crevice.

Don't.

That crack wasn't there before, she thinks as she tugs. The cord pulls back, as if someone else is holding the other end. Goober begins frantically barking below. Her head whips down to the base of the rock where he stands on his hind legs, desperately trying to reach her. With a mighty force, she feels the wreath yank deeper into the crevice. It happens so fast she doesn't have time to release her grip, and her arm is dragged shoulder deep into the darkness. Her cheek slaps against the rock face, forcing a short yelp from her. Goober's barking becomes so frantic it sounds more like one continuous, panicked wail. She looks down at him still struggling to get to her. *My inexhaustible baba*, she thinks, her mind strangely calm. He's jumping up towards her – so hard that his back legs spring free of the ground and for an instant, all four paws seem to scramble up the rock before falling short.

Rose tries to pull her arm out, but her hand won't open and the stone womb seems to have constricted around it. Pragmatic by nature, her mind works to resolve the situation.

This will *not* be another *127 Hours*. 'Nobody's losing an arm today!'

And then, all sound stops.

She can still see Goober barking below; his mouth opens and shuts as he barks, but no sound comes out. Her mouth springs open. She feels her jawbone click in her head as it yawns wide in a scream that makes no noise. She tries to inhale and scream again, but there's no air to inhale. Her eyes roll back into the top of her head. Her back arches as the vibration jangles her vertebrae, growing into a roar full of whispers and moans.

She feels some vital part of herself being loosened, and then torn from her body by an ageless sinew.

She is shown things.

They come in fragments of offal that are forced down into her consciousness. Her mind heaves as it tries to expel them, though finally they stick and play out.

Sometimes she sees them through the eyes of someone else, her view strictly governed by the movement of the eyes she peers out of, as if spying through a submarine porthole. Other times she feels her disembodied self fixed to a particular spot, but free to look where she wishes, as life plays out in front of her in a private performance.

These are memories, she thinks as a loud CRACK! explodes somewhere in her head.

She will come to understand that this is the incompatible sound of her consciousness being forced into a new vision like an eggshell being pushed through a keyhole.

VISIT ME

Rose peers out of porthole eyes at a younger Bunny standing in the doorway of one of the upstairs bedrooms – Lou Lou's bedroom. This Bunny still has long blonde hair and the final, fading rays of a debutante's dewy beauty dancing across her face. Rose almost doesn't recognise the beautiful girl as the same bald scarecrow that now haunts the woods around the house. But the eyes are the same – the idiosyncratic green that also stains Silas's eyes, and all the eyes of his family. Young Bunny pinches her gold crucifix between her thumb and forefinger so tight that her hand shakes. She stares, her face frozen in a terrified rictus, straight into the porthole eyes that Rose peers out from.

A voice that sounds like it inhabits the same vessel Rose is viewing from whispers like ash: *'Visit me I visit you visit me I visit you.'*

The porthole leans in close and sinks into the centre of young Bunny's chest. It pushes against the skin of Bunny's sternum, then moves past it. There's a brief glimpse of bone and meat, like an express train rushing past a station without stopping. It's nauseating and cruelly thrilling. The porthole moves through, and past her, leaping into a storm of multicoloured light that dances like a fire made out of the Northern Lights. The light recedes away from the porthole like a tide, and Rose feels the vessel she's riding expand to fill the empty space.

'Aunt Bunny?' a young boy's voice asks.

The porthole rushes to a space that feels impossibly far away as it speeds through its own mass. There's that feeling of the train zooming by the station again as it re-enters bone and meat. The porthole flashes and Rose sees a view through what she knows to be Bunny's eyes. She feels Bunny's hand still pinching the thin metal of the crucifix. Bunny's porthole eyes turn towards the hall where a little boy stands at the top of the stairs, his green eyes half shaded by the yellow hood of a cape – no, a yellow ducky towel that he wears. It's grimy, like he's run through dirt and mud with it.

Like a lens being changed, Rose then sees him the way the owner of the whispering ash voice sees him; a glowing ball of sparks and dancing lights, much brighter and clearer than Bunny's.

CRACK!

Rose shuts her eyes. Lightning bolt pain tears through her as she's dragged to another vantage point. Her eyes flutter open. She's still in the house, but now she's floating near the ceiling, moored there by an unseen anchor, but free now to see with her own eyes and look where she will. Below is Silas in the hallway, still at the top of the stairs in his yellow ducky hood. There are two Bunnys – one stands in the doorway impassively, and Rose instinctively knows that this is the one her porthole was seeing out of before. The other Bunny lies on the floor, staring at Silas, screaming in terror with her arms outstretched. Rose can't figure out if the outstretched arms are beckoning him or warning him away.

CRACK!

This time the lightning bolt feels like it didn't just rattle something inside her, but snap it.

It's cold now. Rose feels the gentle motion of being suspended under water. She's back in another vessel. She wonders if this is what it must feel like to be a baby inside a womb; floating within yourself but encased in the alien folds of another being. Her eyes open. She floats in the dark water. Her new porthole sways gently as she peeps out of it, just above the surface facing the shore.

There, almost at the water's edge, stands Silas.

She screams, '*Silas! Silaaaas! SILAS! SILAS!*'

Silas's hands and arms are painted in blood. He looks tired. So pale the light of a candle could shine right through him. Goober stands beside him, blood dripping from his snout after a great fight. The little dog looks straight at the porthole, and through the porthole, not at the thing she is encased in, but at Rose.

'*Goob, Goober, get Daddy; get help, Goober. Goober, get help!*'

She is crying, in the portal; she imagines her face resembles that of Bunny on the floor – screaming and unheard.

Goober sees her, he hears her there and is sad – confused – scared. He turns to Silas and barks frantically (but Silas doesn't hear him in this soundless place). He turns to the water and barks, and then turns to her to bark. The little dog hangs his head without taking his eyes away from her. His eyes seem bigger, clearer, more alive. His gaze warms her, but the expression in them makes her feel cut off and alone.

A single pinecone sails out of the woods and lands on the stones near Silas. He turns to look at it. A second lands and rolls past him. A third lands. He turns to look at the trees as a sound like a growing wind roars out of them.

Through the porthole she sees a wall of pinecones break through the tree line like a thick wave of disturbed black flies. They don't follow a normal arc, but fly straight towards Silas and Goober. Silas stands to face them, awestruck by the growing roar, but Goober ignores them, gazing through the porthole at Rose with those clear, deep eyes. The cones speed up as they cover the short distance between the tree line and the shore.

For a millisecond Rose sees Goober and Silas silhouetted against the pinecone cloud rushing towards them, and thinks of *Christina's World*. They saw the painting at MoMA the year before last; the fragile girl sprawled in the dry, barren field, turned away from view, holding herself up on her arms and gazing at the desolate farmhouse and barn that, through disinterested kismet, is her world. Rose did not like the painting. All she could see was the back of the girl's head and she had been bothered by what she would see if Christina turned it towards her. Pain? Fear? Madness? It made her feel heavy and stuck, and she left Silas staring at it while she carried on. Twenty minutes later she found him still staring at the painting with his shoulders slumped forward. Haunted.

Now, from her porthole, she wonders – if Silas turns from the pinecones and looks at her, what will she see?

The wall of cones reaches the two silhouettes, and for just an instant, appears to gently fold around them before both figures pinwheel into a red mist as the cones swirl around them, twisting and tearing their bodies apart.

The porthole Rose looks out of dives into the dark water. She feels a serpentine motion as the vessel swims down into the increasingly black depths. It grows darker and darker until it crosses a Rubicon. A cold, dead, yellow light gently paints the world in a faint glow. Rose sees titanic cliffs on both sides of her as she travels along the bottom of a great flooded canyon. Dead white tree trunks litter the silty bottom like the scrambled ribs of some dead, world-eating creature.

A far-off speck floats suspended in the water ahead of them. She feels the vessel carrying her whip its tails faster – accelerating at nauseating speed. An undulating cloud floats around the dot like electrons around an atom. As she gets closer, she sees that the thing in the middle is her, back arched, eyes closed. The atoms are not atoms, but eels swimming in restless orbit around her as her hand clasps the pinecone wreath.

The vessel swims towards her. The eels shuck away from her like a shoal of startled fish as the vessel breaks their cloud.

Back on the rock face, ripples of water begin to spill out of the crevice in icy rivulets that trickle down onto Rose's paralysed body. A faint glow – the same pallid yellow as the one in the watery canyon – begins to pulse out of the crack, waxing and waning in a breath-like cycle as it shines onto Rose's closed eyes. A bloody tear creeps down her face like an errant pallbearer. The icy rivulets swell into braided trickles that merge into a pulsing rush of water.

The vessel has no interest in the retreating eels; they are moths to a glowing bulb, flies to a swollen corpse belly, scattered by the owl and hyena. She watches from her porthole as the vessel powers through the eels, closing on her body, so gently suspended in the glowing water. It rushes towards the hand clasping the wreath. From within the vessel she feels a great simian mouth yawning below the porthole. It growls. The writhing stone bowels of a black universe unfurl as it strikes.

CRACK!

Rose catapults back into her body on the rock face like broken mirror shards hurled into an empty steel dustbin. Her face contorts as she feels her hand crushed in the stone.

Water explodes out of the crevice in a foaming avalanche. She folds her legs up and under her, bracing them against the rock, before attempting to wrench her arm out of the crevice. Her shoulder pops and grates as ligaments tear like wet newspaper. Her hand comes free from the crevice as she sails out into space before landing on the ground below in a wet, shuddering heap.

And as she gasps – sound roars back into the world.

The first thing that registers are Goober's panicked yips as he fusses over her. Her eyes are still closed. She reaches for him, pulling his warm body into her throbbing arms, before she breaks down and sobs. Her lungs drag in breath after breath. It feels as if she's been held under water until the final stage of drowning – she opened the seal of her lips and throat, inhaling water in a final attempt to breathe. As she gasps in air, the feeling slowly passes like an exhaled shadow.

When her breathing eases, she feels she may be able to open her eyes, which are still welded shut. She inhales, locks the breath in her chest and forces them to open. For an instant all she sees is the pale yellow light bouncing off the underwater cliffs. The nightmare corona fades as she blinks it away, replaced by the familiar light of the natural world as it returns to her. She shivers from cold and fright's memory. The water that soaked her clothes smells like standing water in a swamp – all sulphur and base decay.

Goober's body feels beautifully warm, a loving hot coal in her arms, bleeding life back into her body. He lies pressed against her, his tail taut and still, as if he knows. Which he does.

She can't bring her eyes to look at her hand yet. Her injured shoulder hums with a deep pain that demands a shift in weight. She looks around in disbelief – a shallow puddle of acrid water now rests at the base of the stone. Dead spinach leaves float like empty, burned-out lifeboats on the surface. The water cascades over the chalky soil like mercury, the dead soil seemingly unwilling to absorb it; it either collects listlessly in shallow impressions or retreats towards the edges of the clearing where it disappears into the dark groundcover of the living forest.

Her eyes brush over the rock face again, afraid to linger on any one spot for too long. Telltale drips of water continue to slide down its surface, but the crevice is simply no longer there. The rock is flat and featureless.

As it stares dumbly down at her, the rational part of her mind seizes on the possibility that there is a normal explanation for what she has experienced. She gratefully accepts the notion as fact for several seconds, giving her just enough time to look down at her injured hand. The thought shimmers away like a mirage in a desert of reality. Whatever she was riding in . . . whatever had cracked her mind, and split Bunny . . . whatever had lunged for her in the watery yellow canyon had left its mark on her hand in *this* world as well.

The wreckage begins in the soft webbing between her ring and middle finger, running up her hand, over her wrist and curving halfway up her forearm. It's her forearm that alarms her most. Her eyes trace the deep red impressions of teeth – not quite sharp like an animal, not quite flat like a human, but some place in between.

She tells herself to get up. What she doesn't realise is that she has. She's already stood up, turned and run screaming from the outcrop. She just hasn't registered that her body is moving yet.

Goober follows behind her as she runs down the path. Every footfall ripples pain up into her hanging shoulder, and she wraps her other arm around it to protect it. She's already sprinting when she takes a curve in the path too fast. Her foot searches for the ground but finds a root instead.

The stumble might not have ended so badly if she'd had the use of her arms to break her fall, but when she topples, she hugs her arms tighter instead of flinging them out in front of her. As she sails into the air and off to the side of the path, her head parts a leafy branch and a tree trunk rushes towards her face, hungry for a kiss. All she can do is tuck in her chin like a child avoiding sloppy kisses from a forceful great-aunt as her head slams into it. Her body shudders and turns limp as she slides to the base of the tree.

Goober picks his way through the brush and gently presses his nose against her cheek like he does when he's saying good morning. On those mornings she wraps her arms around him and pulls him into the warm cotton bed sheets.

But today she lies still. He misses her. He licks the blood away from her eyes as it slides down her face from somewhere in her hairline. He smells the shallow, ragged breaths that dart in and out of her nostrils. She's still there, he knows . . . But so distant.

He nuzzles her cheek again and whimpers, as if making a promise to her.

Goober walks back out onto the path with feet that feel heavy with purpose. The clearing can still be seen through the trees. Rose lies less than a hundred yards from its border – he could do it. He must.

He stands protectively in the space between Rose's body and the clearing.

I love MomDad . . . Goober's thought drifts into the darkening woods like a lonely bird aware that it is the last of its kind. He stares into the middle distance, scanning terrain that only the heart can see.

STRAIGHT TO VOICEMAIL

'Hi, please leave a message and I'll –'

Rose's voice flies away as Silas pulls the phone from his ear, hanging up for the fifth time in a row. *She's out walking and left her phone. No, she's taking a nap and it's on silent. Either way, she's fine. She's safe. She's fine*, he thinks as he tucks his phone back into his pocket.

He stands over a crack in the pavement outside Hamner Animal Control and Veterinary Services and peers through the glass door and into the dark interior beyond.

They waited for a call from Dr Singh, and one o'clock had come and gone, leaving him stranded in a lacklustre lunch booth with Lou Lou and Bunny. Finally, he escaped the 'lunch' at Surley's Bar & Grill – which had devolved into Lou Lou ferrying multiple rounds to Bunny, who sat slumped in the booth like a melted wax statue. He was hoping to see Euge at the Animal Control office and have a normal conversation – maybe hear what the vet had found up at Long Lake – but the place is shut, with a small pile of uncollected mail huddled on the interior doormat, white envelopes glowing through the glass door.

He turns away and looks up and down the road. It looks like a film set for a terrible post-apocalyptic movie starring some artiste who was busy transitioning from reality-show *enfant terrible* to movie star. All you needed was to tip two dustbins over, remove the half-dozen late-model pickups, and have the square-jawed idiot walk himself and his show-pony abs down the median, carrying a plastic gun that never fired.

'Fuck, I hate this place.' He isn't sure if he just means Hamner, or the culture it's welded onto like the beat-up wing mirror on an exhausted, Detroit-made Ford.

He checks his watch: 15:42. The doc had said to expect a call around one.

As he walks back to the clinic, he crests the gentle rise in the main road, watching how the incline slices the view of the town into two down-sloping halves. At the end of the slope he spots a white official-looking van parked outside the clinic.

'Finally.' He quickens his pace.

As he arrives, he notes with relief that Lou Lou can be heard in the clinic doorway, which is dutifully held ajar by an orderly/van-driver.

'Now, you get well and I'll see you soon,' Lou Lou says with a liquid shimmer in her voice that hints at their sodden lunch.

He stops short of the doorway to let them exit. Lou Lou gently leads Bunny out towards the van and Silas suddenly remembers that his mother has the ability to be extremely caring if an audience to play to is around. He also notes that Bunny possesses that bizarre ability alcoholics develop where they can appear almost sober despite drinking extraordinary amounts – the flip side of which is that when the rubber finally meets the road, they earn their drunkenness back with interest and a binary switch – skipping 'tipsy' and clicking straight into crying-fat-naked-uncle-at-a-twenty-first-birthday-party kind of drunk.

With less amusement than he'd expect to feel, he witnesses Bunny's switch click as she steps out of the doorway and into the afternoon sunlight. Her knees soften and her legs threaten to buckle as the orderly-cum-van-driver props her up with expert dispassion – he actually says, 'Whoopsie daisy,' as his arms leave the door and swoop under her armpits like he's a trained dancer.

Bunny's ruddy hand gropes for Lou Lou's shoulder as she drunkenly shout-says, 'God bless you, my sister. I will see you soon.' The words bubble out sounding more like 'Gobblesh shishter, eye shee ewe shoon.'

The orderly slides the van door open as Lou Lou fights back tears. She helps Bunny into a passenger seat and buckles her in. Silas feels a brief pang of maddening guilt. He swats it away with a cold rationale that makes him feel less like his mother is a puppy that he's about to kick; this needs to be done, not just for him and Rose, but for Lou Lou, and even Bunny.

There. Much better.

He catches the van driver's eye and nods wordlessly that he'll close the door once the goodbyes are done. The man delivers a social worker's smile before getting into the driver's seat.

Lou Lou drags Bunny's suitcases to the back of the van.

'I'll do it,' Silas offers.

'No,' Lou Lou says, with a shadow of *you've done enough* dancing behind the word.

He turns to Bunny, who's slumped in her seat like a forlorn, drunken toddler. Dr Singh says a momentary, 'Hello, good to see you're off,' before retreating back into the clinic vestibule at the behest of an assistant.

Lou Lou continues martyring herself at the back of the van. The driver is on a phone call. Only Silas sees Bunny slip off her mask. She slowly turns to him, the inebriated cloud in her eyes parting like a backstage curtain as she speaks.

'I'm going to get much stronger.'

He doesn't miss a beat.

'Stay there as long as you need.' It sounds remarkably like *go fuck yourself.*

Instead of reacting to him, Bunny cranes her neck, searching the surrounds behind him.

'Where is Rose?'

He doesn't answer, but his mouth closes and his jaw tightens. The moment hangs in the air. A smile like a straight razor spreads across her face.

'Where is Rose?'

He feels sick. There's a knowing tone in her voice that sticks to the back of his throat, drying the spit in his mouth. Bunny's eyes water as they widen. She looks up, gazing directly into the sun.

'You're too late, Silas . . . God bless.'

Her arm flies out, sliding the van door shut so hard that the driver jumps and Lou Lou squeals a startled 'Ooh!'

Once the *slam* has registered, the driver moves like a wind-up toy. 'Okay, we all sorted?' he asks as he places his phone into the glove box.

'Yes,' Silas yells through the closed door. He looks

through the window at Bunny and she peers back at him – sun-tears streaming, and that straight razor smile still cutting across her face.

The van drives away. Lou Lou wraps her arms tightly around herself like a child self-soothing. Dr Singh has finished with her assistant and sidles up to say something doctorly. Her lips have just parted when Silas spins around.

'One o'clock was three hours ago!'

Dr Singh blinks, the soft skin of her neck collecting under her chin as she jerks her head back, trying to avoid the full force of his voice.

Silas grabs Lou Lou by the arm, leading her to the car.

'You got what you wanted. I'm all alone again!' she wails in a voice set for bad theatre. He fishes the car keys out of his pocket.

'Get in.'

The car speeds away from the wide-eyed doctor, who's now more concerned about Silas's aggressive behaviour than about Bunny's alcoholism. He speeds through the lights at the intersection down the road. Car horns blare and the other drivers erupt in hand gestures and a clarion call of obscene language. Silas doesn't hear them. All he hears is:

'You're too late, Silas.'

I LOVE MOMDAD

Goober watches daylight flee as shadows fatten. It has been hours. Still he stands in the path between MomDad and the approach of The Other.

There are two paths: the earthy one that cools beneath his paws, and another, which is felt but not seen.

He stands in both. Watching.

I love MomDad, his mind speaks. The power of the thought comes not from the words, which like all language, is only a well-intentioned construct; ultimately nothing more than opaque sketches of the actuality beneath them. But when his mind speaks them, they brush an energy source like the end of a copper wire brushing a limitless battery. The battery is love. Not the floral, pink love that people build to keep them warm on cold existential nights, but a primal, molten love that runs through life ignoring logic and reason and sometimes causing great pain. The love that lets a parent choose which drowning child will be saved, and which is given to the river when only one can be carried to shore.

I love MomDad. The thought comes as a white pulse that, for the briefest moment, illuminates the dark of the unseeable path. It rolls over it, crawling over its terrain. A luminescent warning. A weapon.

MomDad stirs. Goober hears her. He wants to run to her, but The Other is too close. Too near to its nest. Its den. The Other made it long ago to weather the eternal winter of its strange existence. Goober's spirit is able to feel it here; he smells it with a second nose he does not understand, but never doubts. Its smell whispers fragmented secrets, gifting the small dog a fractured understanding of it. It tells him that The Other is neither good nor bad – how could it be, when it became itself before those definitions had been created? It is, above all else, simply curious and indifferent – like an ageless and unmanaged child, destroying and creating, following the whims that capture its lonely fancy. But Goober knows that that lonely fancy has now turned towards MomDad.

'Goober?' MomDad mutters, lifting her groggy head from its earthen pillow.

Goober whines and growls, half answering her and half warning The Other.

A stick cracks in the dead clearing.

I love MomDad, Goober says to The Other. The simple syntax of his canine mind expresses its thoughts and feelings in rough-hewn, solid blocks, perhaps better suited for the task they will soon be used for, rather than the complicated syntax of man. White energy ripples out from his small body, unseen by MomDad's eyes. It washes over the lidless pupils that watch them from the stone tabernacle . . . And for a moment, those pupils shrink to pinhead holes that turn away from the light, startled.

The little dog sees The Other flinch – and in it, sees a delicate hope. *I make time*, Goober thinks, as his body tenses like a muscled spring before exploding towards the clearing, head down, teeth bared, throat screaming, towards the stone outcrop.

I love MomDad! His mind-speak smashes the wire to the eternal battery. Love. And this time his will holds it there. He feels a jolt of white energy burst around him, no longer an ethereal ripple, but white liquid fire that turns his teeth to shining silver, and his voice to the war hammer of a dog-headed god. The small size of his corporeal body is irrelevant now; he has run through a threshold to a place where size and time are foreigners.

The Other has been waiting there, preparing itself to cross the stony threshold of its den, into the place where MomDad lies. Goober's charge knocks The Other backwards as the two fight. Silver teeth tear into ageless flesh, the little dog's bark is now a thousand-throated howl that lights and shakes the dark cosmic architecture around them. The Other has teeth of its own that thunder down onto the little dog, only to shatter against the liquid white flames that rise out of him. But its teeth reform and try again and again, searching for weakness.

Goober knows that his time is short. His eternal battery can never be exhausted, but he, the wire, can only stay connected for so long before melting. He releases a howl that bathes The Other in a brilliant light – not enough to show all of its form, but enough to see a throat among the teeth and limbs that bombard him. He springs up and his silver-flamed fangs latch onto the exposed throat; he clamps down in a vampiric crush as he sends the words again, *I love MomDad.*

The liquid light washes down through Goober's teeth and into the maw of The Other's torn throat, and for the first and only time, he hears The Other scream. Even in pain, its voice rumbles with a strength far greater than Goober's silver howl. A hand clamps over his body. The hand's flesh roils, melting away on the white flames like butter on a skillet, revealing obsidian bone beneath. But The Other holds Goober long enough to pull him from its throat, flinging him back and out of the threshold. Goober's body catches the edge as he bounces through. He screams as he is cut on stone.

He lands on the dead earth of the clearing, pinwheeling several times like a ragdoll before regaining his feet. The white flames have left him and his body feels burned and mortally tired. Warmth spreads down his back and runs over his fur, dripping off his undercarriage. His blood will leave a painting of his deeds on the ground for the sun to see in the distant morning.

I live. The thought is an instruction to his own body. His raw paws, burned as if on black summer asphalt, pad away from the stone and down the path towards MomDad. His gait is palsied with pain that stiffens his back, but he wills himself on, and for a moment, it all goes away. He is in her arms again, licking her face and tasting dry blood and tears on her cheeks.

MomDad stands. 'Good boy,' she whispers into his ear as she picks him up.

For this he is glad – he has made time for her to wake. And time for her to run. But maybe not enough.

MomDad holds him in her arms and begins to run from the place. She is unsteady and slow, but running.

The Other was old and strong, and Goober's teeth, though still tingling from tasting its blood, did not drive deep enough to inflict a mortal wound. Nothing can.

A sound of snapping twigs rises behind them as The Other passes through its threshold to give chase.

I love MomDad, he sends his mind-speak out like a ripple again. It frays him to do so; a light steam begins to rise from his fur, but he does this thing willingly, for it keeps The Other at bay for just a little longer – enough time for MomDad to get further away from its den. The Other can only travel so far from its den without its vehicle to climb inside of.

The ripple catches the pupils behind them in a luminescent wave, but this time they do not shrink or turn away. The Other slows for a moment as the white ripple slams into it, but it moves faster to regain lost ground.

He knows he will only be able to send the mind-speak once more before the wire burns away and the connection severs.

The little dog closes his eyes and nuzzles MomDad's neck, drinking in her scent; the scent that, long ago, filled his nose as a pup, chasing away the smell of shit and death and cleaning chemicals in the place he had come from. Her scent had gently calmed him as the ticks were pulled from his ears and snout, leaving scars that still peppered his skin under his short black hair. MomDad had fed him medicine to kill the parasites that ate him from the inside, and stayed with him as they had passed painfully from his body in bloody puddles. MomDad had held him when he slept and loved him when he woke.

Goober fills his lungs with her scent, and in his own simple way says:
Goodbye.

Her mind struggles to understand what happened . . . She had carried him as she ran. There had been a noise behind them like breaking bushes. It had been getting closer but she couldn't look back. Goober was heavy and hot in her arms and the pain in her shoulder was searing, the joint full of ground glass as she carried him. But she would not let him go. She didn't know why or how, but he had done something that she knew had saved her from whatever was behind them. She felt as if there was a pint of clotted blood between the bone and the skin on her forehead; she felt it jiggle with every heavy footfall . . .

And just like that, Goober had nuzzled her neck, then pressed his snout to her cheek like he did in the mornings to wake her, and with a tight whip of his muscled body, wriggled free from her arms and into the darkness behind them.

She had meant to turn and catch him. Had meant to stop. She hadn't cared anymore if the thing behind them caught her. She wouldn't leave him behind.

But a blue-white flash like a lightning strike had exploded behind her and pushed her through the trees with a force that gently cupped her body and flung it forward and away from the clearing. Her legs had felt like they weren't touching the ground as she ran – and she'd run so fast she lost track of the trees rushing past her.

Rose rides the shock wave like a gutter-bound leaf in a summer storm; tears burn her eyes and blur her vision as she screams for Goober, but she cannot stop, and in doing so, a vital piece of her goes away. She feels herself lose time, disassociate. A great distance is travelled. Her lungs heave with heavy, sobbing breaths as she finally slows down, dropping to her knees in the soft carpet of pine needles. Nothing moves behind her. The silent trees loom over her pensively, as if embarrassed by her actions.

'Goober?'

The moon washes the woods in mournful half-light, too weak to cast shadows. She looks behind her, waiting to see his small, stocky shoulders carry him into view. But the woods behind are an empty casket.

An angry buzz fades into her awareness. A few seconds pass before she realises that it's not just inside her skull. She walks towards the sound when she sees a staccato shuttering of headlight beams bouncing along tree trunks, down and far to the left, but getting closer. If the beams stay on their trajectory then she could intersect their path if she hurries. The angry buzz grows clearer; it's a small engine red-lining.

The ground begins to slope downwards as she runs towards the headlights. She frantically tries to guess the exact placement of the road as her feet tear blindly down the slope. She steals a sideways glance at the light barrelling towards her: twin orb headlights. *'Gracias a Dios,'* she whispers.

The thought that she isn't making her way down fast enough begins to nibble at her. Now that she has seen the headlights, the thought of their warm beams passing her by and leaving her in the flat light of the moon looming tangled in the black branches above, makes her squeal. She pumps her legs harder, one foot then the other – then her legs tread empty air as the ground drops away. She floats off the edge of an invisible drop, sailing into the cold air. *I'm getting you help, boy. I'm coming, baba*, her mind lies. Dark branches slap her face and body as she falls. *Don't hit your head again. Do not hit your fucking head again. You have to get him back.* Her head feels like a broken Christmas bauble being held together with tissue paper. If she hits it again . . . She can't. She's the only one who knows where Goober is.

Dark branches part as she drops into the yellow glow of the headlights. Her feet crash to earth, yet somehow, she manages to stay upright. Had she stumbled, the front of the braking vehicle would have hit her broadside and killed her.

Instead, she reflexively jumps as the car's tyres skid on the dirt road, making a dry ripping sound. She has time to pivot away from the car; her head and torso are spared, but the fender kisses her leg, shattering it and spinning her into the night air.

The next moment appears out of blackness, as if Rose's eyes are a TV that has just been switched on midway through a show. Everything glows red. The trees. Her hands.

Her arms stretch out in front of her on the red earth. She thinks it's blood, but her mind slowly begins to work. *Oh, it's the red brake lights on the back of a car*, she thinks detachedly.

A car door opens. Someone is yelling.

'Rosie?! Rosie! No, baby, why were you in the road?! Why were you in the road?!' As her eyes flutter shut, a fresh tide of blood washes over them like a warm comforter carrying her to sleep.

HAIR OF THE DOG

For Silas, the days scuttled along like a carrion beetle over cold skin. His guilt and worry crippled him, disconnecting parts of his mind until he felt unable to make use of the slack muscles that stretched over his face in flaccid bands. He only fully engaged when doctors were sharing information about Rose's broken body, or when Rose woke – fevered and weepy with medicine and pain – before the sedatives pulled her back to rest.

The night of the accident, Lou Lou had sat in the backseat holding his bunched jacket to the gash on Rose's head. It had soaked through in a dark red bloom before finally ceasing. Rose moaned in pain as the car shuddered over bumps on the road. The uneven surface jarred the splinters of bone floating in the flesh of her leg, all bent where it shouldn't have been. The doctors had later said how 'lucky' she was that none of the shards had nicked her femoral. *Lucky.*

Her shoulder had been badly dislocated and the ligaments were torn, but not severed. The doctors said they would heal up almost like new, after a while.

There had been minor head trauma from her headfirst dive into the tree, but no brain swelling or permanent damage, and the gash in her hairline only bled because it had been re-opened by her heavy landing after the car hit her.

The first few days Silas spent by her side at the hospital. He made brief journeys to the canteen or coffee machine when the nurses gently ushered him out of the room in a bid to get him moving. Lou Lou came every day to see them, bringing fresh clothes and an array of wildflowers that she placed in a bright orange vase that seemed out of place in its surroundings.

When she was calmer and not needing to be sedated, Rose woke for longer periods and talked. She told him about clearings and stones and paths; she told him of ancient things and of Goober. She always ended with Goober. Rose desperately tried to remember every detail as she sifted through her memory, which only seemed stranger to her under the stark hospital lighting. She told him how she'd dropped her phone, then she forced him to ring it – if it was still on, then maybe they could track it, she mused desperately. But when he did, it went straight to voicemail, the battery probably already dead for days. She told him of the visions she'd had; of seeing Bunny and then watching her being overrun, or taken, or . . . split. She told him how she saw him and Goober at the lake, and how she had screamed to him, and he hadn't seen her, but Goober *had*. She told him how her hand had been bitten by the thing she was looking out of – the thing that she could see through. The teeth marks on her hand and forearm were gone when she woke in the hospital, but there was an angry purple crescent bruise where they had been. She showed him, but the bruise looked like it could have been from anything. He nodded and looked at her with eyes that didn't know what to say.

When she was a little better, he left her in her room and drove back to the spot where the car had hit her . . . Where *he* had hit her. The fact that it had been by mistake, and impossible to have avoided, made no difference; he would carry it in a deep place inside himself where it would remain, unforgiven.

The accident spot was easy enough to find; the light road traffic meant that the long skid marks still scarred the dirt road. You could spot them if you were looking for them.

He backtracked from the spot, following her footprints up an embankment and through the woods before they simply stopped – almost like she had been deposited there from the air above. From there he picked a different direction each day and walked for hours, looking for paths lined with empty gin bottles, or piles of pinecones, or dead trees in a clearing with a big stone cliff in the middle – or for dead yellow canyons and monsters. He didn't know what he was looking for, he just wanted his dog. When Rose had described the clearing with the stone cliff, faint childhood memories had glimmered somewhere in his mind, but he never found any of them. His voice went hoarse, ground down from calling for Goober every twenty seconds or so. More than once he sat down heavily on the forest floor and cried. He missed his dog. He missed what his family had been before they'd come home to the woods. They should have stayed in the city, he thought to himself, knowing that he had made a mistake; the trouble was, he just didn't know if he was still making one. But he was unsure of what to do now, or where to go. Goober was here somewhere and he needed Silas to find him. Rose was broken and needed to heal. He was racked with doubt and fear and shame.

But he couldn't show her that. Rose needed him to be strong now. He wasn't, but if she needed to believe that he was, then he would lie.

After a week, Rose is allowed to leave the hospital. Lou Lou picks them up in their car as hers is still not starting, nor is there any intention (or much cash) to have it seen to. Rose perches her hip-to-toe plaster cast along the length of the cramped backseat as they drive. Great efforts are made by all not to mention the dog blanket in the front passenger footwell, or the tattered chew toys in the trunk, or the doggy wet-nose marks on the window, or the puppy chew marks on the seat belt, or Goober's hair, which has found refuge in every nook and cranny, or his scent, which is everywhere.

Still not trusting himself, Silas asks Lou Lou to drive. As they reach home, Lou Lou pulls around to the front door, humming a listless tune as she kills the engine. Rose has crutches but requires significant help getting out and getting around. As soon as Silas lifts her out of the car, she thrusts the crutches into her armpits and hobbles determinedly to the edge of the woods.

Silas winces as she does.

'Baby, careful. Your shoulder. Just use the one crutch till –'

'I'm on meds, I can't even feel it,' she snaps at him without turning around.

'Rose, my love . . . let's go inside –'

She turns. Her look silences him. He approaches and gingerly wraps his arms around her good shoulder to help her walk.

'Jesus Christ, just leave it!'

Lou Lou swiftly enters the house, sensing a time for privacy.

'Goober!' The tone in Rose's voice is the same one that she used to use when he was a scruffy puppy playing at the ramshackle dog park near Hell Gate Bridge in Astoria.

'Here, boy! . . . Goober! Come, boy!' The musical tone falters. Silas watches her shoulders hunch over on her crutches as they soften.

'Goober!' Rose screams. Silence. Then a small sob. Silas turns her shaking body into his.

'It's okay, it's okay,' he whispers.

'It's not. I left him behind.' She sobs into his chest.

He holds her tight, soothing the back of her head with calming strokes.

'I will find him. I promise.' *And if that means you only find his bones to bring back, then you walk into those trees for as long as it takes to find them*, he thinks.

'Si, what's happening?' she asks in a wretched voice.

He holds her as he regards the forest. The trees look particularly flat and lifeless, like the poker face of a poorly behaved child who has just been asked, 'Did you do that?'

AFTERNOON

The house looks bright, lived in. At closer examination, nothing much has changed – there are still light layers of dust on most un-trafficked surfaces, but there's a different energy in the house. It reminds Silas of the airy feeling it had before his parents split, and before the sisters turned it into a mausoleum memorialising 'coulda, shoulda' lives.

What was that Churchill quote? If you're going through hell, keep going. That was what the sisters' mistake had been – they'd stopped in the middle.

'Can I get anyone a cup of tea?' Lou Lou offers from the kitchen.

'A glass of water, please. I need to take my pills,' Rose says.

Silas is aware that Rose has begun gradually shaving an hour or so off the end of each dose, and is now taking four daily doses instead of the prescribed three. He has an idea it's to numb something other than her physical pain, so he lets it go.

Lou Lou hands Rose a glass of water and waits for her to take the capsules. His mother's eyes are clearer than they've been in a long time – he's relieved to see authentic humanity expressed in her face. Rose swallows her last pill and lowers the glass with a civil, half-smiling nod as she makes to leave the room.

Lou Lou's hand reaches into the air between them. 'Rose, may I say something?'

Rose's eyes meet Lou Lou as she placidly waits for her to begin.

'Um . . . If Silas wasn't helping this family with problems that he wasn't obliged to fix . . . then he would have been with you that night. I just wanted to say I'm sorry. I really am very sorry.' There was no histrionic lilt in the words, just a heartfelt apology.

Rose nods mechanically as her gaze slowly drifts past Lou Lou. Words wrestle between her lips before she decides to leave her thoughts unsaid, allowing a stony stillness to wash over her face and speak for her.

'I'm tired,' she manages, as she makes her way to the end of the hall to struggle up the stairs.

Silas rests her crutches next to the bedside table and pulls a light blanket over her.

'I don't want you to worry about the deadline, okay? Jerry knows about the accident. He's pretty sure he can take what we've already done back to them in good faith, given the circumstances.'

Rose stares at the empty dog bed in the corner of the room.

'I'll put that away,' Silas says as he gathers Goober's bed.

'Don't. Where will he sleep when he comes back home?' Rose's eyes bear down on him, an angry, pleading indictment on his lack of faith that breaks his heart. All he can do is nod an *of course, silly me* nod and offer up a feeble digression.

'Jerry said he was meeting with the production company today. He'll call when it's done.'

Rose lies down and closes her eyes. Silas stands in the still room, looking at the silhouette of her body under the blanket. Rays of afternoon sunlight wash through the window. On another day they could have been warm and comforting.

'I love you, Rosie.'

'I'm tired.'

'I know, I know, you sleep . . . Rosie, we're going to be okay. I promise.' The next words have been implied and assumed since the accident, but he still needs to say them out loud. 'I'm sorry.'

Silas had drunk before and he had *been* drunk before, about as drunk as people could get, predominantly in college and on sporadic occasions since. But, perhaps from his experiences of living with Bunny, he had never *really* wanted to drink. During his mid-noughties college days, most guys had had topless posters of Carmen Electra, or some young actress's slightly risqué pictures they'd had taken to prove that they were *all grown up*, but Silas had one poster, and that was of Hemingway nursing a daiquiri in Bermuda, his shorts carelessly cinched with a thin leather belt over his drinker's paunch. It had amused him; Hemingway was a legend and one of his idols, but that hadn't stopped Silas from looking down his nose at him for being a drunk.

But as he quietly closes the bedroom door, he wishes he was at Surley's, he wishes he was there with all the other lifers, perched atop a lumpy red stool in a dark corner of the bar, quietly pouring a thin, steady stream of drink onto the little instrument inside his head that makes him feel. He'd keep pouring until he watched the fucking thing fizz and short out in a jig of smoke and sparks.

His sharp yearning is interrupted by the sight of Bunny's bedroom door – no longer perennially closed, but ajar. He stops and prepares for the worst, waiting to see her Gollum-like form perched on its haunches, like a stone gargoyle on the corner of a cathedral. He balls his fist. *What? Are you going to hit her?* he thinks. *Fuck, probably.*

He rounds the corner and peeks inside.

He had assumed some sort of derelict air would waft from the room, but it smells much like the rest of the house: dusty, with a ghostly hint of pine resin from the untreated wood that makes its walls.

The drapes and windows are open, spilling airy sunshine into the room. There's a utilitarian messiness to it; in one corner lies a collection of Silas's boyhood clothes. It looks like Bunny wears an outfit for the longest time possible, then discards it in the corner and leaves it there unwashed as she pulls on the next set of hand-me-downs. Silas discerns this from the rumpled parade of cartoon characters looking out at him from the grimy fabric, as if pleading for a merciful death. The Beagle Boys (which she wore most recently) are on top of Donald Duck (which was her uniform before that). Empty bottles of whatever gin was cheapest at the time of purchase stand four rows deep along the walls, like soldiers in jostled formation. Dead bunches of spinach lie inserted into empty bottles like rare specimens. The exorbitant number of bottles is surely more than most people would drink in a lifetime. *How long did this last you?* he wonders. *A few months? Less?*

The mattress lies bare, with an unused look about it, as if it's been freshly extracted from IKEA packaging. If she had been sleeping on it without sheets, it would have been yellowed with sweat and oils from her skin, but it looks about as used as a store demo model. Nothing hangs on the walls and no personal effects sit on the bedside table. Silas supposes most of her things were burned in the boathouse fire. The only item he sees on a shelf above the bed is a charred cigar-sized wooden box. It stands open. Inside the bottom is a velvet-lined impression, and the top of the inside has the word *Solingen* embossed in cracked gold leaf. He takes it in his hands; the impression is for a cut-throat razor. Below the *Solingen* stamp is a small brass plaque, green with age:

Jonathan,
  A man once stole from your family. With this razor, my father cut that man's throat.
  Remember this every morning that you hold it to yours.
  Your father

Silas tosses the charred box back onto the shelf where it lands with a clatter.

'Oh!' peeps a voice from behind an open closet door.

Silas jumps, barely stifling a scream into a small grunt. Lou Lou steps sheepishly from behind the door. 'I'm sorry, you gave me a fright. I thought I was alone.'

'Ditto,' he says. 'I thought you were *her*.'

Lou Lou slowly shakes her head as she scans the room.

'What are you doing in here?' he asks.

'I came to clean it up. I haven't been in here since Bunny moved in after the fire . . .' She looks about the room before her eyes settle on the bottles. 'I didn't realise it had got so . . . bad.' She steps forward and presses her hand into a corner of the mattress, as if testing it's really there.

'I don't know where she slept.' She chokes. Silas rolls his eyes inwardly out of habit.

'She was hardly ever in here . . . Always out in the woods or God knows where,' Lou Lou says as she picks up one of the gin bottles with spinach in it. She holds it up to the light, shakes it and drops it onto the bed.

'This room wasn't her bedroom. It was just her hiding place. Mine's under the kitchen sink. Do you know why I think alcoholics hide empty bottles? They're the opposite side of the equation – if the glass in my hand just keeps topping up before it's empty, then I can tell myself I'm only having one when it's been five. But those empty bottles the next day, or at the end of the week, they balance the lie. So, I hide them away.' She exhales the words like a stream of consciousness, but they vibrate like shifting tectonic plates.

Lou Lou's eyes well with tears. Silas has never experienced true honesty from her before. He pats her shoulder. The gesture feels foreign between them; too much unsaid and unexpressed means that he long ago bandaged over wounds that needed to see the light of day to be healed. One day he will try and heal them, and he will try to forgive her – but not today. However, he can still try to be kind.

'I think this is called a moment of clarity. A "light bulb moment", as Oprah would say.' He says it with a small smile. As much as Lou Lou frustrates him, he never wanted her to feel this heavy.

Lou Lou nods. 'I love Oprah.'

'Mom, what are you going to do when she comes back?'

Lou Lou frowns at the bottles as if regarding a beloved dog that has gone rabid.

'She can't come back. She has to get better. And so do I.'

Silas lowers his eyebrows back into their normal position before Lou Lou looks back at him.

He gestures around the room. 'You need some help?'

Lou Lou considers things, then says, 'No,' with finality. 'I should do this myself. Oh, Silas, may I use your car to take the bottles away for recycling? The mechanic is coming next week to fix mine and I don't want them hanging around until then . . . While I'm at it, I think I'll throw away the ones under the sink, too. And the ones behind the shed.'

He doesn't bother lowering his eyebrows this time, just mumbles, 'Sure.'

His phone rings in his back pocket. He considers ignoring it, then remembers that Jerry was going to call about the script meeting. He pulls it out, and the blue screen glows with *AGENT JERRY*.

'Sorry. It's our agent.' He runs downstairs, through the kitchen and out into the afternoon air.

'Jerry!' he answers as he closes the back door behind him and strides towards the woods.

Silence on the other end of the line.

For a second his mind explains it away as a bi-coastal

delay, or maybe Jerry hung up just as he slid that green phone symbol of destiny sideways with his thumb. A bristly sigh precedes Jerry's Lawrence Tierney–like growl, which is oddly timid.

'Hey, kid.'

Another silence.

Silas stops walking.

'Say it.'

'I'm sitting in my car in their parking lot. Their whole, ah, their whole division just got absorbed by Walford Media. Walford Media is run by the biggest cunt of a trust-fund baby on the West Coast. They don't make things, they break them into pieces of shit and sell them to streaming services in China as content filler.'

Silas repeatedly runs his finger along the bridge of his nose to the tip, trying to soothe his brain as it rattles in its brackets.

'You told me this was a sure thing, that we were as good as paid. I have no money, Jerry. I have no job. I put Rose through hell to rework this fucking script. We have nowhere to go!'

'He, he's scrapped every project they were looking at!' Jerry says in a colicky grizzle that sits like a cheap dinner jacket over his usually authoritarian voice.

'Do they own the rights?'

Another silence drops like bricks on a skull.

'It's in the contract.'

'I didn't read the fuckin' contract, Jerry. I just fuckin' signed it.'

'Okay, okay, fair enough. Yes, they own the rights in

perpetuity . . . It's an ego thing . . . There's a little money. There *is* a little money!'

'How much?'

'Well, now you gotta remember there's the agency fee and then taxes and this was your first big sell so –'

'How fuckin' much?!'

'You would walk away with three grand. More like two. But you know, kid, it's just not *this* time, but next time.'

Silas closes his eyes and shakes his head.

'We did everything you said,' Silas says, more to himself than to the voice on the other end of the phone.

'Kid, listen, kid, I'm gonna make it right –'

Silas winds up like a pitcher and throws the phone into the woods. He claps his hand over his mouth and bites his palm to stop himself from screaming. He tastes blood.

Rose knows she's dreaming. It's the light; that same diffused yellow dirge light that shone in the underwater canyon. *If a dead animal's swollen stomach was pierced, and the escaping gas was lit, this yellow glow would be the colour of the flame*, she thinks.

Now it lights Silas's bedroom.

Her eyes are still closed, but the light has an oily quality that seeps between her eyelids and eases them open.

A whimper from the corner where Goober's bed lies. Rose hikes herself up on her elbows to see it. Her cast shifts awkwardly, making it hard to move without disturbing the dull ache that had made its home there.

'Goober?'

Tick, tick, tick, tick, tick, tick, tick, tick, the sound of canine claws on the hardwood floor stepping from the dog bed to the foot of *her* bed. She cranes her neck to see him – a flank, a tail, anything! She cranes her neck and catches a glimpse of the corner where his bed lies, empty but for a small brushstroke of fresh blood on the wall – perhaps the kind that a small dog would leave behind after he leaned against it with blood in his fur.

'Goober?'

A cheeky growl emerges from the end of the bed.

The blanket that Silas lovingly draped over her begins to slide off her body in playful puppy tugs.

'Goober?' She pats the top of the bed for him to jump up.

She tugs back and the blanket stops – held taut between her hands and the pulling at the end of the bed. 'Baba, come here!' She tries to yank the blanket back up but every increase in force is met with equal increase on the other side as another playful growl ripples from the foot of the bed. The muscles in her forearms cord with strain, fatigued and filled with painkillers that make her feel translucent. She opens her hands and lets the blanket slide away. She watches the end wash over the edge of the bed and sink out of view, with a feeling that swells up in her throat and makes it hard to breathe.

'Goob–'

Bunny's spider-like body springs into the air from the foot of the bed, sailing towards Rose as her terror turns it all into slow motion. Bunny's face is frozen in a leering rictus of excitement as she closes the distance between them.

'I see you, I see you, I see you, I see you . . .'

Just as her hands rake Rose's bare thigh, she wakes, springing bolt upright as her eyes open to the empty bedroom, which is no longer lit by anything more than the unremarkable light of the dying afternoon. Her hair clings to her face in a cold sweat. For a moment, she mistakes the sweat for the stinking water from the yellow canyon. She wipes it away on the sheet. Her leg sings a thudding melody from under its cast. She leans back on her elbows and grits her teeth as a wave of pain washes over her like a lazy ocean swell. As it passes, she shifts and peers at Goober's bed. Empty.

No smear of blood, no Goober. She looks down and finds the blanket still tightly hugging her body. She reaches for a glass of water on the bedside table, pops four more pills out of the see-through brown bottle with one-handed expertise, and allows them to slide down her gullet. She closes her eyes and breathes and hears Goober's dream-whimper in her head like an echo. *He's dead because of you*, says her head. *No. He's dead for you*, answers her heart as her breath catches again in her throat.

Calm the fuck down, she thinks. She forces herself to be still and loose in her chest, inhaling a meditative breath . . . Better. *Better.*

She reaches for her crutches and wobbles out of bed towards the window. Silas half pulled the blinds, making the room a nest of shadows. Right now, she needs the light of day; anaemic though it is in its late-afternoon state, she needs it to fill the room and chase away the yellow cotton-wool filaments of her nightmare still hanging in the air.

Her gaze falls on the woods as she opens the blinds. A figure darts away, obscured by bushes and trunks.

'No,' Rose whispers as she backs away.

EVENING

Rose almost tumbles down the stairs as she frantically descends them. *Crutch, leg, leg, crutch, leg, leg, ahh, crutch, leg, crutch, leg, crutch, crutch. Mierda!* She hurls both crutches to the bottom of the stairs, hop-skipping the remainder of the way down, both hands shimmying along the banister. The pain in her leg flashes with each hop but she doesn't care.

She retrieves her crutches, hoists them under her arms and jostles outside. She faces Silas's back as he stares into the woods in contemplation.

'Silas!'

He doesn't respond.

'Silas! Silas!'

He turns, startled.

'Sorry, what? Are you okay?'

'Why didn't you – Never mind. Were you back there a minute ago?' She gestures towards the side of the house.

'Huh?'

'Out by the bedroom window! Were you?'

'No. Why?'

'I think I saw her. I think she's back. Someone was below the window – like, you know, how she used to when we first arrived – and I had a dream, I was sleeping and the top –'

A car door slams. Rose turns at the sound and stumbles towards it in jittery bursts. Lou Lou is struggling to lift bags of empty gin bottles into the car.

'Lou Lou?' Rose says, her face half crazed.

Lou Lou looks up at her with a painted smile, but doesn't cease loading the bags. Rose approaches, unkempt in her long nightshirt, hair stuck to the side of her face, dry drool crusted around her mouth, her breath foul and hot, her eyes bloodshot and disoriented.

'Yes, dear?'

'Were you just around the side of the house? The one near our bedroom window?' Rose asks, eyeing her evenly, willing her to answer. *Please God say yes.*

Lou Lou is silent for a moment, lowering the bag and gathering her hands in front of her as if weighing her options. She pinches her index finger with her other hand. 'Oh, I'm sorry, yes. I wasn't sure if you were awake so I was trying to see if there was any movement in your window. I'm heading into town and wanted to say goodbye before I left.' The explanation casually tumbles out.

Rose searches Lou Lou's face for deception, before deciding to dial back the red alert to amber.

'Oh . . . Okay.'

Silas has followed Rose to the car.

'Why are you taking the bottles all the way to town? You can just drop them at the end of Lake Road, can't you?'

Lou Lou offers a vague nod and a slight shoulder raise. 'Yes, but Bunny called. I have to go in for a family counselling session. It's part of her treatment. I might stay at the motel overnight and be back tomorrow. I'll see how things go.

I'll pick up some more food. There's some nice organic soups being sold in town now, artisan stuff.'

Silas purses his lips but says nothing. Rose is relieved; Lou Lou's strange behaviour could easily be explained away if she were nervous about a rehab meeting. The amber light blinks to a shy green.

'She's still my sister,' Lou Lou says with a touch of defensiveness.

'Okay, okay,' Silas says, throwing his hands up in surrender. Secretly, he doesn't want Lou Lou around Bunny so soon after having turned a sober corner; the sisters' co-dependency is a steel cable between them and he wants it severed, even if he has to be the one holding the bolt cutters. *But if the counsellors want to try to take a hacksaw to it, then have at it.*

'Lemme help you. It's gonna get dark soon,' he says, scooping a jangling hessian sack of bottles into the trunk.

'Thank you, sweetheart. Lifting these damn bottles was starting to aggravate my arthritis. Oh Rose, honey, you're gonna make yourself sick.'

Silas turns to Rose and notes her barely covered bottom and dishevelled face. 'Rosie, why don't you hop inside. I'll make you dinner soon.'

'Dinner? Okay. Ah, bye, Lou Lou, drive safe.'

'Oh, thank you, dear. And goodbye. Put your foot up,' she says to Rose with a smile that imprints dimples into her cheeks.

Silas and Lou Lou watch Rose stump back towards the house. He finishes filling the car's small trunk, then moves on to fill the backseats with more bottle sacks. He speaks with a forced casualness he hopes Lou Lou doesn't notice;

she probably won't as she's preoccupied – eager to pack up and get going.

'Mom?'

'Yes, dear?'

'We had a deadline extension. For the script. I was wondering if we could stay a few more –'

'You two stay as long as you like. This will always be your home,' Lou Lou says with a finality that eases his mind. She suddenly hugs him in a tight embrace. He can't actually remember a time when he experienced any ease around her, but this moment was somewhere in that ballpark. The embrace is foreign territory for them both. He awkwardly hugs her back, willing authenticity to transcend his inability to connect with her.

'Thank you,' he says.

The extra time will allow Rose to get better . . . then I'll tell her about the script, he tells himself. Of course, it's a lie; he will never know how to tell her the script is dead, that it was all for nothing in the end, that they came here and lost Goober for nothing and that he doesn't know how to say to her, '*I don't think he's coming back.*'

Silas realises that with all the therapy sessions, the creative outlets, the loving relationship with Rose, his useless bachelor's degree – even with all that, he still doesn't know how to say very much at all.

Silas breaks the embrace. Lou Lou looks at his face and smiles. She smiles the way only a mother smiles at the face of her child: *I made that face*, the smile says. She quickly lifts her hand and places it gently on his cheekbone, as if it might give her a static shock.

'Goodbye, son.'

The hand recedes. She hops into the jam-packed car and drives away.

Silas walks back to the house, filled with a sense of calm. The years of unresolved family discord might finally (maybe) be coming to a close.

But it's fleeting. *Maybe this has all been worth it*, he tells himself, already becoming unconvinced. *Tell Rose about the script now. Do it now before it runs away with you . . . I'll do it when she's a bit stronger.*

As he closes the back door, he spots Lou Lou's purse on the counter.

'Shit,' he says, reaching for his back pocket – the one that usually holds his phone. His hand falters as his mind replays the recent memory of silver plastic flying into the woods. He thinks to ask Rose for hers, then remembers it's also somewhere in the woods.

'Nice throw, fuckhead,' he sighs. *I'll call on the landline after dinner. She'll probably have remembered and turned around by then.*

Rose has made them mugs of milky tea which he carries to the table.

'Jerry called yet?' she asks.

'Yes, they're happy with the revisions. A few details being ironed out but everything's on track.'

Rose half listens to him talk. Silas knows that she's still listening for a distant bark in the woods. They sit in silence until Rose's immobilised leg begins to go numb on the wooden chair.

She battles up the stairs, back to their makeshift den.

Silas offers to help but she waves him off. He rinses out her mug and empties his untouched tea down the drain, watching the steaming brown liquid swirl and escape down the plughole until the basin is bare.

NIGHT

Rose eases herself into the bathroom. She detested using the bedpans in the hospital, but looking at the toilet and then at her immobilised leg, she understands why the nurses were so adamant about her using them; it was the choice of having to cart a soiled bedpan away, or potentially clean pee, poop or both off a plaster cast if she toppled off the porcelain throne.

She leans into her crutch and swings her cast towards the toilet. *Challenge accepted.*

Lou Lou hasn't returned. She probably won't be back from the rehab clinic for a few hours, or she'll end up staying at the monstrosity that is Hamner's Hotel Motel like she mentioned. That'll be hard without her wallet, although Silas is sure that the manager there will remember her well. Silas decides to call just in case – he just needs to figure out where to call.

Jesus, when was the last time you used one of these? Silas thinks, paging through an old phone book. He sits on the armrest of a La-Z-Boy circa 1989. The chair is covered in vertical stripes of various browns, creams and yellows that make it look like a freezer-burned tiramisu in an Italian restaurant that also has a burger pizza on the menu. He finds the rehab clinic's number and dials it on an equally dated phone. The tactile feedback of plastic buttons makes him smile with nineties nostalgia. He pastes the receiver to his ear. The ringing chime hauls up memories of teenage phone calls – stolen moments of relative privacy as he sat in the lounge, tethered there by the phone cord.

Christ, when did I get so old? he wonders as the ring chime chokes.

'Denise Warren Clinic, Mike speaking. How may I help you?' Mike's accent is rough-and-tumble Brooklyn, like a character out of a John Patrick Shanley play.

'Hi, I'm trying to pass on a message to someone.'

'We only accept written correspondence to patients and it gets screened before I'm cleared to pass it on.'

'It's a message to a visitor, actually.'

He hears Mike click into autopilot.

'Visiting hours are over today. Tomorrow's visiting hours are –'

'No, she's coming out of the counselling session this evening. It's my mom, she left her wallet at home. Sorry, I can't call her directly. Would you mind letting her know that Silas has it at home?'

There's a pause on Mike's end.

'No evening counselling sessions. Never have been.' Mike sighs distractedly. 'I mean, I can pass it on to ya ma if she comes in, but there's no sessions to come in to.'

Silas feel his balls tingle like they're about to hit the drop on a roller coaster.

bunny

'Uh . . .' He's lost. Instinct nudges him to check something. 'She's coming in to visit one of your patients – Barbara Burbridge? Goes by Bunny? Shaved head. I'm a family member. She was collected from Dr Singh's practice in Hamner.'

'Oh yeah,' Mike chirps, 'I remember! I picked her up in the van.'

Silas sighs, relieved.

'Yeah,' Mike says offhandedly. 'She ain't here, pal.'

'*What?*' Silas can suddenly see every detail in the La-Z-Boy's armrest: a faded brown stain from a decades-old nightcap; a spot of red nail varnish nestled deep in the fibres – funny what you fixate on during the moments that change your life.

'Yeah,' Mike muses, 'got her back here, opened the door and she did a runner. Literally. She ran straight out the gate, across the road and into the woods – and fast! We aler–'

'Why didn't you tell us?'

When Mike speaks, it's with the measured tone of someone that has just realised they've stumbled into the middle of a private family issue. 'We did.'

If Mike is waiting for a reply from Silas, he won't get it.

Silas is staring at the armrest. The red lacquer spot. Silas remembers Lou Lou wearing it on her dates, the ones she wouldn't come back from until the next day, due to her staying at the Hotel Motel and getting revenge on his father the only way she knew how – through her body and drink. Bunny was wearing the same colour on her nails the night that she drove them into his ribs and he was found catatonic by the EMTs. The sisters had often painted each other's nails in the late afternoons, when they were still on their first wine, and vowels and consonants were still crisp.

Revlon Fire and Ice. He almost says it aloud to Mike.

The brand and range had a cult following among the Burbridge women. Silas's father had known that they loved it. He would buy it for them when contracting in NYC, and had used it as a stocking-stuffer at Christmas.

Silas picks at the red spot. It holds firm to the fabric beneath.

Mike goes on. 'Made the phone call myself as soon as it happened, what – five, six days ago now?'

Silas, answer, he thinks as he stands and slowly drifts towards the kitchen. But something else has caught his attention there.

'Spoke to a lady – Lucy?' Mike says. 'No, Lola?'

'Lou Lou.'

'Yeah, yeah, that's it. Lou Lou.' Mike sounds relieved, like he's off the hook. 'Your, uh, Bunny, she come home yet?' Mike asks affably.

Silas continues towards the kitchen, drawn there by a faint breeze that wasn't there before. The phone cable follows along behind him, its spiralling rings pulling increasingly taut.

Mike barrels on with the confidence of having delivered dozens of 'runner' conversations before. 'Listen, I wouldn't worry. They always find their way home after a while.'

Silas has stopped listening. The phone is still pressed snugly against his ear, but the words are white noise. There is something *in* the breeze. A feeling, like the one that makes people turn around when someone else is watching them. It's a sensation as old as the synapses in the reptilian part of the brain that it crawls along. An echo of violence.

'Rehab ain't mandatory.' Mike is in full swing now. 'You can't *make* her go, but you can always try again.'

Silas stares at the kitchen door. It's open. He looks out into the dark night, and it looks back at him.

'Look, pal,' pontificates Mike, who is becoming nervous at the silence on the other end of the phone, 'I don't wanna alarm ya, but thinking about it, if she ain't shown up by *now*, then you should probably call the police. What did you say your name was again –'

Click.

The taut phone cable has finally been pulled out of the wall. Silas lowers the phone with white knuckles.

A threadbare 'WELCOME' doormat sits just outside the door. The mat has been turned around so the word faces the inside of the house, as if he were the visitor being welcomed home. In a way he always knew *he* was. It had been so the instant that Bunny changed – when she had become Bunny, instead of *Aunt* Bunny. He knew that when she had changed, he had become the visitor in another thing's home.

To whom does the night outside now belong? Into whose house have I now been invited? he wonders.

And then none of that matters. Goober's fluorescent pink bandage lies in the middle of the faded 'O' of the mat. It's wrapped around something, as if still on Goober's leg. He stares into the yawning dark as he creeps forward and stoops to pick it up. He prepares himself to see bone and fur, to see Goober's leg so that Rose won't have to. His hand closes around it as he's overcome with nervous nausea, expecting that what is wrapped in the bandage will crush the fragile hope that Goober would be coming home.

He keeps an eye on the open doorway, raises his hand into his line of sight and opens it. Filling the pink tube and giving it weight is no length of leg, but a pinecone. His breathing eases. He edges the pinecone free and inspects the pink tube. A sparse sprinkling of bristles of black fur coats the inside.

'Oh Goob,' he whispers. For a moment there is relief that it's only a pinecone inside, but the relief quickly flees. He steps into the darkness, no longer concerned with whose house he is entering. 'Goober?! Goober!'

Rose hears Silas's calls as she stands over the bathroom basin washing her hands. She flinches at the noise. A flicker of movement draws her eyes to the small, square frosted window just above her eyeline. She sees two hands pressed against the glass from the outside. Behind the hands, the light from the bathroom bounces off the blurred outline of a shaved head. The hands seem to sense her gaze as its fingers close into its palms like startled sea anemones. The head whips into the darkness with a liquid grace that makes it seem as if the figure is moving through water instead of air. Rose's mind pointlessly attempts to figure out which course of action to take even as her body supersedes the process, sending her hands to her crutches and opening her mouth.

'Silas!'

Silas doesn't hear her scream over his own yelling. He stands outside in the oblong column of light that shines onto the ground from the open door like a yellow brick road to nowhere. He tries not to think about how the kitchen door was open, or who put the bandage there, only that it *was* there.

'Goober?!'

A long shadow swarms up behind him, blotting out the light from the kitchen door. He spins around. Rose stands panting in the doorway.

'I – saw her. She . . . she's here.'

There's no need for either of them to say her name. They know.

'Where?'

'Outside the bathroom window.'

'But that's on the second floor. She can't –'

Semantics don't matter, he thinks. *How she got up there, when there isn't even a windowsill to hold on to . . . It doesn't matter now, she's here now . . . She's home.*

His face turns to concrete. 'Go back inside.'

'You were calling for Goober,' Rose says.

He nods and tosses her the bandage. She catches it and sinks back into the door frame. 'Did you see him?' she asks.

'Go back inside,' he repeats, calm and firm. 'Lock the door.'

He can tell she doesn't want to. If she wasn't on crutches then she'd be right out there with him whether he liked it or not.

Rose peers down at her crutches. She can't help and she knows it.

'Okay, but I'll be right inside if you need me.'

He nods as she stumbles inside and closes the door behind her.

As it closes, the oasis of light he was standing in vanishes. The blackness is absolute as his eyes slowly adjust. A feeling of being stalked settles at the base of his skull like cold mercury; for no reason he can explain, no visual or sound cue to inform the sensation, he knows something is swiftly creeping towards him out of the silken darkness.

He swings his arms in defensive haymakers. *If I touch anything, will it be human? Eel? That wailing, malformed thing that crawled out from the nightmare lake?* He feels the burp of a scream pushing up his throat and fights to keep it inside. A branch snaps nearby. He faces the sound. Another snap. Same direction. Closer. Then another – closer again. He tries to listen over his ragged breaths and the thudding of his heart in his ears. If the noises are regular, then another will surely come in the next second . . .

But before another sound comes, a light switches on behind him. He spins around and discovers he can see the far end of the porch – an old sixty-watt now bathes the house, garden and forest in muted, egg yolk–shaded light. He doesn't see or hear it – but he *feels* it. He knows it has retreated slightly. Yet he knows it's still there, just at the edge of the light's reach.

It's driven back further as another bulb in his peripheral vision flashes on at the other end of the porch. He hears the percussive thumping of Rose's crutches as she hops through the house, searching for more light switches. He hears her slamming windows shut as she does. *Good girl, Rosie.*

The house's eyes blink open one by one as she heaves blinds open, trying to fill the outside with as much light as possible. A handful of outside lights switch on too, turning the house into a small island of light in the otherwise black, moonless night. One or two of the old bulbs flash and die as their tired tungsten coils succumb to age, but the ones that remain glow steadily.

A slight breeze causes an involuntary shiver from Silas. He slowly inhales through his nose and smells the toasted, oaky warmth of freshly sparked tobacco drifting faintly on the breeze.

'Bunny?'

I know you're here.

'Bunny!'

A dry, raw giggle dances out of the darkness. There's no joy in the sound, no amusement, it was simply a wordless reply to his question. A game of Marco Polo in hell.

'Where is my dog? Where is Goober?'

Her voice barks like a dog, giggles and falls silent.

He hears the sound of her body brushing past soft leaves on thin bushes. He follows it, careful to stay in the glow of the light. They slide along the side of the house together: Silas, almost pressed up against the clapboard; Bunny, creeping somewhere, *somewhere*, in the night, beyond the light's reach. The side of the house he finds himself on possesses more than one burned-out globe. Light still shines out of several upstairs windows above him, but it's darker than he hoped for.

She barks again.

Silas thinks he can *almost* see her in the murk. The light

from the house is a blessing and a curse: it makes his eyes less accustomed to the dark when he peers into it, the way stars are brightest when you aren't looking directly at them.

And when he stops trying to see, he sees it: the tiny red dot gently swaying in the woods.

As it's sucked on, the tip of the cigarette glows brighter, reflecting off Bunny's bloodshot green eyes, making them sparkle like two polished marbles nestled in taut grey skin. The burning ember recedes into the filter, fading away as it runs out of fuel to burn.

The air in front of him hisses as an object flies out of the dark towards him. He flinches as glass explodes next to his head. Splintery shrapnel showers the side of his face as he ducks, pointlessly trying to cover it with his hands. Fresh blood squeezes from small cuts on his cheek and temple.

Hatred and rage burn the fear out of his chest. 'YOU FUCKING –'

He looks up to where the cigarette light was, to where he swears he saw those eyes. He drops his hands from his face and halts mid-insult.

Scattered in the darkness in front of him glow *dozens* of cigarette embers. As they're drawn on, their glow waxes and wanes like twinkling Christmas lights. Some are close to the ground, some burn chest height, and others belong to shadows of figures that hang, ape-like, from tall branches.

Bunny barks again, a single bark, but her voice booms from behind every glowing ember in unison.

Silas forgets his bleeding face and runs. The embers speed after him like a swarm of enraged fireflies. They swarm with the sounds of a crowd – a *legion*. The sound of bodies climbing, jumping, running – hurling themselves towards him through the dark woods makes him run faster. He opens his mouth and does the only thing that comes to mind – he screams.

'Rose!'

He rounds the corner of the house and frantically bangs on the door.

'Rose!'

Rose peers out through a peephole before opening it. Silas falls through onto the floor as she swiftly locks it behind him.

'Who's there? I saw lights in the trees.'

'Close them! Close the drapes!' he says, getting back up.

They tear through the house closing every drape and blind that Rose opened. When they steal glances out of windows, red orb embers pulse in and out of the shadows. Bodies scurry and clamour outside.

'It's closed, everything's closed,' Silas calls breathlessly as he finishes his check over the windows. Rose enters the living room, her arms shaking with fatigue and fear.

'Si?'

Silas raises his finger to his lips. 'It's okay, we're going to be okay,' he whispers uncertainly. Dozens of pairs of bare feet pound against the earth and wooden deck outside the front door.

'Call the police,' Silas whispers.

'I lost my phone when I hit my head.'

For the second and final time, Silas's hand reaches for the phantom phone in his back pocket.

'Fuck.'

'Where's yours?'

'I threw it into the woods.'

'Why?'

Silas's eyes dart around the floor. 'The landline. We need to find the landline.'

'It's over there,' Rose says, pointing at the kitchen counter. 'I found it on the floor earlier.'

'Yeah, that was me,' Silas breathes.

He grabs it and rushes to the corner of the room where the wired phone socket is. His hand pinches the jack as he tries to slide it into the socket. It makes a dainty *tik!* as the old plastic cracks and springs apart. The sound of it breaking is so insignificantly small and polite that he can't believe it's happened. His shaking hand dumbly pokes the jack in and out, in and out, as if he expects it to apologise and reform anew.

'I broke it,' he says as he turns to Rose like a bemused child.

He's about to try the jack again when he feels the air grow thin around them; it's as if a giant has inhaled sharply and stolen it away. Silence descends as the moth-wing sound of pattering feet suddenly ceases.

Rose gazes down at her arms and sees her skin bristling with goosebumps. She's not just cold, she's freezing. The house seems to cough violently as a bitter wind ricochets around the room. Rose closes her eyes and envisions herself inside The Other, trapped and encased like Bunny –

Please let it be over. She closes her eyes and thinks the thought as a prayer.

She keeps her eyes closed as every door, cupboard and

drawer in the house flies open in unison and slams shut three times.

On the third slam, the power wavers and the lights go out. They don't snap off, but fade and die, as if the light itself is too fearful to shine.

'Si?' Rose calls in the darkness.

'I'm here,' he says as he moves around blindly, banging into a side table.

'What's happening?' she asks in a small voice. 'Does she have him? Does she have Goober?'

A bright sparking flare lights up the room with a purgatory glow. Silas holds a large fireplace match between them – he offers her the box. Rose hikes her crutches into her armpits to free her hands, then draws out a match, lighting her own tiny torch.

'She didn't go to the clinic,' Silas explains. 'She ran away on the first day. They called Lou Lou and told her about it . . . She lied.'

'Why?' Rose asks the question and instantly realises that it doesn't matter.

'Who else is out there with her? Who are the others?' she asks.

Silas shakes his head as if he's trying to wake from a dream that has exhausted him.

'I think they're all *her*.'

A single female voice barks like a dog outside . . . then another, and another. The noise grows as barks answer barks from all directions. The moth-wing drumming of bare feet starts up again, but this time they don't just circle the house; multiple outliers speed closer to the outside walls, running up and across them while others travel vertically, thumping along under the eaves and over the roof in defiance of physics.

'She's running up the walls!' Rose sobs. 'Si, she's r-running up the walls!'

Rose's wide eyes twitch as they attempt to follow the noises.

The barking builds to a cacophony that assaults the house, bleeding through the timber walls until they almost feel the host in the room with them.

Rose yelps as the turntable switches on. There's no power, but that doesn't seem to concern the vinyl player as it repeats the hanging four-note intro to 'Night Walk'. It warbles in the dark, serenading the couple. Rose's mind travels back to the first time she heard the song, a few weeks ago in the morning – when Bunny had clapped three times behind her, she had jumped in fright, and Bunny had purred, 'That's my song!'

Silas tries to open the turntable cover. He digs his nails into a plastic seam and pulls, but it won't budge.

'It's stuck!' he shouts – unheard over the loud music.

Rose drops one of her crutches and transfers the match to her free hand as she scrambles to the wall. She plunges her arm behind the wall unit in search of the plug, but it doesn't get far before being blocked. Her face twists in confusion as she pulls it back out, holding a handful of dry, dead spinach.

'Geoffrey' Clare's voice sings,

When the day is swallowed by night

Rose reaches her hand back behind the turntable, raking detritus out of the space. A tangle of mummified spinach, pinecones and tiny animal bones cascades onto the floor.

Counting memory lost in moonlight
Silas finds himself listening to the song lyrics.
Foreign hands reaching out to your shadow.
The words to the forty-year-old song feel as if they were written just for them.

Silas throws his match. The small light swirls and hits the wall, halving the already weak light in the room as the flame dies. He grabs the turntable with both hands and tears it out of the wooden unit.

'Shut the' – he heaves it above his head – 'FUCK UP!' and hurls it across the room, where it shatters against the wall.

The music and barking stop. No more movement. He cocks his head upwards, listening. Nothing stirs on the rooftop above. But he can still *feel* them out there – silently frozen in place, crowding around them like hyenas waiting for a wounded prey's limbs to stiffen.

The flame on Rose's match sways half an inch from her fingers. Silas lights two fresh matches and hands one to her. They instinctively huddle by the hearth. Even though it's dark and unlit, by ancient edict, the place of familial gathering suggests a modicum of shelter and safety.

'What are we going to do?' Rose whispers. 'The barking – it feels like they're mocking us.'

'There's no *they*,' Silas says. 'It's all *her*. I don't know how I know, but they're all Bunny. I think they're pieces of her. Like echoes.'

Rose reaches for his hand and her eyes meet his and hold them.

'If she has Goob then we have to get him. That night,

running through the woods – he knew that *thing* behind us was too fast. He didn't fall out of my arms. He jumped.'

Tears wet the lower rims of her eyes.

'I'm not saying that to make myself feel less guilty. He . . . He *knew* he had to buy time. He saved me, Si. And I'm not leaving him with that bitch.'

Silas looks down at his match flame. He can't meet her eyes as he speaks, his voice low and full of secrets. 'He spoke to me in my dream. He told me to eat part of her. To consume her. I . . . I think he was trying to protect me.'

He realises he has never told Rose the contents of that dream on the lakeshore. He opens his mouth again to explain, but stops as a familiar tune floats in from the air outside.

'Is that . . .?'

'Your phone?' she says.

'Stay here and stay away from the windows. I'm going to have a look.' He passes his match to her and places the matchbox on the rough-hewn slab that juts out in front of the fireplace.

Rose sits next to the matches, hugging the knee of her good leg under her chin as she watches Silas creep towards the window. He parts the drapes just enough to peep through.

The backyard is tarry black; no moon. Even the starlight seems reluctant to make the journey down through the night sky. And yet, there in the no man's land of his backyard glows the aqua light of his ringing phone, like the fallen teardrop of an enfeebled god. *Come out*, it whispers, *come out here and fetch me. It will only take a moment.*

Rose holds on to the two lit matches together. She hasn't noticed that the flames are uneven, and thus hungrily creeping along the thin wood that sustains them, travelling much faster than they should.

'Can you see it?' she whispers to Silas's back.

'Yes,' he says without turning around.

'And her? *Them?*' she corrects herself. She now feels as he does about the host outside, that there really is only *one* out there in the woods. One Bunny, who casts many shadows.

Rose stares at a point between Silas's shoulder blades, waiting for a response.

'No . . .' he answers.

She reads the tension in his shoulders in the way that long-time partners can; he's contemplating going out there to get the phone.

'Don't. Don't go out there,' she says with finality.

The twin flames in her hand join themselves, becoming a beast with two backs. If she had not been so focused on making him listen, she might have felt the warm halo of their lovemaking creep towards her finger, but she doesn't.

'It's a trap, Si.'

He turns to her, his face haunted and drawn.

'She's just a crazy fucking drunk. She probably weighs seventy pounds *wet*,' he says.

His words struggle to mask the look in his eyes, which tells the truth. Rose stares into his face and reads the truth back to him.

'No, she's not.'

He looks at her. She looks at him. The flame in her hand kisses the soft skin on the tip of her fingers. She grimaces in pain before dropping the matches. They land on the floor and die. The delicate light speeds away like a child's soul to heaven.

The dark feels like its own animal.

'Rose?'

'I'm here.'

He hears the flat, rolling jangle of matches in a matchbox. A small flash heralds a freshly lit one. Silas's eyes find Rose in the same seated position in front of the gaping mouth of the empty fireplace.

As the match's white afterimage fades, bloodshot green eyes bore into him from behind Rose's shoulder. The scene seems flipped – Bunny's skeletal torso hangs upside down from inside the dark stone fireplace. White hands wrap almost tenderly around Rose's face as her eyes widen behind dirty fingers. Bunny's head leans over Rose's shoulder as she blows out the match. In the last instant of light, Silas sees the top half of Rose's body disappearing up the chimney.

Three voices. He hears three voices: Rose howling like a cornered animal fighting, Bunny growling in a breathless wheeze, and the third voice he doesn't recognise, but it's screaming.

He blindly lunges through the dark towards the sound of Rose's cast scraping against the chimney's guts. His hands find Rose's ankle. It kicks out at him, smashing his knuckles against the rough fireplace wall. He grabs it again and pulls. Rose's body slides down a few feet. He reaches up and discovers her hips, hugs them and yanks. She slides down into the base of the fireplace, kicking and screaming, fighting anything near. Silas still feels Bunny above Rose grappling to pull her back up. He reaches up and his palm presses against her bristly scalp; his hand navigates by touch, his thumb searches and discovers the soft hollow of an eye socket, and curls into it like a knife shucking an oyster. The growling wheeze above him turns to a high, ululating squeal as the eyeball gives way under his thumb and bursts, sending what feels like soft warm jelly cascading down his hand. Bunny's arms retract, and Rose is free. He pulls her out of the hearth as she flails.

He finally recognises the third voice making the alien scream. It is his own.

He stops screaming and scrambles onto the floor, searching for the matchbox. A low growl emanates from high up in the chimney. It begins slowly descending towards them again. He redoubles his efforts, sweeping his hands across the floor as he replays the last moment of light in his mind's eye. *Where was the box? In Rose's hand as she was pulled into the fireplace.* He scuttles on all fours into the fireplace. The growling from the tall void above him is creeping closer. His hands plunge into aged ash and soot as he slides them to the back, running his fingers along the bottom edges until he hears wooden matches jangling in their box. He grabs the box and ducks out of the hearth as the growling vibrates the hairs on his neck. His hands shake mercilessly as he strikes a match and a chance to reclaim the situation.

He glimpses white fingers creep-curling over the lip of the chimney. Bunny's eyes peer over the edge at him – one now gone, ruined by him. And yet, in the depths of the hollow, wet socket, rises another pupil from within her skull – its colour a grey shade of eternity.

A thin, clear stream of fluid sprays into the fireplace from behind him.

'Throw the match!' Rose screams.

Silas follows the instruction without thinking. The match lands in the wet spray and takes off with an airy *whoosh*. The hidden eye recedes from Bunny's socket as she flees up the chimney with a brittle howl. Rose throws the now empty bottle of lighter fluid into the flames, feeding the fire with pinecones from a basket next to the hearth. When those are gone, she finds the cones littered over the shelves and throws them in too.

Clots of chimney debris rain down onto the infant flames, almost extinguishing them as Bunny scrambles up and away. Her feet pound over the roof, sending loose shingles down. Rose follows the sound as it weaves back and forth before reaching the edge of the roof and disappearing.

Silas tends the flames, ensuring they're well fed before leaving them and laying a hand on Rose's shoulder. She jumps at the touch and turns to him.

Her face, shoulders and neck are lacerated with crescent-shaped nail marks and long scratches.

The shoulder he first saw Bunny peering over now has a red, wet crescent of missing skin with scalloped edges.

'Jesus! She bit you?'

Rose looks at her shoulder in a daze. 'I don't know,' she murmurs as she brushes her hand across it and flinches as the pain ignites. 'Ah!' Her voice is weary, scared and filled with sobs. 'Ow, ow, ow, ow . . .'

Silas holds her. He tries to melt courage back into her broken body.

'It's okay. She can't get in again.' He means the words to calm her but they sound hollow.

New footsteps pass over the roof, jolting Rose out of the embrace. They weave up towards the chimney and stop.

Silas cradles Rose in his arms as they listen in silence.

Bunny looses a dog-like bark as something clatters down the chimney. They hear it bounce against the walls as it tumbles down and lands, sending sparks into the room. Something metallic glints in the flames. Rose rushes towards it and looks into the hearth.

'It's Goober! It's Goober! Oh God, no!' she shrieks as she plunges her hands into the fire, ignoring the flames. She holds it in her hands and brings it to her face to be sure, before cradling it as if it were a baby ready to be christened.

The room fills with the smell of Rose's scalding flesh as Silas looks down into her arms. Goober's skull sits nestled in her raw pink palms.

His leather collar and tag bind his lower jaw to his upper. Bunny's gold crucifix wraps around the crown of his skull like a Christian wreath.

Outside, Bunny laughs; great guffaws that only stop long enough for her to bark again maliciously.

'Oh, baba. Oh, no, no.' Rose sways back and forth. A deep, low wail washes out of her, child-like and wretched. Silas slowly reaches a hand towards it. His other is clapped across his mouth. His fingers brush over bone as gently as if it were skin and fur. Giant, heaving breaths fill his lungs. They rock together on the floor, skull between them, holding on to each other as if to steady themselves in a small boat caught in a storm. Tendrils of salty tears and snot hang from

Rose's face. Her mouth hangs open and her shoulders heave and collapse rhythmically as she weeps from the depths of her being.

Silas can't cry. Murder has disconnected something in him and turned his mind and body to cool bronze.

'I'm going to kill her now.' He speaks with a neutral inflection of the sort used to discuss the weather with a vague acquaintance. He stands up stiffly, knowing that he will kill her. Rose, dissolved in her own small corner of hell, does not hear him.

He calmly walks to the door. Above them, Bunny stops laughing. He twists the key and the door unlocks, then he turns the handle with a hand steadied by a singular purpose, flings the door open to let the fire's fading light spill out and steps onto the porch.

I will kill you now. I will kill you now. His mind calmly repeats the mantra, and it will, until he does.

Ting! A sound like a thin metal frisbee bouncing off steel scaffolding seems to come from somewhere inside him. He stops, unsure of what the sound is.

There's a glinting just above eye level in the darkness beside him – the broadside of a cut-throat razor as it catches the meagre firelight. He follows the hand holding it and sees her standing not two feet from him. *Fists are too impersonal for this.*

His hands clap onto the sides of her head. For a moment it appears as if he's going to kiss her. She looks surprised. He sinks his chin into his chest, showing her the top of his forehead, before leaning back and slamming it into her face with the entire force of his body. He feels the crunching of bones vibrating through the top of his head. Bunny sails through the air, landing on the wooden porch and bowling over old wicker chairs.

He stands, not sure what to do next. His body feels light, like it's a spacesuit depressurising. He hears the light drumming sound of liquid dripping onto the floor below him. *Have I pissed myself again?* He takes a step towards her and the light from the open doorway catches the liquid just right. He sees that it's red and wonders why he's pissing blood. His foot drags, then falters as he attempts to take another step . . . And then it makes sense. The sound. The bright metallic sound he heard when he opened the door.

The razor blade in her hands . . . was that the sound it made as it bounced off my bones? He brings his hands up to his stomach. They feel heavy and light at the same time as they slide over his insides hanging from the pristine cut. His hands travel further up, brushing over exposed ribs, then whisk around his upper chest to discover a piece of exposed clavicle. He finds it is much wetter at the clavicle. Far worse.

His hands discover what feels like a pleasantly warm, burbling stream that's sprung up in the soft flesh just below his jaw. He realises that at some point the severed artery would have sprayed instead of burbled, but he was busy attempting to kill his aunt and must have missed that.

I'm cold, he thinks, as he vaguely registers that the side of the house is freshly painted in red spray. His gaze, now fuzzing around the edges, finds her in the spot where she landed. *Don't be alive.*

She lifts her face to him like a lover waking from sleep.

Her face is a ruin: a ragged, deflated mush of gristle and skin now resides where her nose once was, haywire cheekbones no longer sit like a Sharon Tate lookalike, and above her remaining eye is a small crater where there shouldn't be. But still she smiles a toothy grin full of joy and blood.

'It's time,' she whispers tenderly to him as she stands.

He watches her stand, he hears her whisper and still he thinks, *Just don't be alive.* But then he sees her new eye and in it the flashes of a brilliant glow and he remembers the time that he and Aunt Bunny escaped from the endless circling, the land of dead trees and a cave that shook their world with madness. He feels it and for the first time, he sees it how it sees him, and now he understands. *The Little King.*

Bunny clasps her hand over her heart and he knows that she has heard his thought, and is glad.

Before he dies, he sees; he sees what is in the cave, what is beyond the smooth, inward stone. It falls away, and before him lies an eternal sky, streaked with magenta rays and a drowning sun. A lake that drifts in impossible directions simultaneously and a whirlwind of dying stars beneath. Pillars of rock jut upwards in ancient jest, piercing the dancing millennia above. He glances at dead trees and notes every type of animal that has been born behind them, and now him. He searches further beyond the pillars, beyond the trees and sees the peaks of endless black ranges and a roiling, stupid violence that splinters galaxies. He glances back down at his feet and sees a welcome mat, his welcome mat. He steps onto its prickly bristle and as he does so, a silver flash and a silent howl hurtle towards him.

The commotion out on the porch slowly roused Rose from her state of mournful delirium. She heard a sound like a meat tenderiser flattening out cheap steak and then something slid across the porch, bowling over the outdoor furniture. There was a momentary silence and then a resounding THUD. The silence that follows wafts into the house along with the soft, cold breeze that flows in from the open door.

'Silas?' she calls in a half-whisper.

'It's *tiiimmme*!' Bunny howls from outside, her dry, raked voice consumed with blind wonder and joy. It's the voice of the zealot at church, singing in tongues, dancing as souls are promised safe passage by a thin-eyed preacher in cheap shoes, under a rented tent that's paid for in cash.

'It's time, child! Praise!' Bunny screams as she bursts through the doorway, arms waving above her head in exaltation as her bare, bloody feet slap across the timber floor towards Rose.

Rose doesn't have time to react. *She's so fast*, she thinks as Bunny's razor neatly severs her windpipe and the arteries in her neck.

Where is Silas? she wonders as Bunny's mangled face comes close to kiss her forehead. The smell is what does it – that ripe smell of tobacco and ethanolic sweat and madness; a rotten air that seems to ooze out of Bunny's pores like they're the tiny mouths of so many dead and decaying things.

With the last of her strength Rose reaches up to Bunny's face and claws at her remaining eye. The cornea peels back under her fingernail. Bunny doesn't seem to notice, or mind.

Rose is already turning numb, but down below, a prick of pain sears through the numbness like a lightning bolt through fog. She looks down and sees a straight red line where the razor has cut her open in a hillbilly caesarean. Bunny's hand is already inside her stomach, darting this way and that, searching. Rose tries to fight her off, but all she can manage is a shudder from her shoulders as her hands inertly flop against Bunny's chest like dying fish. Bunny's hand ceases moving as her face peels into an enraptured smile. She withdraws, holding her bloody hand up to the blind, empty sockets of her face, as if she still can see. Pinched between her thumb and forefinger she holds a minute red grain, no larger than that of a single sesame seed. The last thing Rose sees is Bunny squatting in front of her, pushing the red seed up and into herself.

CHAMPAGNE BREAKFAST

The morning sun makes dust motes dance sleepily as it warms the air, which feels fresh and new. There's a crisp, cold tang around the edges of the day that make it perfect weather for early-morning walks or large mugs of strong, sweet English tea. It's a morning where one can listen to the world waking up and see fall massaging summer away in a great, pleasant sigh.

The flies wake with the warming sunlight and find the riches that await them in and around the house – cold, clotted, stiff, but still good for a fly. The doors are open, making it particularly easy to follow the blood inside, as they, one by one, enter the house to discover bloody treasures.

Rose and Silas are seated at the table, facing each other as if in pleasant conversation.

They are naked and their eyes are gone, young green pinecones pushed into their place. This, coupled with their hung-open mouths, gives them an uncanny resemblance to surprised cartoon characters, pinecone eyes bulging in fright and frustration as if Tom has caught Jerry but then stood on a nail.

Brave flies trundle in and out of their mouths, testing how far down their throats they can travel.

Upon Rose and Silas's heads rest adornments resembling

two crowns. Rose wears one of pinecones, held together by an aged yellow cord. It was made by a little boy in a ducky hood a long time ago, and left in a place it should *never* have been left, and in that place, it was found and kept for a very special day. Silas wears a woven wreath of spinach leaves picked fresh, made by hands covered in his and Rose's dry blood. They were Bunny's hands, but she is now so deeply enjoined that they're no longer really hers; she's simply a half-awake backseat driver in a vehicle she no longer recognises, having strange visions that are more like dreams as parts of her mind and soul are examined and repurposed while the rest is discarded and slowly digested.

Bunny brings in Silas's phone from outside and it lies on the counter with a voice note blinking on it. She turns her eyeless face towards him, perhaps seeking permission – it is, after all, his phone. She presses the playback button with a finger that leaves flakes of blood on the screen:

> Si, it's Jerry. I tried calling a bunch of times. Now, I understand why you didn't pick up but I hope you listen to this before you delete it. Look, I know a guy who owed me a favour from way back when this town was a little more . . . ah, never mind. Anyway, he's a *Ray Donovan* kinda guy. Bottom line is, we got the rights back – and also that advance-that-wasn't-an-advance. It's more than we talked about so . . . Call when you can. Love ta Rosie, kid. You're both gonna be fine. I promise. Okay, bye now.

Bunny's ruined face slowly starts to beam as she listens to the recording. Her cracked lips part, showing the yellowing teeth behind them. She walks over to Silas and affectionately rests her head against his. Her hand curls into a fist on the table top. *Knock. Knock. Knock.*

The turntable now stands righted. It was in pieces and the Geoffrey Clare record was cracked, so it should not work, but it does. 'Night Walk' flutters out of the speakers, once more filling the house with music.

Bunny's hands plug in the old Mr. Coffee with the nuclear warming plate. The empty glass decanter makes a brittle *dink!* sound as it heats up. She lifts a bowl from the counter nearby and half a dozen flies take off from its rim in a disturbed huff. Most of the blood from her guests paints the walls and floors, but she worked fast last night collecting enough to fill the large bowl. She tips it into an even larger bowl, where it lands with a heavy, half-coagulated *plop.* She opens a bottle of gin, dusty and scuffed from an old outside cache, and pours half of its clear contents into the bowl. She gives the mixture a dozen quick stirs with her bare hand, before licking her fingers clean like a child enjoying a mixing spoon with remnants of cookie dough still on it. She pours the liquid into the coffee urn and a cloud of rancid steam puffs up as the mixture hits the hot glass. So pungent are its contents, even the flies shy away.

Her hand rips open a kitchen drawer to discover a potato peeler. She presses it into the soft inside of her forearm and drags it upwards. A long curl of skin lifts obediently. She pulls it off and drops it onto the counter.

She works quickly, first pressing the peeler against Silas's forehead, just below where the wreath rests, then scuttles over to the opposite side of the table to perform the same diligent action on Rose.

Three strips of flesh lie neatly on the counter. She stands over them in reverie before dropping the peeler and walking over to where Rose bled out on the living-room floor. Goober's skull stares up at her as if he is still fighting. She stomps on it, shattering it into pieces, and picks up a small shard of bone. She returns to the counter, gathers up the three strips, and promptly tosses them and the bone shard into the bubbling coffee urn. Then she sits down to wait.

All this she does without the assistance of her eyes, for they are now gone, but what she possesses now is an intuition and force that gives her *one* profound sight. She does not need her eyes; none of them do, not now.

She sits so still that the flies occasionally crawl into her empty sockets. But they do not stay long, for they sense a corruption there, much deeper than the usual corporeal one they do their trade in.

SHE'S FIXING IT

Lou Lou is hungover and tired as she drives back home.

She had cursed herself for forgetting her purse, but she was a past regular at Surley's, and so (to her surprise) still had a tab at the bar. She'd wrangled a bottle off the bartender before retiring to the Hotel Motel. The night manager remembered her well from years past, so she got by, much like a beloved character from *Cheers*. She had stayed in the room before, but couldn't remember when, or with whom.

Hours were whiled away staring at late-night hosts making political jokes that she didn't understand, while sipping from the bottle of cheap whatever-it-was she was drinking. *Bunny won't hurt them. It's all fine. She's fixing it.* The thought orbited in the background of her mind, making it impossible to think otherwise.

It had started the day she and Bunny had sat for lunch, waiting for the van to take her away. The van that Silas had *made* come and take her away. They had been alone, whispering, or rather Bunny had whispered in her soft, loving voice and Lou Lou had listened obediently. *It's all fine. She's fixing it.*

Bunny had always fixed it before. Silas didn't know about the many times Bunny had fixed it . . . Like when the trucker man who Lou Lou liked had started pushing and shoving her during late nights at the Hotel Motel. She still had a small scar just under her jawline from him. Bunny had fixed it and he went away . . . Or the other man who had somehow found out that Lou Lou had some money, and invited himself to live with them for a time. She had been silly when she'd allowed him to stay. And once or twice she had found him, late at night when he thought they were asleep, rummaging around in desk drawers and filing cabinets – especially interested, it seemed, in the letters to do with bank accounts and insurance policies. He hadn't known, though, that Bunny was more of a night owl than he would ever be. So, she had fixed it and he had also . . . gone away.

Bunny wouldn't hurt them. It's all fine. She's fixing it . . .

Lou Lou rounds the final corner and parks the car in its usual spot. Her eyes are terrible in the bright light; she can see the house, but no discernible details. Music is playing. *Bunny's song. Oh, that's nice. Everyone must be getting along.*

She imagines walking in: Bunny, Silas and Rose will be seated at the table, eating pancakes drowned in maple syrup and butter and berries, each with their own cup of piping hot black coffee. Silas and Rose will have decided against staying for a further few days, having finished their script early. She's loved having him back, but he's made things tense, often unpleasant. Bunny's right. Best if he's on his way. Yes. But hopefully he does get a good deal on the script, perhaps he could even send some money back. This will be a farewell breakfast, a joyous send off before Silas and Rose leave, thankful and happy for the time they've spent here, but knowing that it's time to move on.

She'll help herself to a mug of coffee and let her stomach settle before maybe nibbling a pancake with just a little syrup on top. They will all laugh and politely speak about their plans, before moving along to loving embraces outside by the car. She can envision it now: the two of them with their suitcases already packed and ready to go. The cherry on top will be Goober materialising out of the bushes and bounding up to the car, having returned from his adventure in the woods. As they drive away, they'll all feel refreshed and re-energised, and Bunny and Lou Lou will cheerily wave them away just before 11.30 a.m – in time for an aperitif. Lou Lou will have tears in her eyes as they leave. The tears will be genuine, but dry quickly.

Sounds good to me, Lou Lou thinks, smiling to herself as she walks towards the house in the soft, warm sun.

Her eyes widen when she sees arching jets of black blood sprayed onto the outside of the house. She looks at the congealed blood pool below and the drag marks leading inside through the open doorway. She enters, making small hooting sounds like a startled owl. Her eyes drift to the pool of black blood in front of the fireplace, before sweeping over to the table where Rose and Silas are seated. They are in the seats she had imagined them to be in, but they do not appear as she expected. Not at all.

The smell in the house immediately instructs her guts to start heaving. Hot, bilious foam forms and her empty stomach spills bile out of her mouth and nose, down her front and onto the floor. Even the acidic smell of her insides can't dampen the burned copper smell of blood and meat in the air.

'But, but,' she gibbers, unable to merge the expected version in her head and the abattoir reality of this day.

Bunny's hands gently come to rest on her shoulders. They steer her into a seat at the table. Bunny picks up the coffee urn and turns off the overheated hotplate. The urn's plastic handle has melted in the over-revved heat and it sinks, soft and searing, into her hand. Bunny's free hand gingerly tips Lou Lou's head back, opens her mouth, and pours. Lou Lou screeches as boiling liquid runs down her throat and into her stomach, but she stays put, held there by more than sisterly touch. Lou Lou inhales sharply. The stream of liquid diverts down her windpipe and into her lungs, poaching the twin lobes like eggs in boiling water. Bunny shushes Lou Lou gently and ceases pouring.

She places the urn down, drags one of the table's matching wooden chairs beside her, and sits. A wheezing, pink-bubbled belch escapes Lou Lou's steaming mouth as she dies.

Bunny remains seated at the table for the rest of the day in silence. Her hand occasionally rises to hover over her belly, as if she is judging the heat from a stove element. The flies come and go; she lets them do as they will.

As the sun crawls low and the afternoon loses its warmth, Bunny leaves her seat at the table, removes her filthy clothes and drops them onto the kitchen floor. She switches the Mr. Coffee back on and walks out of the house naked and alive.

Before the sun finally sets, the hotplate pops and bursts into flames. The plastic body turns black and melts; the flames reach up towards the underside of the pine cupboard before licking at the ceiling's wooden beams. The fire moves slowly at first, but eventually finds a good footing in the dry wood.

Days later, after the forest fire had been contained and its origin discovered, police would find three bodies where the kitchen used to be: one male, and two females.

Two more bodies, both male, would also be discovered – dismembered and half mummified – in two large trunks in an unused root cellar under the house.

IT'S TIME

Bunny walks slowly out of the house, knowing it will burn, knowing that the beginning of things has now ended. She walks slowly and with great purpose into the woods and towards the lake, her hands cradling the bulge of her belly. She feels it expand, almost imperceptibly, but unceasingly, under her palms.

At some point in her vigil over Silas, the bright light that so enraptured the one inside her was transferred . . .

It happened one night as she stood watch outside their bedroom window. She was drawn most nights to stand outside and watch him shimmer through the walls of the house like a distant light show.

And through the walls, she observed Silas and Rose join one night – the one inside Bunny understood what this was, because Bunny understood what this was. It was a beautiful thing.

Silas and Rose made love, and the light sank into Rose like an enraptured prophecy. Over the first few weeks, the light became more distinct and separate from both Rose and Silas; a whole that was greater than its parts as it grew.

Bunny walks and walks until she can wade into the cold water as the last light of the day fades away. She is in the same location as Silas after his run all those weeks before. Her emaciated silhouette is black against the rising orange glow of the growing forest fire behind her. The eels wait patiently. They part for her, and follow her like an honour guard as she slowly disappears into the water. They gently pick what is left of the dried blood off her skin. Smaller ones tenderly remove the remains of her eyes from their empty sockets, and nibble away loose skin from the collapsed mound where her nose once was. By the time she wades out of the lake on the opposite shore, her sockets are polished white caves, not unlike the inside of the stone cave in the clearing.

She has been made anew.

Her nose is a crisp clean hole.

Her belly lies full term behind her cradling hands. She continues her passage.

A dull roar rises behind her as the forest fire reaches maturity. There is very little wind. The fire will move slowly through the trees like she does. It waits for her, as she waited for it.

She reaches the clearing, and the stone inside possesses a faint luminescence. The cave opening that, many years ago, invited Bunny inside – and more recently hid itself from Rose – now yawns open like the doorway to a great hall. The one that slumbers inside shifts restlessly as the part of itself that inhabits Bunny slowly approaches. In the countless, timeless ages that it has existed, it has distilled all sensation and experience into nothing more than an eternity of lonely, senseless boredom. Now, it is about to experience something new. (How bright the lights are that shine from inside of her!)

It is going to be a mother.

EPILOGUE

A VIEW THROUGH DIFFERENT KEYHOLES

GLADIATOR, YOU'RE HOME

Donovan, still in his sleeveless Pantera shirt, is too high to move from his tatty armchair on the porch. The sun has slipped away, and he finds himself staring blankly into the gloom of his backyard. Over the last half-hour, the handful of Valiums he dry-swallowed have started to feel like a fresh, pea-sized ball of cotton wool that is slowly expanding in his head. It grows and grows until it ever so gently presses against the inside curves of his skull, sending small wisps of white out to his ears to muffle the world.

The little bottle of pills was a half-assed payment from some mountain slut, who relieved him of the last few crystals of a mediocre batch of meth he'd been hawking for the past two months. He was glad to be rid of it – his supplier had changed cooks and the new guy didn't taste his own cooking. *Like teetotallers makin' fuckin' moonshine*, he thought. He meant to snort approvingly at his own joke, but his stoned lungs could only manage a lazy huff.

She had offered him Valium or a blow job for the crystal. He didn't much like the idea of her toothless mouth (creased and puckered like an old woman's, the way the lips go inwards when there aren't enough teeth behind them) wrapping around his joystick, so he'd taken the pills.

His arm slides off the side of the grease-stained armchair and drops down to where Nellie used to be chained. *Fuck you, Euge, you vetran-er-nerian faggot piece of shit ass-clown*, he thinks as his hand traces empty space instead of Nellie's hulking shoulders. Yes, he beat Nellie on occasion, and maybe bred her a few too many times, but she was a fuckin' *champion*. Dog-fighting rings as far as Georgia knew about Nellie – hell, her pups made him five fucking grand a pop. And when you were talking about some rich football player, or prize-fighter, or jackass hip-hop artist with a face full of tattoos that looked like the inside wall of a middle-school toilet stall, well, they usually paid for more than one pup, and in hundred-dollar bills. He even had a suggested 'fight diet plan' consisting of Winstrol and cocaine (mixed into their feeds) to get the pups ready to fight sooner and harder. Sure, their hearts gave up after a while, but so what – they were fucking *gladiators*, not pets.

But man, Nellie was different. He grew to love her the way Josef Fritzl loved his kids down in the cellar; they were *his* alone, and he was their keeper.

Donovan doesn't hear the low growling coming from the darkness of his unkempt yard. But he sees the eye glisten in the moonlight.

Nellie pads into the space between the porch stairs and the bushes in front of Donovan. He tries to say, 'Nellie. C'mere, you bitch!' but it comes out in a slurred mumble. *Too many Vs*, he thinks to himself.

The dog is still hulking, but there's a starved, lean quality to her. Muscle has shrunk as if she's been freeze-dried, leaving angles in her shoulders that look as sharp and cold as her one eye.

Nellie has been watching him for a while from the bushes. Years of abuse have given her a sense of when he's too slow to beat her and when he isn't.

Tonight, he'll be too slow. And she isn't on her chain anymore.

Weeks in the woods sharpened her senses, and she hunted small and not so small creatures to eat. She found a stream and kept a careful note of how far she roamed from it. It was the only safe water she would go near. She would never go back to the lake where she had watched it take the Good Man away. She had wanted to help him, but her body, so used to pain and violence, had refused and she had run from the thing that had been there in the water. She can sense it in the woods even now, but it's far away, and she's safe to settle what business is left for her to settle.

She pads up the stairs of the porch. Donovan's eyes never leave her one good one; they seem to be smiling a hello to her from his slack face. Her front paws pop lightly up onto his skinny thighs as his numb arms fold her in a soft embrace.

Her scarred nose bobs and weaves across the soft skin of his throat, smelling his narcotic-laden sweat. Finally, her mouth opens, squeezing his neck in an embrace of her own. She presses rather than clamps down, keen not to taste his blood; his sweat smells bitter and poisoned and whatever is in his body might slide down her throat and slow her down too – and the other thing in the woods might find her if she can't sense it and run. A sound like an apple being crushed by a heavy boot resounds from inside Donovan's neck as he stops being anything she needs to ever regard again.

As she's finishing, she hears small whimpers from inside the dark depths of the house. She releases his neck and pushes through the fly-screen mesh covering the front door. She knows her way around the place – it was once her home, after all – and she walks down the corridor to find her old wire crate. Inside, she discovers a single pup wagging its tail, unaware of her size and history, ready to cuddle if she'll let it. Outside the crate is a bowl of food. She sniffs it; it's bitter, adulterated with things that shouldn't be there; things that she had to eat in past years, which made her feel hot and angry and too fast. Her heavy paw tips the bowl over, spilling the mixture across the floor. The little one seems crestfallen. All he knows is that it's feeding time and he's hungry.

Nellie hooks a yellowed, tusk-like canine over the crate door and pulls. It pops open as if made from paper. The little one politely sits back on its haunches. The big new friend smells like the blankets around him, and he knows that he is in *her* den. Nellie delicately edges into the crate and lies down beside the pup. He nuzzles her before discovering a well-worn teat to suckle. After so many litters, she rarely stops lactating, and so she lets him drink his fill.

Tomorrow morning, they will leave, make their way south and eventually out of the woods. For the woods now are sick, and no place for little ones.

TAP, TAP, TAP

Since his granma dragged herself into the woods, Morgan has had dreams. Dreams of hands pressed against windows, and of voices whispering to him from the gap under the bolted front door.

The dreams have slowly crept into the waking light of day, blighting the edge of his vision with flashes of movement he can never quite make out or catch.

Without knowing why, he decides to close the diner section of the gas station permanently. The impact on his bottom line is negligible; nobody eats there anymore anyway. People drive up, buy their gas and go on their way.

The tapping starts a few weeks after he closes up the diner. The big retro slab of bar counter is gone, and he's sold the kitchen stove and fridges. But at night, something *tap, tap, taps*. The first time he hears it, it wakes him and in half-sleep, he yells, 'Enough, Granma!'

The tapping sounds like she's still in the dark, tapping her empty glass, waiting for a refill.

On the last night that he spends at the station, he sits on the steps of the porch where Granma so often talked to trees. He has started drinking to get through the night undisturbed by new noises. He is one beer away from heading back inside and he cracks open a High Life from the ice box next to him – the last one, which he kept for Granma. He isn't much of a drinker, but they're all that's left in the house, and the insomnia is causing him to behave out of character. He takes a sip and lowers it onto the step next to him.

Tap, Tap, Tap.

The sound comes from the woods; it's like an empty glass being tapped against the trunk of a tree. He looks into the murk for a long moment and sees nothing.

He decides to finish the beer inside. His hand goes to take it, but it's not there. He looks down and sees a wet ring of condensation on the old wood where it stood.

The next morning, he drives into town, puts the station up for sale, withdraws his savings and moves to the southern border where no pine forests grow. He marries a plain woman. They have a little girl who is prettier than either of them could have hoped for.

For no reason in particular, they name her Rose.

He never speaks much of the woods, or of his life before, and his friends and family learn not to ask. He lives a long time and never hears the *tap, tap, tap* of an empty glass in the darkness again.

I WILL WALK WITH YOU

To surface from the emptiness of death is a long and dim process. There is no waking because there is no sleep. All there is, is memory. No future – that path is closed to him now – only past.

His definition is no longer his own, but a base sentience shaped by the memories of his life. Limited, but yet here. Over time, the memories that were once Silas relearn a sort of consciousness.

There is a silver presence near him. It is more complete than he is. He does not perceive it as a threat as it waits for him.

But now the presence, perhaps sensing his new consciousness, draws closer.

It selects a memory to show him: a cold, wet nose on the side of his cheek.

'Are you Goober?'

'I am. I am also more.'

'Where is Rose?'

There is a moment of silence.

'Gone.'

He doesn't understand. Why are they here and she is not? The presence feels his thought, and answers, *'Because we took The Other in our teeth. We consumed part of it and now it cannot own us . . . But I could not help both of you in time.'*

The presence sorts through his memories again, and shows him his dream at the lakeshore where they had eaten pieces of it – of Her.

'I must find Rose.'

'She cannot be found.'

'I will find her.'

The presence gazes up at the memories as they become the figure of a man. There is a moment. The presence is thinking. It has a decision to make that is bigger than Silas understands.

'*Then . . .*' The presence resumes its form as a small black dog. '*I will walk with you.*'

They walk there still.

ACKNOWLEDGEMENTS

First and foremost, thank you to you, reader, for picking up this book.

We want to thank our agent Aoife Lennon-Ritchie, who signed two unknown writers back in 2018 off of a screenplay; that screenplay she nonchalantly suggested we turn into a novel. Having never written a novel before, that prospect was terrifying, but yet, here *Bunny* is in the hands of readers. Thank you, Aoife, for your guidance over the years.

We want to mention a thank you to Seth Fisher for reading an early draft of our screenplay *Crepuscular* – your feedback and advice was very much appreciated, as was your genius suggestion to change the title to *Bunny*.

Thank you also to the brilliant team at Pan Macmillan who have shepherded us through what feels like a herculean journey. Special thanks to Alex Lloyd, who read our novel, decided to option it and has guided us through this entire process. Thank you as well to Belinda Huang and Amber Burlinson, who challenged us, and in doing so, made this book better than we thought it could be. And thank you to Allie Schotte and Rufus Cuthbert for all your work on marketing the book. Thank you to writer Maya Fowler-Sutherland, who gave us sound feedback when the novel was still in its early days. Thank you to Henrique Ricky Beirao, who assisted us with the Spanish used in this book. Your Rhubarb is strong. Also thank you to Nicole Cardoni for her help with Spanish phrase questions.

Vere would like to thank three wonderful teachers who helped him keep things weird: Mark de Buys, Lidia Upton and Carol Fields. Emma would like to thank Georgina Makarios, who helped her get through some strange years way back when. And to our family and friends, who have put up with our anti-social ways whilst we were finishing this book – see, we really were writing a book! Thank you to our endlessly entertaining nephews and nieces, Manu, Te Koha, Jessamin and Livia – we thought you would love being thanked publicly in a book (to their parents, please do not let them read this book yet). Thank you to Dean, Daniel, and Deisel Lee-Nayna, who helped us out during a trying time. Thank you to Mary Gardiner, who always reads our work, and to our parents, aunts, uncles, siblings and cousins, we love you.

Thank you to our wonderful dogs, Pepper and Custer, two rescues who came into our lives and brought more colour, randomness and joy than anything before. Goober is based off a combination of these two gremlins, who now live in spoiled luxury. In many ways Goober is the heart of this story, the moral compass, the unbiased love and goodness that we are all capable of but seldom live up to. Goober brings out the best in Silas and Rose, just as our two have brought out the best in us. This book is filled with horror and gore, but there is also a layer that we hope you felt, and that is (in part) a love story showcasing the bond between man and dog. We are convinced that animals are the one true form of magic that is left in this world, and meeting these two dogs has only further solidified that belief. A good part of this book, possibly the most significant part, is a tribute to rescue dogs.

We also need to acknowledge the phenomenal writer that was Caroline Knapp, whose book *Drinking: A Love Story* was a revelation to read for both of us. At the centre of *Bunny* is a family that is reeling from the effects of addiction. Thank you, Caroline, for allowing us to see it from the other side.

Listen to an author-curated playlist of music that inspired *Bunny* by scanning this QR code.